# DEATH OF A MAID OF HONOR

It was time, thought Lucy, as she replaced the dress in the garment bag, to call Beth. She hadn't spoken to her in a long time, and she knew Beth would love hearing about the Bickersons and reminiscing about the wedding. She perched on the side of her bed and picked up the phone, punching in the number she knew from memory.

The voice that answered wasn't Beth's; it was male.

"Is Beth there?" asked Lucy, puzzled.

"I'm afraid not. Who's calling?"

"I'm an old friend. Lucy Stone. Could you please tell her I called?"

"I'm afraid not, Lucy," said the voice, which was close to breaking. "This is Dante."

Lucy knew Dante was Beth's son, whom she remembered as a skinny, mischievous kid. "Is everything all right, Dante?"

"No. It's not. Everything's wrong." He gasped, letting out a sob. "My mother is dead . . ."

Books by Leslie Meier

Published by Kensington Publishing Corporation

A Lucy Stone Mystery

# SILVER ANNIVERSARY MURDER

## LESLIE MEIER

**KENSINGTON BOOKS**
www.kensingtonbooks.com

KENSINGTON BOOKS are published by

Kensington Publishing Corp.
119 West 40th Street
New York, NY 10018

All Kensington titles, imprints, and distributed lines are available at special quantity discounts for bulk purchases for sales promotion, premiums, fund-raising, educational, or institutional use. Special book excerpts or customized printings can also be created to fit specific needs. For details, write or phone the office of the Kensington Special Sales Manager: Attn. Special Sales Department. Kensington Publishing Corp., 119 West 40th Street, New York, NY 10018. Phone: 1-800-221-2647.

Kensington and the K logo Reg. U.S. Pat. & TM Off.

ISBN-13: 978-1-4967-1034-5
ISBN-10: 1-4967-1034-7
First Kensington Hardcover Edition: September 2018
First Kensington Mass Market Edition: August 2019

ISBN-13: 978-1-4967-1035-2 (ebook)
ISBN-10: 1-4967-1035-5 (ebook)

10 9 8 7 6 5 4 3 2

Printed in the United States of America

*For John Scognamiglio*
*Editor Extraordinaire*

# Chapter One

"**H**onestly, I'm surprised he hasn't killed her," whispered Harry Nuttall, leaning over the deli counter at the IGA in Tinker's Cove, Maine. He was speaking to one of his regular customers, Lucy Stone, who was doing her weekly grocery shopping.

Lucy was a part-time reporter for the *Pennysaver*, the local weekly newspaper, and had developed the habit of shopping after the paper's Wednesday noon deadline, taking advantage of the free afternoon, which also happened to be a time when the usually crowded supermarket had few customers.

"So is it the usual?" Harry pulled on a fresh pair of plastic gloves. "A pound of ham, sliced thin, and a half of Swiss?"

"I guess I'll live dangerously," said Lucy, turning to watch Warren Bickford, Harry's potential murderer, presenting his wife and likely murder victim, Sylvia, with his wrapped cold cuts. Then remembering the task at hand, she turned back to Harry. "Throw in a half pound of turkey breast, too."

"Do you want it sliced like the ham?" asked Harry. Lucy's attention had returned to the Bickfords; Warren's deli purchase had clearly not satisfied Sylvia. She glared at the label on the package through heavily made-up eyes, ran her red-tipped nails through her obviously bleached blond hair, pointed at the label, then roughly thrust the packet back to Warren. "Black Forest, Warren. I told you Black Forest! Honestly, how many times do I have to repeat myself?"

Warren bent his head and seemed to offer an apology, then trotted obediently back to the deli counter.

"Same thickness as the ham?" Harry asked again, the grin on his face revealing his amusement at Lucy's fascination with the Bickfords.

Lucy considered asking him to slice the turkey a bit thicker than the ham, but aware that Warren was under the gun to deliver the correct order, changed her mind. "Same," she said, turning to give Warren a big, warm smile. It seemed the least she could do for the poor, henpecked husband. "Nice day," she said, referring to the lovely, mild, May weather that was such a treat after the bitter cold Maine winter, which this year had been followed by an especially blustery March and extremely muddy April.

"Sure is," replied Warren, unzipping his jacket. Lucy guessed he was in his early fifties, and like most middle-aged men in Tinker's Cove, he was wearing khaki pants and a sports shirt topped with a light sweater. His thinning hair was combed in the standard left-parted barbershop cut and he was developing a bit of a paunch. That growing tummy was probably the result of an occupational hazard; as owner and operator of a limo service he spent a lot of time sitting behind the wheel. "Sorry to bother you, Harry, but I got the wrong ham. I should've asked for Black Forest. I hope it's no problem."

"No problem," said Harry, placing Lucy's three packages on the counter. "It's already wrapped. I'll save it for the next customer who wants Virginia ham."

Warren let out a relieved sigh. "Thanks, Harry." It seemed he was about to say something more, perhaps a reference to his wife, but thought better of it and bit his lip instead, rocking slightly from one sturdy Timberland shoe to the other while waiting for Harry to slice his Black Forest ham.

Lucy put her packages in her cart and pushed it along, heading for the meat counter, which ran along the back wall of the supermarket. She paused at an island displaying English muffins—buy one get two free, a deal that was hard to pass up—and witnessed Warren rejoining his wife and presenting the correct ham, rather like a little girl offering flowers to the queen.

"Warren, you always do this. You don't speak up and people take advantage of you. Just look—this ham is sliced much too thick. Not that I blame Harry. He isn't going to shove that slicer back and forth any more times than he has to, if people don't speak up and ask for thin slices."

Warren stood like a statue, letting his wife's criticisms rain down on him. "Do you want me to take it back, *dear*?" he asked, with the slightest note of sarcasm in his voice.

Sylvia expelled a large sigh. "No, Warren. We don't have time. We have a big order this week." She flourished her shopping list. "Do you think you could manage a simple task like getting the coffee while I look over the meat? Beef chuck is supposed to be on sale, but I'll be amazed if they have any left this late in the week. They probably sold it all on the weekend. Not that they'll get away with it, not with me. I'll insist on a rain check."

"You do that, dear," said Warren. "Quite right. Now, do you want decaf or regular, and what brand? Or should I go for price?"

"It never ceases to amaze me, Warren. How long have we been married? Twenty-five years next month, and you don't know what brand of coffee we drink?"

"Well, it's usually the one in the red package, but sometimes it seems to me we have the blue kind."

"*The red kind? The blue kind?* Honestly, Warren, you sound like a child." She rolled her eyes. "Get the Folgers, unless Maxwell House is on sale for half price. And don't fall for that foul French roast stuff. Can you do that for me?"

"Yes, dear." Warren trotted off in the direction of the coffee aisle, and Sylvia, as promised, attacked the meat counter. Lucy, hoping to avoid witnessing any more of Warren's humiliations, slipped off into the cereal aisle. Distracted by a special on canned soups on the end cap, where she was searching for chicken noodle but only finding minestrone and vegetarian vegetable, she wasn't quick enough to miss Warren's presentation of a green can of coffee.

"Green is decaf, Warren; everybody knows that," declared Sylvia, in a voice that could probably be heard on Metinnicut Island, ten miles across the bay.

"But it's Folgers, like you said." He attempted a weak defense. "They could have changed the package, you know."

"No, Warren, they haven't changed it." Sylvia paused to sniff a cello-wrapped piece of chuck, then replaced it. "Now, take this back and get the red Folgers. And do hurry. We've got a lot to do and I'm going to have the butcher cut me a fresh piece of chuck. The nose knows—you can't fool my nose. This meat has probably been sitting out here since Sunday."

"Right, dear," said Warren, obediently hurrying back to the coffee section to complete his assignment. Watching him go, Lucy thought Harry might have a point. Some day, maybe some day soon, Warren was bound to snap.

Diverting as that thought was, Lucy had a long shopping list that demanded great concentration as she frequently consulted the weekly ad for specials, checked prices, and thumbed through her coupon file. From time to time she heard Sylvia's strident voice berating Warren for something or other, but she didn't actually encounter the Bickfords again until she reached the checkout counter.

Warren was busy bagging their order when Dot Kirwan, the cashier, announced the amount due.

"A hundred and forty-seven dollars!" exclaimed Sylvia. "We don't want to buy the store, do we, Warren? We just want to eat for a week."

"Should we put this back, dear?" suggested Warren, who was holding a large bottle of expensive olive oil. "We could get a smaller one."

Sylvia shook her head. "The larger one is a better value, Warren. You ought to know that. It's cheaper per ounce. Now pay the bill and stop grumbling."

"Yes, dear," said Warren, pulling his wallet out of his back pocket and handing a credit card to Dot.

"Let me see that!" demanded Sylvia, snatching the card out of Dot's hand. "Just as I thought. It's the wrong card!"

Dot's eyes met Lucy's, and they both struggled to maintain neutral facial expressions while Warren fumbled with his wallet. The two women were of like minds and Lucy had great respect for Dot, who was the widowed matriarch of a large family. Most of her kids and grandkids worked for the town, filling positions in the fire and police departments, which made Dot a valuable source of inside knowledge for Lucy.

"Oh, give me that wallet!" demanded Sylvia, losing patience. He obliged and she flipped it open, pulling out a wad of plastic cards. "My word! What is all this? Exxon, Sears, Shell, Visa, Plenti . . . Ah, finally! This is the one that gives us rewards, Warren." She waved the colorful bit of plastic underneath his nose. "Only use this one, from now on, only this one. You don't need the rest. You might as well cut them up and throw them away."

"I'll do that, dear," said Warren, who had continued packing the groceries and was holding the disputed can of Folgers coffee.

"Just slide the card on the keypad," urged Dot, and Sylvia complied, signing with a flourish. Warren carefully placed a plastic bag containing their eggs on the child seat and pushed the cart toward the door, followed by Sylvia, who was checking the register tape as she walked.

"Thank you and have a nice day," said Dot. Unable to stifle her laughter any longer, she burst into a fit of giggles. "I call them the Bickersons," she whispered to Lucy, as the automatic door opened and the Bickfords exited the store.

Lucy felt a certain sympathy for Sylvia as Dot finished ringing up her order, which amounted to nearly two hundred dollars despite her coupon clipping. Sylvia was right about one thing, she decided, as she pushed her heavily loaded cart out to the parking lot, and that was the price of groceries. The sun this afternoon was very bright, and she paused in the shady overhang to put on her sunglasses only to find they were missing. They weren't in the usual pocket on the outside of her purse, and they weren't inside, along with her wallet, granola bar, numerous pens, phone, and reporter's notebook, either. Sighing, she gave the cart a shove and stepped into the sunlight, squinting. She'd almost finished loading everything into her trunk when it came to her: she'd pulled the sunglasses off when she got to work earlier that day and set them down on her desk. They were most likely still there, so she'd have to swing by the *Pennysaver* office to retrieve them.

Lucky for her, there was a vacant parking spot

right in front of the weekly newspaper's Main Street office and Lucy swooped right in, then dashed into the office, setting the little bell on the door to jangling. Somewhat to her surprise, she was greeted not only by the receptionist, Phyllis, but also by her editor, Ted, who didn't usually stick around the office after deadline. The two were standing at the reception counter, heads bent over a press release.

"What's up?" asked Lucy. "Breaking news?" Late breaking news was a problem for a weekly, which had to wait an entire week before printing stories that by then had become stale.

"Not hardly," said Ted, chuckling. He was not only the editor, but also the publisher and chief reporter for the paper, which he'd inherited from his grandfather. That celebrated New England journalist's rolltop desk still dominated the old-fashioned newsroom and was Ted's most prized possession.

"You've got to see it to believe it," said Phyllis, laughing so hard that her sizable bosom was jiggling as she handed the press release to Lucy. Phyllis was celebrating spring's late arrival by wearing a pink bouclé sweater that matched her pink reading glasses and her hair, also dyed pink.

Lucy quickly scanned the press release, which announced in bold capitals that Sylvia and Warren Bickford were soon to celebrate their twenty-fifth wedding anniversary in June by renewing their vows, that joyous ceremony to be followed by a reception to which the whole town would be invited. And that was not all, promised the press release, which went on to invite all the ladies of the town to participate in a fashion show of wedding gowns from the past by modeling their own dresses. All those interested should contact Sylvia at her shop, Orange Blossom Bridal.

"This is so funny," said Lucy, when she'd finished reading. "I just saw the Bickfords, who Dot Kirwan calls the Bickersons, at the IGA. She picked on him mercilessly; the poor guy couldn't do anything right. Harry, the deli guy, said he was surprised Warren hasn't murdered Sylvia. A divorce would be more appropriate than renewing their vows. The whole town is going to be laughing at them."

"It's pretty smart, if you ask me," said Ted. "It's great publicity for her bridal boutique, and also for his limo company."

"It could backfire," said Lucy. "Everybody knows it's an unhappy marriage. Nobody'd be surprised if Warren bailed out, or worse."

"Oh, I don't know," said Phyllis, in a thoughtful tone. She was a bit of a romantic, having found her great love, Wilf Lundgren, rather late in life. "There must be something that keeps them together, despite outward appearances. I think it's kind of sweet."

Lucy spotted her sunglasses, exactly where she had left them, and grabbed them, perching them on top of her head in Jackie Kennedy style. "Speaking of sweets, I gotta run before my ice cream melts—see ya tomorrow!"

Lucy thought about marriage as she drove the familiar route through town, down Main Street, and out to Route 1, then turning onto Red Top Road and up the hill to the handyman's special she and Bill had restored and in which they'd raised their four children. Sometimes the glue held, even for couples like the Bickersons, who didn't seem terribly happy, and sometimes that glue dried up and crumbled, like the stuff she'd spent hours scraping off the back of an antique picture frame she'd recently picked up at an estate sale. There had been rough spots in her marriage to Bill—she remembered fights but not exactly what caused them—but she'd never seriously considered divorce. Maybe, she admitted to herself, that was because she was far too practical to attempt to raise four children by herself, especially considering the mostly low-wage jobs available to women like her in coastal Maine. She didn't want to spend her summers juggling a couple of jobs, chambermaiding by day and waitressing by night as many local women did.

That wasn't quite fair to Bill, she thought with a smile, pulling into the driveway. She loved him. She'd been distant at first, when he began chatting her up in college, but through sheer persistence he'd gradually won her over. Now, after the house and the kids and grandson Patrick, he was so much a part of her that she couldn't imagine life without him.

Though, she admitted to herself as she began toting the heavy recyclable bags of groceries into the house, she could use a little help from him right now. What was it her mother used to say, when her father was nowhere to be found? Something about wishing she could put on her hat and walk out the door, though that didn't quite take into account the fact that Dad was just going to work. She knew that Bill, who was a restoration carpenter, was hard at work on a big project, transforming an old, abandoned church into a vacation home for a successful Portland restauranteur and his family.

Still, it was a big job, toting all the groceries that would feed herself and Bill, and their two daughters who hadn't yet flown the nest. The fact that Sara, now a graduate student at nearby Winchester College, was a vegetarian, and Zoe, an undergraduate at the same institution, was avoiding gluten, didn't make things any easier. Her grocery list was now filled with the special foods the girls demanded: quinoa, kale, organic yogurt, free-range eggs, hormone-free milk, on and on it went. She dropped two heavy bags on the kitchen table and went out for more, eventually making three trips to get everything inside. And then there was the unloading, the sorting and the storing.

When she'd finally folded the last bag and tucked it away with the others in her bag of bags, she sat down at the round, golden oak kitchen table and considered making herself a cup of tea. Entirely too much work, she decided, opting instead for a glass of water. She sipped it thoughtfully, thinking of Sylvia's challenge: could she possibly fit into her wedding dress? Setting down her glass, she decided she had to find out.

The dress, shrouded in a garment bag, hung in the back of her closet. She hadn't looked at it in years, had almost forgotten about it. Like most mothers, she had a vague hope that one of her daughters might wear it for her wedding, but so far that hadn't happened. Even Elizabeth, her oldest, who worked for the tony Cavendish Hotel chain and was currently living in Paris, hadn't shown any interest in marriage, much less in wearing her mother's dress. It probably wouldn't suit her, thought Lucy, climbing the steep, back stairway that led from the kitchen to the bedrooms on the second floor. She would surely want something more high fashion.

Entering the bedroom she shared with Bill, Lucy opened the bifold closet doors, which stuck a bit and which Bill kept meaning to fix. She slid the clothes along the rod until she came to the long garment bag, which she pulled out and laid on the bed, then unzipped it to reveal the white dress.

It was a simple design with short sleeves and a jewel neckline. The bodice was made of Alençon lace, ending in a slightly raised waist. The full skirt was heavy satin ending in the slightest suggestion of a train, and fastened with a wide ribbon sash at the waist. It was slightly crushed from hanging in the closet all these years, and the veiled headpiece, which she had tucked into the bottom of the garment bag, was flattened.

She took it out, reshaping it with her hands, and set it on her head, fluffing out the white tulle veil, and looked in the mirror. She was much older now, but if she brought the veil forward, over her face, she almost looked like the young woman in the wedding picture that stood on Bill's dresser. But not quite, she decided, snatching the coif off and tossing it on the bed.

Picking up the dress, she held it at arm's length and studied it. It was a pretty dress but nothing like the strapless sheaths the girls wore these days, and not like the heavily beaded and hugely skirted cream puffs that had been fashionable for a while.

Turning to the full-length mirror on the back of the bedroom door, she held the gown against her body and sighed. It was obvious, without even trying it on, that she could never fit into it. She wasn't fat, not by a long shot, but she'd given birth to four children, and she'd breast-fed them all. Her body had changed and she was no longer the little slip of a thing who had worn that dress.

Standing there and studying her reflection, she thought it wasn't just her body that had changed; she had changed, too. She was much more confident these days and much more assertive than she had been as a young bride. She was more open-minded, too, and less opinionated. Back then, she thought, she'd been a bit of a prig, convinced there was a right way to do things and a wrong way. Nowadays she was no longer convinced that food colorings were poison, that childbirth had to be natural, and all plastic should be banned.

She realized now that her strongly held beliefs had been a defense against an uncertain world. That had become obvious when she stepped inside the church vestibule on her wedding day and panicked, completely terrified to take that first step down the aisle to the altar where Bill was waiting for her.

"Ready, sweetie?" her father had asked, cocking his elbow and inviting her to take his arm.

*Not at all*, she'd realized, wanting only to turn tail and run right out the door. She would have fled, she remembered, except for the fact that everything was going black and she was about to faint. It was Beth Gerard, her best friend and maid of honor, who had produced from somewhere a brown paper lunch bag, which she gave to Lucy, instructing her to breathe into it.

Dad had held her up as Lucy breathed in and out, deep breaths, into the paper sack. "I thought this might happen," said Beth.

"I can't do this," said Lucy. "The wedding's off."

"It's rather late for that," said her father.

"Look, if it's no good, you can get a divorce or an annulment. But today, you have to get married," said Beth.

"It's not Bill, it's me. I can't go down that aisle."

"Oh, yes you can," said Beth. "Just imagine they're all naked."

Standing there, in front of her mirror, Lucy smiled, just as she had on her wedding day when she followed Beth and the other bridesmaids down the aisle on her father's arm. Afterward, everybody said they'd never seen such a radiant, happy bride.

It was time, thought Lucy as she replaced the dress in the garment bag, to call Beth. She hadn't spoken with her in a long time, and she knew Beth would love hearing about the Bickersons and reminiscing about the wedding. No time like the present, decided Lucy, knowing that unless she made the call immediately the moment would pass and she would be distracted and forget. She perched on the side of her bed and picked up the phone from the bedside table, punching in the number she knew from memory.

The voice that answered wasn't Beth's; it was male.

"Is Beth there?" asked Lucy, puzzled.

"I'm afraid not. Who's calling?"

"I'm an old friend, Lucy Stone. Could you please tell her I called?"

"I'm afraid not, Lucy," said the voice, which was close to breaking. "This is Dante."

Lucy knew Dante was Beth's son, whom she remembered as a skinny, mischievous kid. Now, from his deep voice, it was clear he was all grown up. And it was also clear to her that something was wrong. "Is everything all right, Dante?"

"No. It's not. Oh, Lucy, everything's wrong." He gasped, letting out a sob. "My mother is dead."

# Chapter Two

Dead? Beth dead? That couldn't be right. How could that be?

"I can't believe it," said Lucy, feeling her world turning upside down. "What happened? When? Was she sick? She never mentioned . . ."

"They say it was suicide. She jumped off the balcony yesterday morning. . . ."

Lucy knew Beth lived—no, had been living—in a high-rise penthouse in New York City. Sitting there in her bedroom, phone in hand, Lucy envisioned Beth taking that final leap, falling through the air and landing in a crumpled, bloody heap on the sidewalk, and was horrified. She could only imagine what Dante was going through.

"Oh, Dante, I am so sorry." Lucy gripped the handset so tightly that her knuckles turned white. "I can't believe it."

"I wish there was a better way to tell you."

"There's no good way for something like this." Lucy choked back a sob as tears filled her eyes.

"I know you're upset so I won't keep you. It looks like the funeral will be Saturday morning at St. Andrew's."

Lucy had grabbed a wad of tissues from the box on her nightstand and was wiping her face. "I'll try . . ." was all she managed to get out before breaking down entirely, hitting the end button and collapsing onto the bed. Lucy wasn't a crier, although sometimes she did have to blink back a few tears. But she hadn't really cried in years, not like this, sobbing and wailing and producing floods of tears. She couldn't fight it . . . she simply had to go with it until the storm ceased, leaving her aching and empty. Moving slowly and painfully, like an old woman, she finally got up off the bed only to find herself standing on the little hooked, bedside rug without a clue what to do with herself.

She moved to the window and looked out, surprised to see that nothing had changed in the yard. The neat rows of vegetable seedlings were still sprouting in the garden, the grass needed mowing, and a couple of robins were busy hunting for worms to feed their nestlings. Beth had died and nothing had changed. Beth had died and everything had changed.

Beth had been her first and best friend. Lucy couldn't remember how or when they'd first met; it seemed Beth had always been there. They'd been in the same classes all through elementary school, they'd gone to the same church and Sunday School, and they'd gone to the same high school, where they both adored French and hated algebra. They went to different colleges, but the first thing they did when they got home for vacation was get together to compare notes on everything: boys, classes, clothes, hair, music, movies. Lucy never quite knew what she thought about these things until she'd thoroughly discussed them with Beth.

Beth was the leader of their gang of two; she was the one who initiated things. She was the one who convinced Lucy to skip school in favor of a ride on the Staten Island Ferry one early June day when the weather was simply too beautiful to miss. And it was Beth who dared Lucy to shoplift a pair of earrings from Fuhrman's Department Store, earrings Lucy still had and always felt guilty about whenever she caught sight of them in her jewelry box. But Beth was also the one who knew which bands were cool and which were not, who would share her lunch if you forgot yours, and who would keep a secret forever.

That's why she'd felt quite lost when Beth suddenly announced she was quitting college to join a religious cult, the Angel Brigade. Lucy had suspected at the time that Beth's sudden religious awakening was less about a genuine conversion to the Brigade and more about the cult's remarkably handsome and charismatic leader, Gabriel Thomas. Whichever it was, it meant that Beth had dropped out of her life, essentially abandoning her.

Beth only stayed with the cult for a year or so, long enough to become pregnant with Gabriel's son, Dante, and much too long, as she put it, to tolerate his infidelity. But although the divorce meant she was back in Lucy's life, it was never the same as before. They stayed in touch, through annual Christmas cards and occasional phone calls, but there was never the same closeness as they followed their own diverging paths. Lucy married Bill and they moved to Maine and raised a family; Beth stayed in the city with her only child and proceeded to work her way through three more husbands. In truth, Lucy had never really gotten over Beth's sudden decision to join the cult, which felt to her like desertion.

And now, suicide. That was the ultimate betrayal, thought Lucy. Suicide was a huge slap in the face to everyone who loved you, to family and friends who would forever wonder why their love wasn't enough. It left survivors with a huge burden of guilt, always questioning what they could have done differently, and whether they could have prevented that final, desperate act.

Still standing by the window, Lucy noticed a flash of color, a male robin who was fighting with his reflection in the shiny, black Weber grill. What foolishness, what vanity, she thought, as the little fellow strutted and flapped and feinted at his own image. It reminded her of Beth, the way she never passed a mirror without checking her appearance. Her first act upon arrival anywhere, was a quick stop in the ladies' room to check her hair and apply fresh lipstick. There was no way, she thought, that Beth would hurl herself to destruction off a twenty-two story building. She was impulsive and emotional, sure, but she had recently invested many thousands of dollars in a face-lift and Lucy knew her friend would never risk damaging that newly firm chin line.

Lucy sat down on the side of the bed and reached for the phone once again, this time calling Sam Blackwell, another childhood friend who had also been one of her bridesmaids. Sam still lived in New York and had remained friendly with Beth, occasionally meeting her for lunch or an art exhibit.

"I was just going to call you," said Sam. "I guess you've heard."

"I can't believe it."

"I can't make any sense of it either. Beth was emotional—she had lots of highs and lows—but I never thought she'd do something like this. I saw her just a week or two ago...."

"Was she depressed?" asked Lucy.

"Not at all. If anything she was kind of up. We were having lunch at this new soup place and she was really excited that they had mulligatawny soup." Sam paused. "Maybe too excited, now that I think about it. Maybe she was losing her grip and becoming unstable. I just thought it was Beth being Beth. Now I wonder if I could have said something or done something that would have made a difference."

"Don't blame yourself. It doesn't change anything." Lucy remembered reading somewhere that people who were considering suicide often became remarkably cheerful and upbeat once they'd made the decision to kill themselves. The article went on to say that this change often fooled others, serving as a smoke screen.

"I just keep going over and over everything she said, trying to remember if there was some indication...."

"Even if there was, what could you have done?"

"I know," admitted Sam. "I fantasize about grabbing her and carrying her off to safety. I see myself pulling her back off that awful balcony. Last night I had nightmares about nets and trampolines and bungee cords, anything that might have saved her, but they always failed and she ended up smashed on the sidewalk."

"Maybe you should talk to a therapist," said Lucy.

"Brad's been suggesting that for years," admitted Sam, referring to her husband. "It's been a bit of a running joke."

Lucy decided it was time to get serious. "Are you going to the funeral?"

"Of course. Are you? It's probably going to be Saturday or Sunday."

"I spoke to Dante and he said probably Saturday. I'll fly down, but I need a place to stay. . . ."

"Oh, sorry, Lucy, no can do. We're not in our apartment; it's being renovated. We're getting rid of those old moldings on the walls. I've hated them for years, you know. New floors, updated kitchen and baths, the whole shebang. Everything's topsy-turvy, the furniture's in storage, and Brad and I are in an extended stay hotel." She paused for breath. "I don't think it's full. I could make a reservation for you, if you want."

Lucy was flummoxed. She hadn't anticipated this. She'd just assumed she could stay at Brad and Sam's roomy prewar apartment on Riverside Drive. Now she was faced not only with the cost of a last-minute airplane ticket but would also have to pay an exorbitant rate for a New York hotel room. "I guess so," she decided, swallowing hard.

"Consider it done," said Sam. "I'm so glad you're coming, Lucy. We can have a good cry together."

"Something to look forward to," she said wryly. "See you soon."

After ending the call, Lucy tried to focus on everyday chores like emptying the dishwasher, making supper, and setting the table, but found herself standing like a statue, plate or pot in hand, wondering what she was supposed to do with it. Sara and Zoe came home, but were occupied with cell phones and didn't notice their mother's odd behavior. Bill, however, was immediately concerned, puzzled by the lack of dinner preparations.

"What's for supper, Lucy?" he asked, sitting down on one of the kitchen chairs and proceeding to unlace his work boots.

"Supper?" repeated Lucy.

"What's the matter?" he asked, looking at her suspiciously.

"My friend Beth died," she said, wiping her eyes. "It was suicide."

"That's terrible," he said, hopping up with one shoe on and one off and taking her in his arms.

Lucy nestled against him, feeling his beard on her forehead and resting her head on his shoulder. It was at times like this, she thought, that she really appreciated her husband. He was a rock, someone she could count on to support her in times of trouble. She slipped her arms around his waist, hugging him.

"So," he said, clearing his voice and pulling

away to hop back to the table, where he sat down and started unlacing his remaining boot. "I guess this means it's pizza for supper."

Next morning, Lucy's friends agreed that husbands and children were not reliable sources of emotional support. That was one reason the four women had continued their weekly Thursday morning breakfasts at Jake's Donut Shop, setting aside time for sharing good things and bad, offering advice, and sometimes simply listening and caring. This morning, Lucy had found her friends reliable as ever, offering sympathy and clean tissues.

"Sara and Zoe never knew Beth, so I didn't expect them to understand," said Lucy, who had wiped her eyes, blown her nose, and recovered enough to take a sip of coffee. "And Bill never much liked her, back when we were dating."

"That's typical, when a romantic relationship becomes serious," said Rachel Goodman, who'd majored in psychology and never got over it. "He would have seen her as a rival for your affection and attention."

"Men have two speeds," said Pam Stillings, whose experience as a cheerleader in high school had given her a rather jaundiced view. "Sex and sports. The rest is uncharted territory for them."

"I still can't get over the fact that she jumped off that terrace. Not after all that plastic surgery you said she'd just had," said Sue, tucking a lock of glossy black hair behind her ear with a freshly manicured hand. Sue was the fashionable member of the group, whose husband, Sid, claimed that he went into the customized closet business when faced with the need to accommodate his wife's ever-expanding wardrobe.

"And now I've got to go to the funeral, which is turning out to be very expensive," said Lucy, looking up as Norine, the waitress, approached with their breakfast orders. "It's not just the airplane ticket; I've got to stay in a hotel. My friend Sam can't put me up. She's having her place renovated."

"Here you go, ladies," said Norine, passing a Sunshine muffin to Rachel, granola-topped yogurt to Pam, and hash and eggs to Lucy. "As for you," she said, giving Sue the evil eye, "I suppose you'll want more coffee."

"If it's no trouble," said Sue, smiling sweetly. As far as Lucy could tell, Sue existed on a diet of black coffee and white wine.

"I'll be back in a mo'," promised Norine, who returned promptly to top off all their cups.

"You know," said Sue, tapping her coffee mug, "I bet you could stay with Sidra. She has a big new place, with a guest room."

"I wouldn't want to impose," said Lucy, who had seen Sue's daughter Sidra grow up, marry, and establish a career as a TV producer in New York.

"She and Geoff would love to have you," said Sue, taking out her cell phone. In a matter of minutes she'd arranged the whole thing, including having Geoff meet Lucy at the airport. "It's no trouble for him," she insisted. "They live in Brooklyn, which is practically next door to LaGuardia."

"Brooklyn?" asked Lucy, whose teen years had been largely spent riding the subway between her home in the Bronx and her high school in Manhattan, and thought of newly fashionable Brooklyn as possibly bordering Outer Mongolia.

"Is that a problem?" asked Sue.

"Oh, no," said Lucy, who had been brought up to never look a gift horse in the mouth. "I'll take the subway." What she didn't mention was the fact that the trip from Brooklyn to St. Andrew's in the northernmost reaches of the Bronx would entail a very long subway ride. "Thanks for setting this up for me."

"No problem," said Sue. "That's what friends are for, and we've been friends for, could it be? Over twenty-five years?"

"Speaking of which," said Pam, scraping the last bit of yogurt with her spoon, "what do you think of Sylvia Bickford's Silver Anniversary Weekend?"

"It seems like years ago," said Lucy, "but I was grocery shopping yesterday afternoon and Sylvia and Warren were there, too. Poor Warren couldn't do anything right. Sylvia was all over him. Dot told me she calls them the Bickersons. It's hard to believe they've stuck together for twenty-five years."

"They're quite a pair," said Pam, smiling naughtily. "Maybe the sex is good."

"I don't want to think about it," said Lucy. "Sylvia and Warren—yuck!"

"Something's holding them together. . . ." began Rachel.

"Yeah, and that something is called business," said Sue. "She's got the bridal shop, he's got the limo service, and this is just a publicity stunt. Renewing their vows and having a fake wedding reception, asking all the ladies in town to parade around in their wedding dresses—clearly mutton dressed as lamb—well, it's absolutely disgusting and I hope nobody falls for it."

"Well, I'm all for it," said Pam. "I pulled out my dress and it still fits! Of course, it's not a traditional white one. I had a sort of orange caftan. We had one of those barefoot-on-the-beach weddings. I'm not at all sure Sylvia will want me to model it for her fashion show." She looked down rather sadly at her empty yogurt bowl. "Oh, well, Ted and I can still go to the reception. What about you guys? Are you all coming? It'll be fun. I'm sure there'll be dancing and cake!"

"I think I'll skip it," said Sue. "I never liked cake."

"What about you, Lucy?"

"I do like cake, which is why my wedding dress no longer fits. . . ."

They all laughed.

"Although in my defense I was a tiny slip of a thing, practically a child when I got married."

"Likely story," scoffed Pam. "What about you, Rachel? You've been strangely silent today."

"Oh, sorry. I've been thinking about friendship and how relationships change through the years, but sometimes there's still a really strong tie, even when people go in separate directions."

"That's true," said Lucy, thinking of Beth.

"And I've been thinking about the Bickersons," continued Rachel. "It's clearly an unhealthy, abusive relationship, and I don't want to celebrate or encourage that sort of marriage. Marriage should be based on respect and shared values, and it should be a partnership of equals. I'm very uncomfortable when I hear one partner picking on the other and I can't imagine how Warren and Sylvia are going to get through this celebration without embarrassing themselves and everybody there. If you ask me, they should take whatever amount they're planning on spending and use it instead to consult a qualified marriage counselor. This so-called Silver Anniversary Weekend is nothing more than a diversion, a way of avoiding the hard work of addressing the problems in their marriage."

"So nobody's going?" asked Pam, disappointed.

"Don't be silly—we'll all be there," declared Sue. "Nobody's going to miss this show."

# Chapter Three

The Friday evening flight from the Portland Jetport to New York's LaGuardia Airport was only supposed to take ninety minutes, but when she added in the extra time needed to get to the airport from Tinker's Cove, park the car, and get through security, it turned out that Lucy had plenty of time to reflect on Beth's life and her untimely death.

With more than an hour on her hands before boarding, Lucy chose a seat in a row of connected black leather chairs, considerately slid her carry-on roller case beneath it, and prepared to wait. She had bought today's *New York Times* to read, intending to acquaint herself with the city's news, but the paper remained folded in her lap, unopened. Ever since she'd learned of Beth's death she had found it hard to concentrate on anything else, and kept playing and replaying the same memories in her mind.

In some ways, she thought, it was like picking at a scab, which behavior, as her mother had frequently reminded her, only served to prevent the wound from healing, and might even cause it to become infected. Beth's death was indeed festering in her mind, bringing all sorts of uncomfortable emotions to the surface.

Regret was a big one. Why hadn't she fought harder to keep her relationship with Beth alive? Why hadn't she done more to keep Beth from joining that crazy cult? Looking back, it was clear that had been the turning point, the moment when their paths began to diverge. Lucy had stayed in college, opting for the safe and conventional, while Beth had veered off into the fringes.

She remembered meeting Gabriel Thomas and had to admit he was very good looking and had a charismatic personality, if you went for that sort of thing. During that time Lucy herself had been a popular coed mostly occupied with fighting off the advances of oversexed frat boys, but she had learned in a comparative religion class that sex, either overtly practiced or strictly repressed and controlled, was an important factor in a number of religions. Hearing this theory, she was quite sure that Miss MacIntyre, her Methodist Sunday School teacher, would have offered a strong rebuttal. But looking back, Lucy doubted that even Miss MacIntyre could have prevented Beth from embracing Gabe's fervent faith, or Gabe himself, for that matter. And, thought Lucy, it was entirely possible that Beth was already pregnant with Dante when she joined the cult.

Once Beth had disappeared into the Angel

Brigade, Lucy had lost all contact with her. She'd
mourned the loss, but she'd also felt resentful at
being suddenly dropped after so many years of
friendship. That resentment had lingered, color-
ing their relationship when Beth emerged, after
about a year, and their on-again, off-again friendship resumed. Beth hadn't offered much information about the cult or her experience there,
preferring to focus instead on her adorable baby,
Dante. Their meetings had been infrequent, but
Lucy remembered some pleasant afternoons spent
with mother and child, often in a park or play-
ground.

It wasn't too long, however, before Beth disappeared again, this time into the artistic underground of Manhattan and the arms of artist Tito
Wilkins. Wilkins was the flavor-of-the-month at the
time, and Beth had enjoyed mingling with celebrities and glitterati at openings and parties. She'd
also enjoyed the easy availability of drugs like co-
caine and heroin, which led to addiction and a
near-fatal overdose. She'd been fresh out of rehab
when she called Lucy, ready once again to renew
their friendship, and by the way wondering if Lucy
wouldn't mind occasionally babysitting Dante.

Lucy hadn't minded. She'd come to accept her
new status as Beth's sometime friend. She was
looking forward to graduation and her upcoming
marriage to Bill and was thinking of starting her
own family. She enjoyed spending time with the
energetic little preschooler, and had been pleased
when Beth began dating Colin Fine, a chiropractor devoted to healthy living and natural foods,
marrying him in a humanistic ceremony at the

Ethical Culture Society. It couldn't last, of course; she should have seen the handwriting on the wall. Dr. Fine was rather like a big bowl of brown rice, good for you but lacking in flavor, especially for someone like Beth, who was used to more exotic fare.

After announcing the divorce, Beth had vowed to Lucy that from now on she was done with marriage. She was going to concentrate on being the best person she could be, if she could only find that person, and was determined to provide Dante with the best upbringing possible. By then Lucy was living in Maine, and Beth had remained in New York City, but they made an effort to get together once or twice a year, occasionally called each other, and exchanged annual Christmas cards with newsy, handwritten notes.

Lucy noticed people around her getting up and realized she must have been so occupied with her thoughts that she missed the call for boarding. She tugged her carry-on out from under the seat and got in line, digging out her ID and boarding pass. Once she'd made her way through the aggressively welcoming gauntlet of unhelpful crew members and found her assigned seat, stowed her case in the overhead bin, and settled into the cramped window seat, she was having second thoughts about this trip. The aisle seat was occupied by a very large man who spilled over onto the dividing armrest, and their nearest neighbor, the woman across the aisle, appeared to be a nervous flyer who was already holding the barf bag.

*Beth, I'm not sure you're worth all this*, thought Lucy, immediately ashamed of herself. It was a short flight and the discomfort was temporary, certainly nothing to compare with whatever hell Beth had been going through when she decided to take her own life. But that was the frustrating part—it was very hard to understand what exactly had been the problem during these last few years of Beth's life. She was married to a billionaire, Jeremy Blake, who doted on her and made sure she had everything any woman could possibly want. There was the penthouse apartment in Manhattan, the house in the Hamptons, the pied-à-terre in Paris, and a private jet to travel between them all. There were servants and daily deliveries of floral bouquets, freshly washed and ironed sheets on the bed every night, huge walk-in closets packed with designer clothes and more Manolos and Louboutins than anyone could possibly wear, and lots of huge bathrooms, bigger than most people's bedrooms. Beth's calendar was packed with charity galas, Broadway openings, and appointments for massages, facials, and coiffures as well as discreet visits to the best plastic surgeon in Manhattan. It was a life that anyone would envy, and Lucy admitted to herself that she'd had a few struggles with that particular green-eyed monster.

Maybe, she thought with a sigh, she'd understand better after this weekend. But for now, she turned her attention to the flight attendant's instructions on how to use the emergency oxygen mask, just in case. She wasn't taking any chances. You never knew when such knowledge might be necessary. The safety lecture at an end, she made sure her seat belt was tight and settled back for takeoff.

Geoff Dunford was waiting for her when she got off the plane, dressed in a flannel shirt and jeans. It seemed you could take the boy out of Maine, but not the Maine out of the boy. He was the principal of a highly regarded charter school that focused on science, but Lucy couldn't help seeing him as the kid who was always roaming the woods around Tinker's Cove, studying birds and fishes and everything that moved.

"How was your flight?" he asked, taking her roller bag.

"Cramped," admitted Lucy, who had been greatly relieved when the lady with the barf bag managed to avoid using it. "Thanks for meeting me. You must have better things to do on Friday night."

"Not really," he said, with a smile. "Sidra usually has a project for me. We're trying to turn our little patch of yard into a garden. So far I've dug up a couple of old tires, numerous concrete blocks, and a bedpan."

"You should get your brother down to help," suggested Lucy, referring to Fred Dunford, an archaeology professor at Winchester College, the liberal arts college in Tinker's Cove. "Tell him it's an opportunity to research urban life."

"I tried," admitted Geoff, leading the way to the parking garage. "I'm afraid he saw right through me."

"That's the trouble with siblings; they know you too well."

Traffic was light and they made good time in Geoff's little Fiat, though Lucy found the car's small size rather unnerving. She was used to tooling around the back roads of Maine in her compact SUV, which was huge compared to the Fiat. Parking took a bit of time, as Geoff searched for a spot, but that gave her a chance to get a sense of the neighborhood. The narrow streets were lit by streetlamps, a rarity in Maine, and she could see that they were lined with brownstone town houses, some of which still had quaint gaslights burning in their tiny front yards, and there were lots of trees. When a spot opened up, Geoff quickly swerved into it, which Lucy realized was one of the advantages of a small car. She could never have fit her CRV into a spot that small.

"We're right across the street," he announced, a note of triumph in his voice. "And this spot is good until eleven a.m. Tuesday, so I hope Sidra doesn't have any weekend plans that involve driving." How ridiculous, thought Lucy, to have the expense of maintaining a car but not feel able to use it for fear of losing a parking spot.

Moments later they were ducking under the stoop of a newly renovated brownstone and entering the "garden level" apartment, which Lucy thought was a rather precious way of referring to the basement. Geoff paused in the entrance and removed his shoes, adding them to a rather large collection that was neatly stowed in a wooden cubby. Lucy followed his example, which she guessed was one way of coping with the city's dirty streets.

Then the door opened and they stepped into a light, bright space where she was welcomed by Sidra with air kisses on both cheeks. Sidra had inherited her mother's good looks and a good deal of her furniture, thought Lucy, glancing around and recognizing several pieces.

"Are you hungry? Thirsty? What can I get you?" asked Sidra. She was freshly showered and dressed in an oversized T-shirt and yoga pants, without makeup and her damp hair combed back in a simple, short style.

"Nothing, thanks," said Lucy, struggling to stifle a yawn.

"You're tired," said Sidra. "I'll give you a quick tour and show you your room, okay?"

"Sounds perfect."

The apartment was roomier than Lucy expected, with exposed brick walls in the large living and dining area. A compact kitchen was tucked beside a long hall, which led to two bedrooms. The larger contained a double bed and a couple of dressers, the smaller guest room was only large enough for a futon, lit by a pin-up lamp on the wall. The hall also contained a large closet with a stacked washer and dryer. "That's what sold us on this place," said Sidra. "Now we don't have to go to the laundromat."

"You mean I don't have to go to the laundromat," teased Geoff.

"Well, admit it, Geoff. You love these machines."

Lucy couldn't help smiling, amused by the couple's enthusiasm for what appeared to her to be very tiny, toy-like appliances. Back home in Maine she had heavy duty machines with extra-large capacity, able to deal with Bill's filthy work clothes.

"And here's the bathroom," announced Sidra, flinging open the door to a truly tiny space, where the toilet was squeezed next to, and almost beneath, a pedestal sink. "With a full-size tub," proclaimed Sidra, proudly. "And it's all yours for the next twenty minutes."

"Sidra's on a tight schedule," explained Geoff. "She has to get to bed by nine-thirty at the latest for her job." Lucy knew Sidra was a producer for an early-morning news show and had to get up very early.

"It's so boring, I know, but if I stay up late on the weekend it throws me off," she said.

"I understand," said Lucy, who had learned the value of a good night's sleep when her kids were small. "I'll be quick."

"I'll stow your case in the guest room," said Geoff.

Lucy was good as her word, taking only a few minutes to use the toilet, brush her teeth, and wash her face before tucking herself into bed in her tiny room. There was something odd about it, she thought, looking around as she opened her book. Suddenly she had it: there was no window. There couldn't be. The apartment was in a row house, with other houses on either side, which meant there could only be windows in the front and the back. For a moment she struggled with claustrophobia, hoping there was enough oxygen to sustain life through the night in the windowless room. Oh, to be in Maine, where her house had two full baths as well as a powder room and the pine-scented breeze blew through the open windows and lifted her gauzy bedroom curtains. Setting her book aside, she clung to that image as she turned off the light and closed her eyes.

Next morning there were no instructions about the bathroom. There wasn't even any sign of Geoff or Sidra, so Lucy indulged in a long shower. When she emerged from the bathroom the young couple had returned and were sitting at the kitchen table in running clothes and drinking coffee from take-out cups.

"We usually go for a long run in Prospect Park on Saturdays," said Geoff, as Sidra hopped up and claimed the bathroom. "We got you some coffee—I hope black's okay. We weren't sure how you take it."

"Thank you." Lucy took Sidra's vacant chair and wrapped her hands around the cup containing the magical elixir. "Black is perfect. Just what I need."

"What time is the funeral?" asked Geoff.

"Eleven."

"How are you getting there?"

"Subway, I guess."

He glanced at the clock, which read a few minutes before nine. "You'd better get a move on, then. It's going to be a long ride."

Lucy took her coffee into her room, where she sipped at it while dressing in her funeral clothes: black pants, a black and white polka dot shirt, and a gray blazer. A pair of pearl earrings and plain pumps completed her outfit.

She carried the empty cup back to the kitchen to put it in the recycling bin, and saw that Sidra was back at the table. "Where's the nearest subway station?"

"On the corner—you can't miss it," she replied. "Will you be back for lunch? Or dinner?"

"Dinner. I'd love to take you guys out, if you'd like."

"Thanks, Lucy. We're going to work in the garden so that would be great. Oh, and Geoff says you're taking the subway, so here's my pass. I won't need it today."

"Thanks," said Lucy, taking the bit of bright yellow plastic. "See you later."

Stepping out to the street, Lucy discovered it was a gentle spring morning, with the newly leafed trees creating dappled shade on the sidewalk. She quickly spotted the subway entrance and walked toward it, wondering what connections she would need to get to the church in the Bronx.

Descending the stairs, she was assailed by the smell of the subway, a mix of soot and who knows what all—maybe it was ozone—produced by the electrically charged third rail. Lucy was no stranger to the New York subway; she'd taken it from the Bronx to Manhattan every weekday when she was in high school. She was surprised, however, to discover that it hadn't changed since then. The station was in poor repair, with broken and stained tiles on the walls, and a couple of the same scarred, heavy wooden benches she remembered occasionally sitting on. There were never enough for everyone and even if she managed to grab a seat, which only happened during the afternoon ride home when there were fewer commuters than during the morning rush hour, she usually had to give it up to a pregnant woman or an elderly person.

The train rolled into the station, the brakes screaming as they always did, and she stepped aboard. It was pretty empty—she knew it would fill up as it got closer to Manhattan—and she was able to sit opposite the illuminated map that indicated the train's progress toward Bleecker Street, where she would change to the 6, then change again at Union Square for the 5. It was amazing, she thought, how millions of people had used the subway system through the years. Her mother and father, her grandparents even, had ridden the subway and it was still the same. If by some miracle she could resurrect Poppop, he would be able to count off the stations along the way to Woodlawn. The decades passed, the people came and went, and the subway trains rattled on as they always had.

The subway had become an elevated line in the Bronx and Lucy descended a long flight of iron stairs at the Nereid Avenue station. The elevated structure shaded the street below, and as she crossed the street she noticed the little storefronts of the bodegas, liquor stores, and newsagents clustered around the station. Then she stepped out into the sunlight, following the path she'd trodden so often in her youth to Katonah Avenue, which led to the church at 241st Street.

She had been christened and made her confirmation in St. Andrew's, had the papers to prove it, and she had a clear memory of attending Summer Bible School there and playing the Farmer in the Dell. She'd been the cheese, standing all alone, and she hadn't liked it one bit. Now, she thought, the little stone church seemed a bit shabby—the woodwork needed a fresh coat of paint and the stone could use some pointing. These were tough times for traditional denominations and she assumed the congregation had shrunk since the days when her family worshiped there. But today, Beth's funeral was drawing a large crowd and Lucy joined the line of mourners entering the church.

Once inside she smiled at the huge stained glass window of Jesus suffering the little children to come to him; as a kid she always wondered why he was supposed to be suffering. He seemed perfectly pleased, dressed in lovely robes with his longish blond hair styled into a pageboy and his blond beard neatly trimmed, surrounded by a group of small children and woolly lambs.

"Lucy! You made it!" exclaimed her friend Sam Blackwell, giving her a big hug. "We saved you a seat—we're right down front."

Sam had put on some weight, but her head of flaming red hair remained as bright as ever, without a trace of gray. Lucy followed her down the aisle to the pew where Sam's husband, Brad, was sitting, saving seats for them with the printed orders of service. Lucy picked hers up and paused, struck by the photo of Beth on the front.

"I still can't believe it," she whispered to Sam as they sat down.

"I know," agreed Sam as the organist began playing the prelude.

The service was brief and impersonal, a few prayers and hymns, a short eulogy that could have described almost anyone, delivered by a very young minister, and then they were all on their feet singing the final hymn, "Amazing Grace." As is customary, the congregation waited for the principal mourners to leave the church, and that's when Lucy got a glimpse of Jeremy Blake, Beth's billionaire husband.

He looked exactly like a billionaire ought to look: tall and fit, well-groomed with a full head of wavy hair, expensively clad in a very white shirt, subdued gray tie, and a charcoal gray suit that fit so perfectly it had to have been tailor-made. He walked alone, occasionally giving a somber nod to someone he recognized, followed by a prosperous-looking group that Lucy presumed were family members. The only person she recognized was Dante, who had grown into a handsome young man. He bore a slight resemblance to his father, as Lucy remembered Gabe, but he definitely got those dimples and hazel eyes from Beth. Whatever he was doing, she thought, he must be doing well, as he was wearing a designer suit that was almost as well-tailored as Jeremy Blake's.

Nearing the end of the aisle, Dante caught up with Jeremy and tapped him on the shoulder. Blake whirled around, glared at him for a moment, and then marched off before Dante could say a word, effectively cutting him dead.

Many people had witnessed the interaction and there was a shared reaction, gasps of shock and hushed murmurs of disapproval, that traveled through the church. Then people picked up their things and began making their way out, pausing to offer consolations to Dante and thanking the minister. As for Jeremy Blake, he was noticeably absent.

# Chapter Four

Lucy didn't have much time with Dante, due to the crowd of mourners, so she offered the usual consolatory "I'm so sorry," but in a sudden surge of emotion managed to add, "I've known you since you were in diapers. I can't replace your mom but I'm happy to try. You've got my number." Dante reacted by hugging her warmly and thanking her, and then he turned to greet the people behind her.

Lucy caught up with Sam and Brad, who were waiting for her on the sidewalk. Since there had been no invitation to a reception following the service, Sam suggested they grab some lunch on nearby McLean Avenue. Brad made his apologies, saying he had a big case coming up on Monday and needed to work. "Besides, you two probably have a lot of catching up to do and I'd be a third wheel."

"See you later," said Sam, offering her cheek for a quick parting peck.

"There used to be a good pizza place," suggested Lucy, as the two old friends walked along. "Do you mind? I miss New York pizza up in Maine. Pizza there's okay, but it's not the same."

"Fine with me," agreed Sam. "Funerals always make me hungry."

"I wonder why they didn't have a collation afterward, as we call it in Maine. Funerals are very popular in Tinker's Cove, and you've got to have a pretty lavish spread or people will talk."

"Even the service was pretty minimal and impersonal. I could've given pretty much the same eulogy for my cat."

For the first time that day, Lucy laughed. "Golly, you're terrible."

"Well, it's true," insisted Sam, defending herself as they turned the corner onto McLean Avenue. Lucy was happy to see the pizza place was still there, and when they stepped inside she was greeted with the heavenly scent of tomato sauce, heavy on the oregano.

The two friends ordered a large, with pepperoni, and sat down at a table with Diet Cokes to wait for it to come out of the oven. Lucy looked around the pizza place, amazed at how little it had changed. The tables appeared to be the same worn Formica, the benches were covered in red Naugahyde, repaired here and there with duct tape, and the same huge painting of smoking Mount Vesuvius still hung on the wall. One thing was different, however: the prices. Pizza was now a lot more expensive than she remembered.

"So, Lucy, how are the kids?" asked Sam, running her hand through her curly hair.

"Everybody's great, but we don't see much of Elizabeth or Toby. Elizabeth's still off in Paris. She's an assistant concierge at the Cavendish Hotel there."

"Oh, to be young," said Sam, sipping her cola.

"Toby's married, and he and Molly have a little boy, Patrick. He's my only grandchild, so far, and he's far away in Alaska. Toby's researching salmon propagation, something like that, and Molly's working as a teacher's aide." Lucy sighed. "I really wish I could see more of Patrick, but we do Skype once a week."

"It's not the same. . . ."

"No, it's not, but it's all I've got, unless I can convince them to send him back to me for the summer. So far that's not happening."

"You could go to Alaska."

"I'm working on it." Lucy popped the top on her can of cola. "Sara and Zoe are still home. They're both at Westminster College. Townies get a discounted tuition, and since they're living at home we don't have room and board expenses." Lucy paused, screwing up her mouth. "That's not exactly true—they're eating me out of house and home with their organic this and all-natural that."

Sam smiled. "What are they studying?"

"Sara's doing graduate work in geology and Zoe hasn't really picked a major. I think she's going to end up with a degree in communications or something like that. So what about you? They haven't managed to shut down Planned Parenthood yet?"

"Not yet, but they're sure trying," said Sam, who was an executive director. "I've been working hard on fund-raising, just in case. But there's no question we'll have to cut back on services if we lose federal funding. It's a disgrace, really, because we're the only provider for cancer screenings and contraceptives for a lot of low income women."

"I remember that gala fund-raiser we went to all those years ago," said Lucy, remembering a special charity event at the Metropolitan Museum of Art. "That was so amazing."

"It sure was," agreed Sam. "But sad to say, my focus is now on grant writing. Not nearly as much fun."

They looked up as a good-looking young kid wearing a white apron over his T-shirt and jeans delivered their pizza.

"I've missed this. I dream of this," said Lucy, pulling a huge triangular piece loose and folding it in half, New York style, so she could bite off the pointy end. She took a bite and closed her eyes, sighing with pleasure. "Soooo gooood."

Sam laughed. "It's funny what you miss, when you leave the city. I always get a strange longing for the subway. The smell, the rattle of the trains, the dingy stations and that screeching noise the brakes make."

"Me too," admitted Lucy. "Bill doesn't understand it at all."

"Neither does Brad." Sam took a bite of pizza. "You know, he handled all of Beth's divorces, including this last one, from Jeremy Blake. It wasn't finalized—it was still in the works. I assume it was pretty complicated, considering his wealth, but Brad never talks about his cases with me."

"Did you see much of Beth?" Lucy was reaching for her second piece.

"For a long time I didn't, but one day a year or so ago she called me up at work, out of the blue, saying she wanted to become involved. She made a big donation and she also started volunteering. She did a lot of fund-raising, but she also helped out in one of our clinics, escorting clients through the antiabortion protestors."

"Wow. That's real frontline stuff."

"It isn't easy, that's for sure. Some of those people are very, um, vehement. I thought she'd do it once and that would be it, but she was one of our most faithful volunteers."

"What do you think caused this change? Back in college she was never one for social action, unless you consider a frat party social activism."

Sam chuckled. "So true. I think maybe she got more reflective, looking back on her life. This was divorce number four, you know, and I imagine she was beginning to think she'd spent too much of her life depending on men to define her. She dropped a few hints—nothing precise, mind you— but she told me she'd learned the hard way not to trust men. They were always hiding something, she said."

"Like what?" Lucy was considering eating a third piece of pizza and thinking that she really shouldn't.

"We could split another piece," suggested Sam, reading her mind.

"Okay." Lucy got up and asked the guy behind the counter for a knife, which he gave to her.

When they were each started on their half slice, Lucy returned to her question. "What did Beth think her husbands were hiding? Affairs?"

"Maybe, probably. But I think it was other stuff, too. Gabe, the cult guy, could've been doing just about anything, right? He exerted a lot of power over the Angels, and he never struck me as being saintly, to say the least. Then there was Tito Wilkins, the artist. He came straight out of the 'hood,' complete with gang tattoos."

"Okay, but what about the chiropractor? He was so boring. . . ."

"Dr. Colin Fine. Beth used to call him 'Dr. Colonoscopy' because he had a fixation with her, well, um . . ."

"I get it," said Lucy, after struggling to swallow a mouthful of cola while laughing. "What about the billionaire? Blake?"

"Well," said Sam, leaning closer across the table and lowering her voice, "I happened to overhear Brad talking with Beth one night and he was saying she was asking for too large a settlement. He seemed really uncomfortable and withdrawn afterward, like he was troubled about it, and I don't think it was just about the money. He's used to shaking people down all the time, going after big settlements for malpractice or fraud or whatever. It's usually the bigger the better, but he was cautioning her, telling her it was a dangerous game, messing with someone like Blake."

Lucy felt a chill run down her back, and she knew the air conditioning wasn't on yet. "You don't think . . ."

"I don't know what to think. Jeremy Blake sure didn't seem overcome with grief this morning."

"Well, they were in the midst of a divorce. You could hardly expect him to be heartbroken."

"And he's saving a lot of money now that she's dead and he doesn't need the divorce."

"But he's really rich," said Lucy. She wasn't ready to let go of the fantasy she'd nurtured about Beth's life as the pampered wife of a billionaire, the life she'd sometimes envied, especially when she was struggling with the monthly bills. "He could afford dozens of divorces."

"Trust me," said Sam, a steely glint in her green eyes. "Jeremy Blake loves money more than anything or anyone. That's how he got to be a billionaire and that's how he's going to stay a billionaire."

"You don't really think he pushed her off the balcony, do you? Just to save a couple of million dollars?"

"Doesn't matter what I think. The cops have determined that Beth was alone in the apartment, so it had to be either suicide or a tragic accident," admitted Sam, pausing to wipe her mouth with a paper napkin. "What they didn't take into account is the pressure she was under from Blake that could have driven her to do something desperate. He might not be legally guilty, but I do believe he bears some responsibility for her death."

"Point taken." Lucy was thoughtful, staring at the three remaining pieces of pizza. "Do you want them?"

"Brad might like them for a late night snack."

"You take them then." She smiled ruefully. "You'll be saving me from myself."

Sam waved the waiter over and asked him to box up the leftovers. She gathered up her handbag and scarf, then turned to Lucy. "How are you getting back to Brooklyn? I've got my car and can give you a lift to midtown."

"That would be great." Lucy sighed with relief. "It took me close to two hours to get here, which included a rather long walk from the station. And I have to admit, the actual experience of riding the subway didn't quite match my nostalgic memories."

Lucy still had a fairly long subway ride after Sam dropped her off at Grand Central, and plenty of time to think about the funeral and mull over Sam's theories. As the train rattled through the dark underground tunnel she struggled to understand the pressure that Beth was under from her husband. Was she like some nineteenth-century tragic heroine, say Madame Bovary, who was deep in debt? Or maybe, like Anna Karenina, she had an illicit affair? Those stories took place in a different time, when morals were much more rigid. These days, attitudes about affairs and debts were more relaxed. Even a criminal conviction and a jail sentence, like Martha Stewart's, was just a bump on the road to even more success and wealth.

The train finally screeched to a halt at Seventh Avenue and Lucy got off and made her way through the long, tiled tunnel to the exit. Climbing the stairs to the sidewalk above, she concluded that the person most likely to provide insight about Beth's final days was her son, Dante. She'd love to have a good long talk with him, but how? She realized she had no idea how to contact him;

she'd called Beth's number when she spoke to him. She didn't even know where he lived. He could have flown into the city from anywhere. And if she did manage to get a message to him, say through the church or the funeral director, would he really want to talk about his mother with her? Would he be ready to speak openly about such a painful loss, or was it too soon?

Lucy had almost reached the corner of Thirteenth Street when she paused to admire the display of fresh flowers in front of a small bodega, one of the little neighborhood shops that sold almost everything anyone could need: groceries, toilet paper, newspapers, and magazines. She decided to buy a bouquet for Sidra and chose an enormous bunch of mixed flowers, amazed at the low price. In the city, it seemed, the things you had to have, like toilet paper, were expensive, but luxuries, like fresh flowers, were cheap.

Geoff and Sidra were both home when Lucy arrived at the brownstone, and Sidra was only too happy to abandon the IKEA bookshelf they were attempting to assemble and take a break to put the flowers in water. "Thanks, Lucy. These are just gorgeous."

"I can't get over the flowers," said Lucy, slipping off her good shoes and adding them to the collection by the door. "There seems to be a huge display on every corner."

"Well, you certainly chose wisely. I love lilies and hydrangeas." Sidra was fussing with the blooms, arranging them to suit her style. "Do you want something? Coffee? Tea?"

"A glass of water would be lovely." Lucy sat down

at the bistro table and wiggled her stockinged toes. She usually wore sneakers and wasn't used to walking long distances in heels.

"How was the funeral?" Sidra placed a tall glass of cold Pellegrino on the table for Lucy.

"Okay. It was sad, of course." Lucy took a long drink. "If it was supposed to provide closure, I'd have to say it was a big failure. I feel more confused now than ever."

Sidra put the vase of flowers on the table and took the other bistro chair. "Was Jeremy Blake there?"

"Oh, yes. So was her son, Dante. He tried to speak to Blake, but Blake brushed him off. No love lost there."

"Blake's an occasional guest on the show, you know. The makeup girls call him 'Hands' because he can't keep his off them. He even asked one to lunch in a hotel room."

"A working lunch?" quipped Lucy.

"He promised champagne."

"Did she go?"

"No. She told him she doesn't take lunch so she can leave early to get home to her kids. She said that mentioning the kids kind of cooled him down."

"Why do they have him on the show? I thought he was in real estate."

"He's newsworthy, involved in a lot of charities. Lately he's been doing a lot with the Central Park Conservancy, restoring some of the structures in the park."

"So he does have a conscience. My friend Sam doesn't seem to think such a thing possible."

Sidra smiled ruefully. "He doesn't do it out of the goodness of his heart. It's good PR and a big tax deduction for him."

"You New Yorkers are all so cynical," observed Lucy.

"And lazy, to boot," added Geoff, handing Sidra an Allen wrench. "I'll hold the shelf while you screw."

"Geoff loves it when I screw," said Sidra, smiling naughtily as she got up from the table. "Was Dante at the funeral?"

Lucy leapt on the question. "Do you know him?"

"Sure." Sidra was on her knees, busily twirling the little wrench. "Everybody knows Dante. Just the one name. Like Beyoncé. In fact, he does a great imitation of Beyoncé."

"Dante does?" Lucy pictured the slim young man in the tailored suit she'd seen at the funeral and tried to imagine him decked out in one of Beyoncé's minimal, sexy costumes. She failed.

"He sure does. He's got a terrifically successful act impersonating all the divas. People flock to see him. I think he's performing at the Ridgway bar."

"He probably won't be performing tonight, right after his mother's funeral. . . ."

"I can find out." Sidra hopped up and pulled out her phone, quickly reaching the hotel and asking if the show was going on as scheduled. "He's on at nine and eleven tonight."

"I don't suppose you could stay up late and go with me?" asked Lucy. "I'd really like to see him."

Sidra was reluctant, and gave Geoff a questioning look that seemed to say, "How about it?"

"Don't look at me," he protested. "Female impersonators are not my thing."

Sidra sighed. "I've heard he's fabulous and I've never seen him, and I can probably get comped if I say I'm from the TV show." She shrugged. "Actually, it's a good idea. I don't know why we haven't had him on."

"Great." Lucy's expression grew puzzled and a hand flew to her mouth. "What should I wear?"

Lucy had heard of the Ridgway bar, with its famous murals picturing Dorothy Parker, Ernest Hemingway, and F. Scott Fitzgerald among other twentieth century literati, but she'd never been there. It was tucked away in the exclusive Ridgway Hotel, located on a quiet residential street off Lexington Avenue. Places like the Ridgway always made her feel uncomfortable, as if someone with $1532.67 in her checking account didn't really belong in such a ritzy place, but the doorman greeted her as if she were indeed a member of the one percent. She figured it was because she was accompanied by Sidra, who had inherited her mother Sue's unerring taste in clothes, as well as her confidence. It was Sidra who had transformed Lucy's funeral suit into an evening outfit with the loan of a sparkly sequined top.

Sidra's attitude upon entering the lounge, where she paused and glanced around as if she were the queen reviewing the troops and not finding them quite up to snuff, got them a desirable table next to the stage. After they were seated and had ordered their herb-infused martinis, Sidra filled Lucy in on Dante's act.

"You never know who he's going to be impersonating—that's part of the attraction," Sidra said. "I read in *New York* magazine that he sometimes doesn't even decide until a few minutes before the show, depending on his mood. Beyoncé is a big favorite, but he does Katy Perry, Marilyn Monroe, Liza Minnelli, all the divas. I wonder who we'll see tonight."

"I guess performing is an escape of sorts," suggested Lucy, who was struggling to understand how Dante could manage to face an audience on the same day he buried his mother.

"You know what they say—the show must go on." After Sidra bestowed a smile on the waiter who delivered their drinks, she tapped glasses with Lucy. "To life."

"To life," repeated Lucy, taking a cautious sip of her drink. She rarely drank anything as strong as a martini and was wishing she'd stuck to her guns and ordered a familiar glass of chardonnay.

The lights dimmed and Judy Garland appeared on stage—at least that's how it seemed. The handsome young man she'd seen earlier that day at the funeral had somehow transformed himself into the fragile waif with a big voice. The lounge fell silent as the people in the crowded room took a moment to realize that Judy Garland had not risen from the grave, but had instead been recreated by a supremely talented performer. Suddenly, everyone was on their feet, welcoming Dante with a standing ovation.

The set flew by as Dante flawlessly performed

Garland's beloved tunes, one after another, accompanied by a small band. The act sometimes bordered on caricature as he mimicked Garland's awkward stance and jerky movements, but the audience got the joke and loved every minute, often laughing, and always applauding loudly after each number. Then the mood became somber as the stage was darkened, save for a single glowing lightbulb dangling from a cord. Dante stood beneath it, partly in shadow, and said simply that "this song is for someone special who is now no longer with me." He then sang, very simply and without affectation, "Somewhere over the Rainbow." Everyone in the room, audience and servers alike, was riveted and quite a few people had to dab their eyes. Then it was over. The applause was thunderous, but Dante had left the stage without taking a bow. Only that dangling lightbulb remained.

"Wow," was all Lucy could say, as she struggled with her emotions. What a filthy, rotten shame that Beth couldn't see her son's amazing performance in her honor. Now was too late. It was wrong. It wasn't fair. She wished with all her might that Beth wasn't dead.

"That was extraordinary," said Sidra, pulling her out of her thoughts.

"I really want to talk to Dante, but maybe this isn't the time. . . ."

"Let's try," said Sidra, signaling a nearby waiter. "Could you possibly do me a huge favor?" she asked, pressing a twenty-dollar bill into the waiter's hand. "I'd so appreciate it if you'd let Dante know that an old friend, Lucy Stone, is here tonight."

"It will be my pleasure." He nodded and disappeared, returning a few moments later and offering to escort them backstage.

Lucy and Sidra followed him, walking down a narrow hallway lined with boxes of liquor and other supplies, eventually reaching a black door with a glittery star hung askew and fastened with masking tape. The waiter knocked, a male voice yelled "Come in," and they stepped inside a small room where most of the space was taken up by racks of glamorous costumes. In the rear, seated before a mirrored dressing table, they found Dante, sans wig and dressed in tight bike shorts and a T-shirt. He was wiping the makeup off his face, but quickly dried his hands with a towel and stood up.

"That was an absolutely amazing performance," said Lucy, as he engulfed her in a big hug. "It's so good to see you." She stepped back and studied the face she'd known since he was a baby, noticing the dark circles beneath his eyes. "God, this must be awful for you."

"Pretty bad," admitted Dante, turning to acknowledge Sidra.

Lucy was quick to offer an introduction. "This is my friend Sidra Dunford. I'm staying with her and her husband in Brooklyn."

Dante smiled politely and took her hand. "Nice to meet you, Sidra."

"Same here." Sidra returned his smile and got right to business. "Actually, I've been trying to meet you for some time. I produce *Rise and Shine America* and I'd love to have you on the show. Not necessarily right away—I know this isn't a good time—but sometime. Keep it in mind."

Dante was nodding, clearly interested. "I will," he promised, taking her card.

"I don't want to keep you. I know you have to get ready for another set," said Lucy in an apologetic tone. She suddenly felt as if she was being an intrusive nuisance. "I just wanted to stop by and let you know . . ." She paused, not knowing what to say. Finally, she blurted out, "Oh, gosh, is there any chance we could have a real talk, maybe tomorrow?"

He nodded. "Sure. I'd like that. Brunch tomorrow? I usually treat myself to a big Sunday breakfast at Kasanof's. Do you know where it is?"

Lucy knew the famous deli. "Great. What time?"

"I usually go around ten, to beat the crowd."

"I'll see you then." Lucy impulsively hugged him. Sidra smiled a good-bye, and they left.

"You know, I think that was a one-time thing, the Judy Garland tribute," said Sidra, as they exited out the back door. "I bet that costume gets put away forever."

"Why do you think that? It was a fantastic performance."

"Yeah, but he'd taken off the wig and costume and was removing the makeup, even though he still has another set. I think he'll do a different character at eleven."

"That was really special." Lucy's voice broke. "It was for his mom."

"Yeah."

Sunday morning and Lucy was back on the subway, eerily empty of the weekday crowds as the train rattled along carrying her and a handful of others into Manhattan. Kasanof's Deli was on Third Avenue, in the Upper East Side, a stubborn holdout against encroaching designer boutiques. Lucy could never quite understand the appeal of the place, which was frankly rather grubby and run down. It was known for its sandwiches, especially the pastrami, which was piled four inches high on enormous slabs of rye bread with a slice of sour pickle on the side. Lucy didn't approve of such excess, especially so early in the day, and ordered black coffee and a toasted everything bagel with butter.

"Buttah?" inquired the chubby, gray-haired waiter, sounding as if he'd never heard of such a thing. "No schmeer?"

"No schmeer," repeated Lucy, smiling at the Yiddish word for cream cheese. "Butter."

"Okay." He shrugged. "Have it your way."

Lucy settled in at her table by the window, watching the occasional passerby and keeping an eye out for Dante. Dressed in jeans and a Yankees sweatshirt, he arrived just as the waiter delivered her coffee.

"Sorry I'm late," he said, taking the other chair.

"You're not late—I was early."

The waiter had stayed at the table, recognizing a regular customer. "The usual?" he asked, and after getting a nod from Dante, he offered his condolences. "We're all sorry about your mother; she was a real lady."

"Thanks, Irving."

"I'll be back with your coffee in a mo'."

"Great." Dante turned to Lucy. "I've been coming here for ages. I don't know what I'd do if it closed. It's my Sunday morning ritual."

"You don't go to church? What would your father say?" Lucy knew it was a provocative question, since his father was the cult leader Gabriel Thomas.

"No way." Dante shook his head. "I don't remember anything about my father or the Angel Brigade. I was only a babe in arms when Mom managed to get away. That's how she always said it, like she'd escaped from a really bad situation. She had nothing but scorn for religion, any religion. She said they were all the same, all about control." He shrugged. "Far as I know, he's still terrifying people with fire and brimstone sermons."

Lucy was thoughtful. "I'm a little surprised he let her go. Didn't he try to get her back?"

The waiter set down a mug of coffee for Dante and said their orders would be up in a sec.

"I think she must've had something on Father Gabe." Dante added some cream to his coffee and gave it a stir. "I was about eight I think, something like that, when I found a stamped letter addressed to the *New York Times*. We were packing to move— one of Mom's many moves—and it was taped to the back of a mirror. I asked her about it and she said it was an insurance policy. She tore it up, said she didn't need it anymore. That was when she was leaving Tito, the artist. Happiest day of my life."

"Why was that?"

"He was a filthy pig. We all lived in this squalid loft in Soho. This was before it was fashionable, long before. The streets were full of litter and discarded syringes . . . there was graffiti everywhere. The place was a shambles. Of course Mom had enrolled me in a fancy uptown Montessori school and all the other kids lived in regular apartments with normal moms and dads." He laughed. "You might not believe this, but I was a very conservative little guy. I kept my toys in a certain way and if they got moved I got really upset. I'd only eat peanut butter and jelly for lunch, no crusts, cut into perfect squares. I guess I had it every day for a decade or more."

Dante smiled as the waiter delivered his order, a huge platter filled with a mushroom omelet, bacon and sausage, hash browns, and a smaller plate piled with several slices of toasted challah bread. He also had Lucy's bagel, accompanied with a couple of squares of foil-wrapped butter.

"Gosh, I shouldn't eat all this," said Dante, lifting his fork and spearing a sausage.

"You must burn a lot of calories on stage." Lucy buttered her bagel and took a bite.

"Not enough. I run, too." Dante was moving on to the fried potatoes.

"So what happened after Tito? Beth married the chiropractor, right?"

"Dr. Colin. I thought he was going to be great. We moved to Riverdale, up in the Bronx, and I went to public school, which I loved. We went everywhere in lines. The desks were in neat rows, and we had spelling tests and multiplication drills. The only problem was the doctor—what a freak. Poor Mom. He had Mom constantly scrubbing and washing. The apartment smelled of Clorox. It was too much even for me, and I was really into being clean and neat. If anything was out of place, if you forgot to take off your shoes, all hell broke loose. He'd go into a tirade."

"As I recall, that marriage didn't last too long."

"No, thank goodness." Dante cut into his omelet, releasing a stream of melted cheese dotted with mushroom bits. "That was a good time. It was just Mom and me. She got a job in fund-raising at the Bronx Zoo. I used to stop by after school and wander around, looking at the animals and waiting for her to get out at five. Then, when I was older, I got into a performing arts high school. For the first time in my life I finally felt as if I was in the right place, that I belonged."

Lucy was biting into the second half of her huge bagel, the half she had vowed she would not eat. "And then came Jeremy Blake?"

"He came on the scene when I was in college, up-state. If I'd been around more I could've warned her." He bit into a piece of bacon. "No, that's not quite fair. I had high hopes for her happiness, at first. It was like a fairy story, you know. The handsome prince, with his high-rise castle on Lexington Avenue."

"I admit, I was pretty jealous." Lucy signaled for more coffee. "There I'd be, struggling to pay the mortgage, and she'd call from Paris or some other fabulous place. It was Thailand that really rankled. She was going on about the birds and flowers and I was snowbound with a case of the flu."

Dante nodded. "I know. Same here. I was in the snowbelt, freezing on my way to class, and she'd send me these postcards of fabulous beaches."

"What about vacations?" asked Lucy, as the waiter refilled their cups. "Didn't you get to join her?"

"She'd invite me but I never really took to Jeremy. I went once and I saw the way he treated people. He was obnoxious and overbearing. . . ."

"I saw the way he brushed you off at the service yesterday."

"That's how he is." Dante shrugged. "I don't think there was ever a real relationship between them. He got a beautiful wife, a social asset, and she got rich. It's no wonder she slipped into depression."

"So you think it was suicide?" asked Lucy, in a soft voice.

Dante shook his head. "No way. She'd never do that." He leveled his hazel eyes on Lucy's. "About a year ago I tried to get her into treatment and I told her I was afraid of losing her and she promised me—she said I shouldn't worry, that she'd never do anything crazy, like suicide. That's what she said and I believed her." He paused, looking around at the shabby deli, with its worn linoleum floor, the discolored walls, and the framed photos of celebrities and politicians hung every which way, and took a deep breath. "I still believe her." He smiled, blinking hard. "She wasn't perfect, not by a long shot, but she never lied to me. Never."

"But if she didn't kill herself, that means somebody must have killed her."

"Exactly." Dante raised his eyebrows and nodded.

"Aren't the cops investigating? Your mom was a high profile person; her death got a lot of press.

The police would be under a lot of pressure to conduct a thorough investigation."

"That's what they claim, but you can't always believe them." He paused and pulled out his wallet, producing a business card. "The investigating detective gave me this," he said, pushing it across the table.

"Don't you want it?" Lucy picked up the card, which had Detective Lieutenant Tim McGuire's name printed on it, along with his precinct and contact info.

He shook his head. "Never trust a cop. That's what Tito always used to say, and I think he was right." He snorted. "Only on that one thing, mind you. Everything else was crap."

Lucy smiled, tucking the card into her pocket. "I hope you'll stay in touch, let me know how you're doing."

Dante gave her a dubious glance. "That sounds suspiciously like a promise you must have made to my mother."

"Nope. I've always been fond of you, ever since you were in diapers. And I can't help it—I admit it—I have this strong mothering urge."

He stood and gave her a hug. "Well, thanks. You can be my de facto mom."

"You've got a deal," she said, returning the hug.

Lucy thought over what Dante had told her as she walked toward Lexington Avenue and the subway, and found she wasn't as convinced as he was of Beth's honesty. There had been times when

Beth lied to her, mostly little fibs about borrowing a pair of pantyhose or skipping an arranged meeting, usually because some guy asked her out, and claiming she'd forgotten it. Lucy also knew that people who were planning to commit suicide could be quite cagey, and often were careful to give no hint of their intentions to loved ones, who were completely taken by surprise. But even bearing all that in mind, she doubted that Beth had taken her own life.

Lucy was marching along Sixty-Ninth Street, which was lined with large apartment buildings, when the jutting canopy of one caught her eye. She'd seen it before, she thought, trying to remember where or why it suddenly seemed so important to place it. Then it hit her. It had been pictured in a news story about Beth's death. She stopped in her tracks. This was it. . . . This was Beth's building. She looked up, past the rows and rows of windows, but couldn't see the penthouse, which was set back. Her eyes fell and she quickly scanned the sidewalk, looking for what? Traces of Beth? She shuddered and, feeling rather woozy, began to sway on her feet.

The doorman, who had just stepped out of the building, noticed and caught her before she fell. "Come on in and sit down," he urged, supporting her and leading her into the lobby. There he placed her on a nubby gray sofa, next to a ficus tree, and went to get a glass of water.

Lucy sat with her head between her knees, taking deep breaths. When the doorman returned, she was sitting up and feeling well enough to sip the water.

"I'm so sorry," she said. "It's just . . . you see . . . I knew Beth Blake. She was an old friend."

"That was terrible," said the doorman. He was a pleasant-looking guy in his sixties, and Lucy suspected he was a retired policeman, or even military. Or maybe it was just his uniform, with its double row of brass buttons. "Everybody in the building is pretty upset."

"I'm just sick about it. I'm at a complete loss." Lucy had a sudden brain wave. "Was she close to anyone here? Is there anyone I could talk to?"

He pressed his lips together and shook his head. "I'm sorry, but I doubt anybody here could tell you anything. The Blakes were up there, in the penthouse, and it's not like she bumped into her neighbors in the hall or anything. This is New York—people keep to themselves."

Lucy suspected she might have gone too far. The doorman was there to protect the privacy of the building's residents and he wasn't going to allow her to intrude on their peace and quiet. "I wonder," she asked, thinking aloud. "Did you see anything odd that day, the day Beth, I mean Mrs. Blake, died? Anything out of the ordinary?"

He was clearly losing patience with her. "You mean apart from the fact that one of the residents took a dive off the twenty-second floor?"

Lucy sniffled and dabbed at her eyes with a worn tissue she found in her pocket. "I just can't believe she killed herself."

He sighed. "I wish I could help you, but the fact is, I wasn't here. It was street-cleaning day, and some of the tenants have me move their cars for them, so they don't get parking tickets. I heard the sirens, of course, but I never guessed it was all for my building. When I got back all hell had broke loose and the street was full of cop cars and flashing lights and ambulances. Too late for the lady."

Familiar with tragedy, Lucy could picture the scene. "It must have been awful."

"You said it." His voice had a definite note of finality.

"I'll be going. Thanks for your help."

"Here," he said, pulling a lollipop from his pocket. "I keep 'em for the kids. It'll raise your blood sugar."

Lucy unwrapped the pop as she left the white brick building, and when she tucked the cellophane into her pocket she found the business card Dante had given her. She pulled it out and studied it as she walked along, sucking the lolly, only to discover the precinct was on the next block. It was worth a try. Cops worked on Sundays, didn't they?

The precinct was a squat brick building, squeezed between a couple of town houses that had been subdivided into apartments, and Lucy wouldn't necessarily have identified it except for the blue light over the door. Stepping inside, she noted the reception area was grubby and smelled of sweat and disinfectant. A uniformed officer was sitting behind a thick sheet of Plexiglas, which had a few holes drilled in it to allow communication with the public, if the public yelled. Lucy didn't feel up to yelling, so she slipped Detective McGuire's card through the little slot at the bottom of the Plexiglas barrier.

The officer apparently didn't feel up to speaking either, but returned the card and tilted his head to the side, indicating a man in plainclothes who had just stepped through a scarred metal door and was closing it behind him.

"Excuse me," said Lucy, showing him the card. "I'd like to speak with you, if you have a moment."

"A moment's all I got," he answered in a gruff voice. Detective McGuire was in his fifties, with a broad, freckled, Irish face and a graying buzz cut. He was dressed in loose track pants, a dark blue windbreaker over a black polo shirt, and running shoes.

"It's about Beth Blake, the woman who fell to her death last week."

"Yeah. I remember."

Lucy sensed she'd better be brief and go straight to the heart of the matter. "Well, I was talking with the doorman and he said he wasn't in the building when it happened. That means somebody could have gotten into the building, somebody who shouldn't have been there. Maybe a thief and she discovered him, something like that, and he pushed her off the balcony?"

"Look," he said, meeting her eyes with his baby blues, "I'm sure you want to be helpful and all, but we investigated thoroughly and the lady took her own life. If you need some help dealing with this, we have a list of resources that I can give you."

"You say you investigated thoroughly, but I know family members who say—"

"I'm sure they don't think we did enough. I understand that. Suicide is hard for families to accept. But take my word for it, there is no evidence of any foul play. The building has CCTV, and nobody came or went while the doorman was moving cars, except for one elderly woman with her little white dog." He scratched his head. "I don't think Mrs. Feinstrom from twenty-two A has a habit of pushing people off balconies, do you?"

Lucy was willing to explore the idea. She knew some pretty tough old ladies back in Tinker's Cove, but Detective McGuire was clearly impatient to be on his way.

"Thanks for your time," she said, as he brushed past her. He was pulling the door open when she had an idea. "Oh, wait. Could that CCTV tape be tampered with? That happens in TV shows all the time."

McGuire turned and glared at her. "Didn't happen here," he growled, turning on his heel and letting the door close behind him.

# Chapter Five

There was a lot of turbulence on the Sunday evening flight home, which matched Lucy's emotions. The days following a death of a friend or family member are always something of a roller coaster, and Lucy's emotions rose and fell with the plane's altitude. It was time to put it all behind her, she thought, as the jet cruised serenely through fields of clouds. Then there would be a sudden lurch and she'd wonder if there was some conspiracy afoot, some reason the police were so eager to close the case. Then there were the drops through thin air, accompanied by panicked screams and grabs for the armrests that filled her with despair. Beth was dead and it didn't make any sense. They said she killed herself, but she had everything to live for.

But if she hadn't killed herself, somebody else had to have hurled her off that balcony. Unless, thought Lucy as the plane rose through the clouds and burst into the pink glow of the setting sun, it was a terrible, dreadful accident. That was really too much to bear, she thought, with an involuntary gasp. Beth falling because she reached too far, or because a railing gave way? But that couldn't be right—the investigators would have found the broken railing. Maybe she had plants growing on the balcony . . . maybe she was plucking off dead leaves and lost her balance.

Not Beth, thought Lucy. Beth didn't care the least bit about plants or gardening, and if there were decorative plants on the balcony they would most certainly have been tended by a professional gardener. Beth wouldn't have risked her manicure, much less her life, to tidy up a few brown leaves.

Lucy turned and gazed out the little window, noticing that the sky was darkening. She didn't want to see her anxious reflection in the glass, so she closed the shade and opened the book that had been lying in her lap, unread. She turned on the overhead light and settled back to read, but the words made no sense to her. Instead of paper and ink, she saw Beth's husbands, one by one. Husbands were always prime suspects and, from what Dante told her, Beth's husbands were certainly not above suspicion. There was Gabe Thomas, apparently still running that crazy Angel Brigade outfit, which Beth claimed was all about control. The artist, Tito Wilkins, had burst onto the art scene straight out of the crime-ridden projects in the South Bronx. As for the chiropractor, Lucy had always harbored a suspicion that chiropractic bordered on quack medicine. But of the four, Lucy tended to think that Jeremy Blake had the most to gain from Beth's death because he was still deeply involved with her and stood to lose not only money, but perhaps even his reputation in the divorce.

The captain announced that passengers should prepare for landing, and Lucy checked that her tray was securely latched, her seat was in the upright position, and her seat belt was fastened. She leaned back, took a deep breath, and came to the conclusion that Beth must have been murdered by one of her husbands. But which one? And why? And most difficult of all, Lucy had to make peace with the fact that she would probably never know.

Lucy got to work bright and early Monday morning, happy to be back in her familiar routine. Phyllis was at her desk behind the reception counter, almost hidden by an enormous bunch of pink and magenta peonies. She was wearing a blouse in an unusually subdued shade of pale rose, but had gone with magenta for her hair and nails.

"Oh, peonies," moaned Lucy, leaning in for a sniff of their lovely scent. "I have peony envy—I'm lucky if I get one or two blooms on my bushes."

"Wilf grows them," said Phyllis, referring to her husband. "He's got some secret formula. He won't even tell me what he does."

"Probably horse manure," offered Ted, who was pouring himself a cup of coffee. He was adding some cream when he turned to Lucy and, as if suddenly inspired, asked, "How was your weekend?"

Lucy was taken aback, since Ted rarely bothered with small talk. "Not great," she replied. "I was in

New York, at the funeral of one of my college friends."

"Uh, sorry." Ted sat down at his desk, chagrined that his effort to be sociable had backfired. "I didn't know."

"You would if you paid attention," observed Phyllis. "Lucy left early on Friday to catch a plane."

Ted was quick to defend himself. "I guess I had other things on my mind, like our falling subscription rate and the rising cost of newsprint."

"It's okay," said Lucy, seating herself at her desk and turning on her computer. "I'm okay. It's all behind me now and I'm a forward-looking person."

"Good. I want you to give the harbormaster a call. I heard there was some vandalism at the herring run and . . ." He stopped in midsentence as the door flew open and the little jangling bell announced the arrival of Corney Clark. Corney, as executive director of the Tinker's Cove Chamber of Commerce, was a frequent caller at the paper and a reliable source of news.

"What's up, Corney?" asked Lucy. She was wondering how Corney, who wasn't getting any younger, always managed to look so good. It was her huge smile, Lucy decided, and her youthful, sporty clothes. Today Corney was wearing a striped French top and light cashmere cardigan, skinny black pants, and sporty red driving shoes.

"You may well ask," she answered, with a sigh, as she sank into the chair Ted kept for visitors next to his desk. "Sylvia Bickford is driving me insane."

"She tends to do that," said Phyllis. "Just ask Warren."

"I don't know how that poor, sweet man manages to put up with her," said Corney, who was digging in her tote bag.

"He's either genuinely sweet and good, or he's amusing himself by thinking up various ways of killing her," said Lucy.

"I vote for the latter." Corney produced a sheaf of paper, which she waved about for emphasis. "This is Sylvia's plan for Silver Anniversary Weekend, which she expects the chamber to organize and support. She wants ads, she wants banners— the works—but so far she hasn't come up with a penny." Corney paused and batted her heavily mascaraed eyelashes at Ted. "Te-e-ed, I don't suppose you could give us some free coverage, like maybe a special supplement? A lot of businesses are going to have twenty-five percent off sales. The Queen Vic and some of the B and Bs are offering special anniversary packages."

"It depends on how many businesses buy ads," said Ted. "The more ads, the bigger the supplement."

"Could you give the advertisers a break on rates?" asked Corney.

"How about this? I'll cut the rates for the bigger ads. The more space they buy the better the deal."

"I knew I could count on you." Corney patted his hand. "And maybe Lucy could write some feature stories about couples who've been married for twenty-five or more years?"

"Whose idea is that?" Lucy wasn't enthusiastic about adding a series of lengthy interviews to her already full work schedule.

"Sylvia's, of course. And she wants her marriage to be the focus of the story."

Lucy was incredulous. "Sylvia wants me to write a glowing story about her marriage? I can't do it. I'll be a laughing stock. I'll lose all credibility, right, Ted?"

Ted was chewing his lip thoughtfully. "I dunno, Lucy. Think of it as a challenge. It could be hilarious, if you do it right. Tongue in cheek, you know? Besides, we don't have space for it this week. You've got a whole week to work on it."

"Oh, Lucy, I know you can do it. You've got such a way with words," exclaimed Corney, hopping to her feet. "I gotta be going. Sylvia wants to see me at nine a.m. on the dot." She handed the news release to Ted. "This is the schedule, and some suggestions for coverage from Sylvia. See ya!" With those parting words she breezed out the door, leaving the little bell jangling in her wake.

Ted watched her leave, then turned his attention to the papers she'd given him, saving the schedule and tossing the rest into the circular file.

"So, Lucy, who are you going to interview? Who are the happiest couples in Tinker's Cove?" Phyllis was grinning mischievously.

"I dunno. How about you and Wilf?"

"Oh, no. We're practically newlyweds." It was true. Phyllis and Wilf had found each other rather late in life and had only been married for a few years.

"Too bad. I'm open to suggestions, if you can think of anybody."

By the time the deadline rolled around on Wednesday, Lucy had a list of four couples to interview for her story. Instead of taking the afternoon off, as she usually did, Lucy headed to the Community Church to interview Reverend Marge Harvey and her husband, Hawley. When she arrived at the simple clapboard building she found Reverend Marge and her husband out on the lawn, working on the sign that announced the upcoming sermon. Reverend Marge was holding a large box of black letters and was handing them, one at a time, to Hawley, who was placing them on the sign.

"Marge, this doesn't look right," said Hawley, stepping back. He was a rather short, chubby man, who wore his long, gray hair in a ponytail. Like most of the men in town, he favored khaki pants and plaid flannel shirts, and was wearing a sturdy pair of hiking shoes. "I don't think *redemption* has two *p*'s."

"I think it does, like exaggerate has two *g*'s." Reverend Marge was dressed similarly, in khaki pants and a polo shirt, with matching hiking shoes.

"Let's ask the expert," suggested Hawley, greeting Lucy with a smile. "She's a writer, after all."

"And I rely on spell-check," admitted Lucy, with a smile. "But I do believe there's only one *p* in *redemption*."

"It's two to one, I yield," said Reverend Marge. "Is Redemption Possible?"

"I'm sure it is," said Lucy, somewhat shocked at the question. It was only a matter of spelling, after all.

"Of course it is. It's the title of my sermon. And the theme, too."

"Marge's sermons are brilliant," said Hawley, adding the final question mark and stepping back to admire his work.

"Good job, Hawley." Marge gave her husband a loving pat. "Let's go in and have a cup of tea and chat with Lucy. And behave yourself. We're supposed to be an example of a loving couple."

"So far, so good," said Lucy.

They gathered in Reverend Marge's study, which was a small, book-lined room. Instead of a desk, Marge worked at a table she'd placed in the center of the room, which was surrounded with a half dozen chairs. The table was covered with books and papers, arranged in neat piles. A plate of cookies was added, and they were soon seated in a cozy group with their mugs of tea.

"So how did you two meet?" asked Lucy, beginning the interview.

"At a civil rights march," said Hawley. "Some cops were dragging Marge away rather roughly and I—"

"He punched one of them," said Marge, smiling at the memory, "even though it was supposed to be a nonviolent demonstration."

"I don't know what got into me." Hawley's round face was glowing and his eyes were gleaming naughtily.

"The next time I saw him we were in court. We'd spent the night in jail. I was terribly worried they'd charge him with assaulting an officer or something, but he apologized and the judge let him go with a warning."

"She came over to make sure I was okay. By then I had a black eye thanks to the cops, and I asked her out."

"I wasn't thanking him. I told him he should be more restrained in the future. . . ."

"But you did agree to have coffee with me."

"Only because I felt sorry for you."

Hawley chuckled. "It worked. We've been married for twenty-five years."

"What's the secret?" asked Lucy. "They say almost half of all marriages end in divorce."

"Well, we have the same values, the same beliefs, and we treat each other with respect," said Marge.

"It's the sex," said Hawley, with a wink. "I'm in it for the sex."

"God's plan," said Marge, grinning and reaching across the table to take his hand. "Allelulia."

Lucy was smiling when she left the Harveys to go to her next interview. They were a cute couple, she thought, and not at all what she expected. But then, Reverend Marge was nothing like the stern minister of St. Andrew's when she was growing up, who focused on sin rather than redemption. And the thought came to her, Reverend Marge was nothing like Beth's first husband, Father Gabe, who demanded complete obedience from his flock of believers and his wife.

Next up was the optometrist Phil Shahn and his wife, Betty, who Lucy had arranged to interview in the comfortable antique house built by Captain Isaiah Cook in 1823. Dr. Shahn's office was in an ell on the back of the house, but Lucy was invited into the kitchen, where Betty was browning a pot roast.

"That smells delicious," she said, seating herself on a stool at the kitchen island. "Is that your secret? The way to a man's heart is through his stomach?"

"Sure is," said Phil, joining her at the island. "Betty's a great cook and we've been married for forty-seven years." He was wearing a white lab coat over a button-down oxford and a pair of gray flannel slacks, and had a pair of chunky, black eyeglasses perched on his nose.

"Phil does a lot of the cooking," said Betty, setting the lid on the pan. She took off her apron, revealing a blue jean skirt and pale pink polo shirt. "He often pops in from the office to stir a pot."

"You must be together a lot since the office is in the house. Does that pose any special challenges?"

"It did when the kids were little. They'd wander in when he was examining someone, which some people didn't appreciate. But now they're all grown and I have to admit, I like having him close by. It's good to know that if I have a problem, like a spider in the sink, I can call him."

"When I walk through the door"—Phil indicated the connecting door with a tilt of his head—"I leave work behind. Whatever problems I've been dealing with stay on the other side, in the office and examining room. Home is home."

Lucy looked around the newly renovated kitchen, with its white cabinets, quartz counters, and pendant light fixtures, noticing the family photographs arranged on the wall and the childish art displayed on the double-doored stainless steel refrigerator. "You have a big family. . . ."

"Four kids and seven grandkids," said Phil, a note of pride in his voice.

"We're going to be great-grandparents soon,

thanks to Lulu. She's the one with the big bow in her hair."

Lucy saw a photograph of a smiling blond toddler, dressed in overalls and cradling a large marmalade cat.

"She's all grown up now, and is going to have a little boy," continued Betty, clearly pleased as punch with this exciting development. "I can't wait."

"Any tips for newlyweds?"

"Get a good pot roast recipe," said Betty.

"And when she's not looking, doctor it up," said Phil, grinning and ducking the dish towel his wife tossed at him.

As she drove to her next appointment, with artists Ben Melfi and Willa Stout, Lucy thought about the Shahns' marriage. She suspected that their devotion to their family, their kids and grandkids, was a major reason for the success of their relationship. Or maybe, she thought, it was the other way round. Maybe it was their easygoing, accepting attitude that allowed them to produce their large and much-loved family. Money also played into it, she decided. It wasn't the answer to all problems, but it was an undeniable fact that a professional with a specialty like optometry made a very good income and that income made life a lot more pleasant. The photos of the Shahn family included numerous vacation snapshots at ski resorts and expensive theme parks. She didn't doubt that they'd had their share of difficulties—everybody encountered problems, especially when kids were involved—but having the financial resources to deal with those hurdles made a big difference.

Artists Ben and Willa obviously had a much different lifestyle, she decided, as she pulled into the driveway at their combined home and studio and braked beneath an enormous wooden sculpture that was a modern version of a totem pole. Instead of the naturalistic images on a traditional totem pole, this version featured the faces of various advertising mascots including Ronald McDonald and Mr. Clean.

Willa greeted her, emerging from the garage that served as a studio, dressed in paint-spattered jeans and shirt, and wiping her hands on a rag. "Hi, Lucy. I'd offer to shake hands but I'm elbow deep in paint."

"No problem," said Lucy. "What are you working on?"

"C'mon in and I'll show you." Lucy followed Willa into the studio, which was cluttered with paintings and props. The work in progress stood on an easel and depicted a household angel, a harried woman with wings and halo attempting to cope with a sink full of dirty dishes, a squalling infant, an angry husband, and numerous cats. An easel with a half-finished self-portrait stood in the corner. "I'm calling it *Herding Cats*."

"It's very clever." Lucy grinned ruefully. "It could be my life."

"Let's go in the house. Ben is taking a break from sculpture today. He's got tennis elbow and it's acting up."

"I love the totem pole," said Lucy, as Willa opened the door leading to the kitchen. The room was a colorful riot, with kitchen cabinets painted in various bright colors, patchwork curtains, and dozens of plates hanging on the wall in no particular order.

"How 'bout some tea?" offered Ben, rising from his chair at the kitchen table, where he was sketching.

"Lovely." Lucy sank into the old-fashioned chair he offered, thinking it was exactly like the ones in her grandmother's kitchen except that Nanny's were painted black and one usually had her enormous gray cardigan hanging on the back, handy in case she had to run outside. This chair was purple with pink polka dots.

Soon the three were gathered at the table, sipping on chamomile tea and chatting like old friends. After agreeing to disagree on the virtues of a proposed wind farm, and agreeing on the fire chief's decision to refurbish rather than replace the town's aged ladder truck, Lucy got down to business. "Does the fact that you're both artists pose special challenges in your marriage?" she asked.

"We work in different media," said Willa. "He sculpts and I paint, so it's easy to be supportive of each other. It's not like we're competing, y'know?"

"Your styles seem to complement each other. You both seem to be interested in critiquing modern life."

Ben nodded and grinned, a twinkle in his eye. "Some folks see Ronald McDonald and think I'm making a statement about consumerism. Others see Ronald as a beloved figure from their childhood. I'm okay with either, if it gets them to buy the darn thing."

"Righto," agreed Willa. "It's not easy making a living in the arts. We seem to be either madly rich or completely poverty stricken."

"But we're talented and inventive." Ben pointed to the rainbow-colored cabinets. "Willa's idea. She used some leftover paint."

"That was my cheap and cheerful phase," admitted Willa. "Nobody was buying my work—my studio was filling up with unsold pictures and it was too discouraging to paint more—so I took a break."

"You have control of your time. . . ."

"Absolutely," said Ben, interrupting her. "That's the best part. We have plenty of time to be together."

"For the record, how long have you been married? And how did you meet?"

"Gee, it's close to thirty years now," said Ben. "We met on the overnight train from Paris to Nice. We were both kids, backpacking in Europe."

"We still love traveling," added Willa, bestowing a loving look on her husband, "and since we've got a credit card that gives us free miles and now we've discovered Airbnb we can stay at all these fabulous homes. We've been meeting other artists, getting lots of inspiration and ideas. It's very affordable and it's opened up the world to us. We're going to Morocco next month, staying at some English antique dealer's place. I can't wait."

"I'm jealous," said Lucy, envying the artistic couple's freedom.

"I have a question for you," said Willa, turning the tables on Lucy. "Are you going to be in the Silver Anniversary fashion show, wearing your wedding dress?"

"Uh, no. I'm sorry to say it doesn't fit. Are you?"

"Yeah." Willa was beaming. "I don't have that problem since I wore a sari. Bright pink. But I'm not sure Sylvia will approve."

"She issued an open invitation to all women married for twenty-five years or more. I don't think she can stop you." Lucy was closing her notebook and picking up her bag, ready to go. "She's my next interview. Do you want me to ask her?"

"No," said Ben, squeezing his wife's hand. "Let's surprise her."

Back on the road, Lucy wrestled with the challenging problem that faced her. How was she ever going to portray the Bickersons—no, the Bickfords—as a happily married, loving couple? It was clearly an abusive relationship, with Sylvia constantly belittling and scolding Warren, and she didn't want to give readers the impression that such behavior was acceptable.

True to form, Sylvia was quick to take charge when Lucy arrived. Warren had greeted her at the kitchen door—nobody in town ever even thought of knocking on the front door—but Sylvia quickly intervened and insisted on being interviewed in their living room. Lucy was whisked through the antiseptic operating room that was their kitchen and quickly installed on a vinyl-covered couch in the very formal living room.

She hadn't been in a room like this in years, she thought, noticing the white rug, the crystal sconces, and the stiff arrangement of sofa and two chairs placed with mathematical precision on either side of a coffee table adorned with a bouquet of fake flowers. She bent down to retrieve her notebook from her bag and was embarrassed when the movement resulted in a fart-like noise as her skin on her thigh pulled against the sticky vinyl slipcover.

"It happens," said Warren, with an apologetic grin. "I've asked Sylvia to get rid of that sticky vinyl, but she always says—"

"'Do you want to have nice things or not, Warren?' That's what I say and he knows it's because he's such a slob that we need the covers." Sylvia was perched on a rather stiff armchair, also covered with clear vinyl, and was wearing a tailored dress with a straight skirt. Her stockinged knees were pressed tightly together and her ankles were crossed. "Men!" she exclaimed, rolling her eyes and patting her tightly curled hair. "They just seem to bring dirt with them. Raised in a barn, that must be it. If it weren't for us ladies, insisting on civilized behavior, they'd just wallow in beer and pizza and girlie magazines. Don't you agree?"

Lucy didn't want to impugn the men in her life, her husband and son Toby, so she merely shrugged. "They do produce a lot of laundry, but so do my girls."

"Laundry! Don't even get me started. Warren's got a limo business, you know, and sometimes he has to change a tire or fiddle with the oil gizmo. Sometimes there's nothing to do but throw his stained clothes in the trash."

"I have to look nice for the customers," said Warren, by way of explanation.

"And you have both been remarkably successful in business and in marriage," said Lucy, resorting to flattery. "Will you share your secret with our readers?"

Sylvia was quick to answer. "Hard work and determination, that's all there is to it. People blame failure on everything and anything but themselves. It's the economy, or the weather, or discrimination. That's my favorite. Blacks and Hispanics don't get a fair shake. . . . Women can't get credit to start businesses. . . . The system is rigged against them, on and on they go. Well, I'm a woman and I've done very well, if I do say so myself."

"Yes, you have, dear," said Warren.

"And it's no thanks to you," she replied. "Warren is a big wet blanket, always disparaging my ideas. He said a bridal shop would never succeed in a little town like this, but I said if it's good, people will come from miles away. And they do. Just yesterday I had a lovely girl from New Hampshire. Came all the way, she said, because she heard Orange Blossom Bridal has the most beautiful dresses."

"Your two businesses complement each other. . . ."

"Absolutely. It was my idea. Warren was hesitant. He didn't want to take on such a big, expensive commitment. . . ."

"That's not quite true, dear."

"Oh, shut up, Warren. You know that I'm right."

Warren repeated what must surely be the mantra of his marriage. "Sorry, dear."

"But I told him you have to spend money to make money, and the limo business is doing very well, though I do have to keep on top of things there, too."

"What about your relationship? What is the secret to a long marriage?" asked Lucy.

Sylvia studied her husband, reminding Lucy of a

dermatologist examining a suspicious mole. "You
have to make it clear from the beginning who's
boss."

Warren cleared his throat and it seemed for a
moment that he was going to say something, but
he clearly thought better of it.

Sylvia gave Warren a little pat on the shoulder.
"Warren's a good husband, though like all husbands he's a work in progress."

"Thank you, dear."

Sylvia insisted that Lucy leave through the front
door, which allowed her to show Lucy the large
portrait of herself that hung in the hallway. Sylvia
paused beneath the very flattering painting that
depicted her in a beaded lace wedding dress with
padded shoulders and invited Lucy to snap a photo.
Lucy obliged, managing to restrain the laughter that
was building and threatening to erupt in a hysteri-
cal outburst, and dutifully took the picture. Only
Sylvia would choose a wedding portrait that omit-
ted the groom, she thought, as she dashed to her
car and finally released the hoots of laughter she'd
been bottling up.

# Chapter Six

As she drove back to the office, Lucy thought about the interviews and the story she had to write. The four couples were very different, but they'd all found a way to make their marriages endure. She wondered if there was any one thing they all had in common, but all she could come up with was the sense she'd gotten that for better or worse they'd committed to the success of their marriage. Even poor Warren, henpecked as he was, must have made a decision at some point that life with Sylvia was preferable to life without Sylvia.

As often happened these days, her thoughts turned to Beth. Why hadn't Beth been able to make her marriages work? Was it some failure on her part, or had she simply made a series of bad choices? Lucy remembered reading the confession of some oft-married celebrity, she couldn't remember who, saying that she entered every marriage absolutely convinced that this time it would be different, this time it would work.

That was probably also true of Beth, as she careened through life, bouncing from one relationship to another. The problem with that, thought Lucy, was that Beth had expected to find a Prince Charming to save her, and had only come to the belated realization that she had to save herself after her fourth marriage. She would have liked to get to know this older and wiser Beth, and suspected she would have preferred her to the old, dependent Beth, but she'd never had the chance. Beth was gone, but the question remained whether she'd died by her own hand or someone else's. If only Lucy could get back to New York. Maybe then she could figure out what had really happened to Beth. But that was out of the question since she didn't have the money or the time necessary for a real investigation.

She reached the *Pennysaver* office and slid into a vacant parking spot right in front; it was late afternoon and the little town was emptying as people headed home for the night. She wanted to take advantage of the fact that she would have the office to herself to get a head start on the happy couples story, which she knew would be challenging. She unlocked the door and went in, flipping on the lights and powering up her computer. But when she faced the empty screen she realized she didn't know where to start.

Writer's block was not something she was familiar with, but she had come across a few tips in the course of her career. *Just start* was one piece of advice she'd heard, and she tried typing in a few random thoughts but soon ran out of steam. *Start with a quote* was another bit of advice, so she reached for the battered office copy of *Bartlett's Familiar Quotations* but didn't find anything that seemed to suit. Shoving the thick book aside, she thought enviously of Ben and Willa's upcoming trip to Morocco, which they were able to take thanks to saved air miles and Airbnb.

On impulse, she Googled *Airbnb* and much to her surprise found a reasonably priced studio apartment in Beth's neighborhood. Well, not quite Beth's posh district, but close enough, on the other side of the park, the West Side. That left the problem of airfare, but after a bit more poking about on the computer she found a travel site that offered some very low fares, although her itinerary required taking a very early Saturday morning flight and involved changing planes in Cleveland for some crazy reason. That left her with the problem of time. She was going to have to beg Ted to give her some vacation time and, even more challenging, she would have to convince Bill that she needed some time to herself. She suspected that taking a vacation from her marriage was going to be a lot trickier than taking one from her job.

Now that she had a plan, she found she was able to write the story. "There's no single recipe for a long and happy marriage," she began, going on to write sympathetic portraits of three of the couples she'd interviewed. She struggled a bit when she got to Warren and Sylvia, but discovered that if she deleted Sylvia's negative comments about Warren from her quotes she could present them as a contented couple united in their complementary businesses. Sylvia did say, after all, that "Warren is a good husband" and "the limo business is doing very well." She just left off the parts about him being a "work in progress" and having "to keep on top of him."

Finally satisfied with her story, Lucy hit SAVE. She stood up, stretched, and headed home for the night. Home to her husband, who she hoped wouldn't mind pizza, again.

Next morning Ted welcomed Lucy with a big smile. He was already at his desk when she arrived, fresh from a gossipy breakfast with her friends. "Super job on the happy marriages story, Lucy. I don't know how you did it, but you managed to make the Bickersons seem like a relatively congenial couple."

"Sounds like mission impossible," said Phyllis, settling herself like a broody hen at her desk. Maybe it was just the reddish orange tint to her hair and the matching sweatshirt that made her look like a Rhode Island Red today.

"I hope it doesn't sound phony," said Lucy, remembering the breakfast bunch's skepticism when she told them about the story. "Everybody in town knows what they're really like."

"No." Ted shook his head. "It's like you're presenting another side to this couple that most people don't see. You're showing the stuff that keeps them together, like their businesses."

"Well, we'll see. If there's one thing I know it's that Sylvia isn't shy about making her displeasure known."

"You've got a week's grace," said Phyllis, pointing out that since the deadline had passed, the story would run in the next issue.

"That reminds me, Ted," said Lucy, working up to requesting the time off she so desperately wanted. "I've been working pretty hard lately, and I'm really having a difficult time coping with my friend Beth's death, and I was wondering if you could get along without me for a week."

Ted swung around in his swivel chair and adopted a serious expression. "I know, Lucy, that must be tough. I lost a golf buddy a while ago and it's still bugging me. He had a sudden heart attack—came out of the blue—and left his wife with three young kids. "

"They say Beth killed herself, but I can't believe it."

"When do you want to take off?"

"Next week?"

"Are you sure you're not trying to avoid Sylvia?" asked Phyllis.

"That would certainly be a benefit," admitted Lucy.

"Okay," said Ted. "But you'll have to finish up the assignments I've already given you."

Lucy bit her lip. There was quite a lot on her desk, including revised fishing regulations, a proposal to construct a new water tank, and a planning board hearing about a controversial proposal to demolish one of the town's oldest structures. "I can work late tonight," she said.

"Okay then." Hearing the little bell announce a visitor, Ted swung his chair the other way in time to see Corney Clark arrive. "Hey, Corney, what's up?"

"I just wanted to stop by and let you know that the Silver Anniversary Weekend is really taking off. I placed two tiny ads—it was all we could afford—in the *New York Times* and *Boston Globe*, and several local innkeepers have told me they're already getting reservation requests. The town is going to be buzzing with well-heeled empty nesters, looking for things to buy and places to eat."

"That's good news," said Ted.

Corney had seated herself in the visitor's chair next to Ted's desk and crossed her legs. "I'm thinking of dying my hair silver for the weekend," she said, twirling a lock of hair. "What do you think?"

Phyllis was quick to jump aboard. "Great idea! We should all do it!"

Lucy wasn't quite so eager. "No way. I'm doing everything I can to cover up my gray hair."

"Some women look really cool with gray hair." Corney turned to Ted. "What do you think?"

Ted held up his hands in protest. "I don't think, not about hair color anyway."

"I think Lucy's right. I think going gray is going a step too far." Corney shrugged. "I'm actually wishing I could wash my hands of this entire shindig. After all I've done for Sylvia she reamed me out when she heard about the ads. She was actually yelling at me, saying they were tiny and cost far too much. It was the best I could do, with the money I had. It's not like she's come up with any financial support. She wants the chamber to pay for all the publicity, but she's insisting on being in charge. I told her it doesn't work that way and she threatened to take her complaints to the board."

"I wouldn't worry if I were you," said Lucy. "The board members think you walk on water, Corney."

"I am pretty fabulous if I say so myself," said Corney, only half joking. "But it's still annoying to have to deal with unnecessary negativity."

"That should be Sylvia's middle name," said Phyllis, and they all laughed.

Corney went on her way, and Ted turned to Lucy. "Hey, Lucy, before you go could you check out how the Silver Anniversary Weekend is coming along? Call a few of those innkeepers that Corney mentioned, okay?"

Lucy sighed, only too aware that this was yet another assignment on her to-do list. "Okay," she said, and reached for the phone.

Her first call was to the Queen Victoria Inn, commonly called the Queen Vic. This venerable old establishment had stood on a leafy knoll in the center of town, from where its patrons could sit in rocking chairs on the porch and watch the local goings-on. It was the town's only three-diamond inn, a fact that the rates reflected.

Lucy's call was answered on the first ring. "Queen Victoria Inn. How may I help you?"

Lucy recognized the voice as belonging to the manager, Bill Pusey.

"Hi, Bill," she began. "It's Lucy from the *Pennysaver*. I'm just doing a little survey for a story on the upcoming Silver Anniversary Weekend."

"We're booked solid, and frankly, I'm amazed. June is usually very quiet for us, but this Silver Anniversary Weekend is putting us on the map. I've had to turn people away. And money's no object for these folks. There were lots of requests for suites, more than I can handle. I'm looking for extra help, too. Anybody you know who wants to pick up a few bucks for a weekend's work changing beds?"

Lucy filed that thought away, thinking that Sara and Zoe might be interested. "I've got two able-bodied daughters."

"Have them stop by. I need waitresses, too, if they're squeamish about cleaning rooms."

"I sure will. Any idea where these people heard about Silver Anniversary Weekend?"

"The *New York Times*. It's all from that teeny little ad."

"Interesting," said Lucy, typing as she talked. "Thanks."

"No, thank you," said Bill. "We appreciate all you do for us at the *Pennysaver*."

Unused to such sentiments, Lucy blushed. "Just doing my job."

After making a few more calls, Lucy was able to whip through a story reporting that hotel bookings were very positive for the upcoming Silver Anniversary Weekend. She called the state fish and game department and got an explanation for the changes in the freshwater fishing regulations, and spent all afternoon pursuing members of the water commission about the expensive proposal to build a new water tank. Then she headed home, intending to whip up a quick supper so she could attend the planning board meeting at seven o'clock that evening.

She was dumping a bag of prepackaged salad into a bowl when she got a call on her cell phone and she was surprised to see it was from Dante.

"How's it going?" she asked.

"Some days are better than others," he said in a thick voice that made Lucy wonder if he'd been drinking.

"That's to be expected. It gets better with time."

"That's what they tell me." He sighed. "Some days I really feel like I can't go on. I mean, I find myself heading for the Brooklyn Bridge and I'm afraid what I might do."

For a moment, Lucy thought her heart had stopped beating. "Oh, no, Dante, please don't. Don't do anything rash."

"I shouldn't be bothering you like this," he said.

"It's not a bother. I'm your ad hoc mom, remember." Lucy collapsed into a chair at the round, golden oak kitchen table and leaned on her elbow, bent over the phone. "You're such a special person and so many people love you." She was so focused on the call that she didn't notice Bill had come home and was standing behind her, expecting his usual welcome.

"It's just so hard. I don't even want to get out of bed in the morning. She was my mother, you know? Why wasn't that enough for her?" Dante's voice broke and he sobbed. "She used to say we were the Dynamic Duo. The husbands came and went, but she promised that didn't change anything between us, that she would always be there for me. Turns out it was all a big lie. It's like she didn't love me."

"That's not true," said Lucy. "I know that for a fact. And I love you, too. And I'm working on coming to the city, probably on Saturday. Can you hang on that long? Just a couple of days. For me?"

Getting a mumbled assent, Lucy ended the call. She laid the phone on the table and stood up, wiping her eyes. Still blinking back tears, she turned, intending to continue fixing supper, and encountered her husband. Bill did not look pleased.

"What was that all about?" demanded Bill. "Who is this guy?"

"I was talking to Dante. Beth's son."

"Likely story." His face was red and he was clenching and unclenching his fists. "Are you having an affair?"

Lucy couldn't believe what she was hearing. "Are you crazy?"

"Don't call me crazy! I come home from a hard day at work and you're crooning sweet nothings into the phone—*I love you, can you hang on a couple of days, for me?* That's pretty suggestive stuff."

"He's grief stricken. His mother killed herself. It's a terrible thing for anyone to have to deal with, and he's an only child. They were very close."

Bill's expression softened, but he still wasn't convinced. "So you want to rush back to New York to console this kid? What about me? What about the girls? You've got responsibilities here."

Lucy rolled her eyes. "Oh, give it up, Bill. You're a big boy and the girls consider me more of a nuisance than anything else. . . ."

"What do you mean?" he demanded. "They don't think you're a nuisance. That's not true."

"That just shows how little you know," declared Lucy, as a little seed of anger and resentment began to sprout. "I'm the one always throwing a monkey wrench into their plans. They'd both love to get out of this house and on their own in some off-campus apartment where they could do Lord-knows-what. Boys, booze, and probably drugs."

Bill was not about to hear his daughters, his little angels, maligned. "Now you're going too far, Lucy."

"So you'll accuse me of infidelity, but you think your daughters are little sweethearts, pure as the driven snow?"

Bill let out a huge breath. "I'm sorry. I can't help being jealous, even after all these years."

Lucy went to the sink and poured herself a glass of water, which she drank slowly, hoping it would dilute her warring emotions. Setting the glass down, she sighed. "I'm sorry, too. Dante is really suffering, and to tell the truth, so am I. This Beth thing has thrown me for a loop. I'm all at sixes and sevens."

"And you want to go to the city for the weekend?"

Sensing she had Bill on the ropes, Lucy resorted to a tactic she saved for extreme cases: she pouted. "For a week."

"A whole week? Where will you stay?"

"I found an Airbnb. It's cheap, and I checked my credit card and I've got miles I can use if I fly to New York via Cleveland."

Suddenly, Bill was laughing. "Cleveland?"

"Yeah." Lucy was laughing, too. "Go figure."

Then they were in each other's arms, and Lucy was pressing her cheek against Bill's soft flannel shirt, hearing his big heart thumping away. "I love you."

Then Bill was pressing his lips against hers, and she melted into a lovely kiss. It ended, and she stroked his beard, wishing they could scamper up the stairway and into bed. But they couldn't, because the girls were due home any minute. Then she had an intriguing thought. "You could join me in the city for that last weekend. It would be nice to be together, just us two."

"It would," said Bill, coming in for another kiss as the door flew open.

"Oh, yuck!" exclaimed Zoe.

"Aren't you too old for this sort of thing?" demanded Sara.

The two sisters marched through the kitchen and thumped up the narrow back staircase, headed for their rooms.

"I'll check on flights tonight," said Bill as they stepped apart.

"But don't tell the girls until the last minute," whispered Lucy. "We don't want them to know they'll have the house to themselves for the whole weekend."

Bill's eyebrows rose. "Why not?"

She patted his cheek. "When the cat's away . . ."

"Not our girls," he insisted.

"I hope you're right," she said, going back to her salad.

# Chapter Seven

Once she'd made the Airbnb and plane reservations, Lucy was eager to be off, but she had a whole day to get through. Friday turned out to be a very long day indeed, beginning with the ring of the alarm, which woke her out of a deep sleep. She'd been up late the night before at the planning board meeting, which didn't end until after eleven, and then she'd had trouble falling asleep. When she finally did doze off she slept fitfully, waking every few hours with the uneasy sense that she'd had a nightmare but unable to remember what had frightened her.

Bill was already up. She could hear the shower running. When he came in, his hair still damp and wearing only a towel, he greeted her with a sexy smile. "I love the way you look in the morning, with your hair mussed and your eyes still sleepy."

"And my breath all stinky and my bladder ready to burst," replied Lucy, throwing back the covers and groping around the rag rug beside the bed for her slippers.

"You sure know how to dash a fella's hopes." Bill had dropped the towel and was pulling on his briefs. "Patrick called last night. He was sad he missed you."

"Patrick!" Lucy loved chatting via the computer with her grandson who lived in Alaska. "Patrick called and I missed him?"

"Yeah. He looked good. He's all excited about soccer. He got his first goal. We've got the video, and Toby posted it on Facebook."

Lucy grabbed her phone and took it with her into the bathroom, where she replayed the goal several times while seated on the commode. She considered watching one more time while she brushed her teeth, but decided that perching the phone on the edge of the sink probably wasn't a good idea.

Pulling on her robe, she headed down to the kitchen, where she found Sara and Zoe arguing over the last container of yogurt.

"I'll take that, thank you," she said, plucking it out of Zoe's hands and ending the argument. She poured herself a cup of coffee and sat down at the table, placing the unopened yogurt in front of her.

"Aren't you going to eat it?" demanded Sara.

"Maybe." Lucy took a long swallow of coffee.

"Mom, you always say that we shouldn't take food unless we're going to eat it," protested Zoe.

Lucy sighed and took another long drink of coffee. "I'm really not up to arguing this morning," she said. "There's cereal, English muffins, bagels, juice, eggs. I'm sure you can find something to eat.

Or if you really have to have yogurt you can pick some up at the Quik-Stop on your way to class."

"You're always running out of food," grumbled Sara.

"Sara's right, Mom. If we had our own place we wouldn't be eating up all your yogurt."

"And how exactly do you plan to pay rent and buy groceries?"

"We'd get jobs," said Sara.

"College is your job," said Bill, coming up from the basement, where he'd gone to get a set of drill bits.

Something clicked in Lucy's fuzzy brain. "Actually, you could pick up a few bucks, if you want. Bill Pusey at the Queen Vic needs temporary help for the Silver Anniversary Weekend next month. He said to stop by."

"What kind of work?" Sara was skeptical. "I won't do toilets."

"He needs waitresses, too."

"Well, maybe," she grumbled.

Lucy's eyes met Bill's in a shared acknowledgment of their daughter's inconsistency. Sara wanted independence, but not if it meant working at a menial job.

"I'll talk to him," said Zoe, who was always the more practical one. She was buttering a slice of whole-grain toast. "Who knows, it might lead to a summer job."

"Elizabeth worked there," said Bill. "And now she's in Paris."

"Humph," was all Sara had to say, as she slipped on her jacket and grabbed her backpack. "I've got to go. I've got an eight o'clock."

Lucy was late for work; she'd gotten distracted by packing for the weekend when she was dressing and somehow the time got away from her. She still had to write up the planning board meeting, and was finding it difficult to make sense of the convoluted discussion about an eighteenth-century barn that had been converted to a slaughterhouse in the nineteenth century and then became an auto body shop sometime in the early twentieth century, but had actually been abandoned for several decades and was now in imminent danger of collapsing, which the town building inspector determined made it a dangerous nuisance. He wanted the building demolished, but members of the historical commission argued for preserving the structure, which featured a unique adaptation of post and beam construction.

She was saved, temporarily, from attempting to elucidate what exactly made this ramshackle building unique, by a rare phone call from Elizabeth.

"*Comment ça va?*" she crowed, employing one of the few French phrases she knew.

"*Très bien, Mama,*" replied Elizabeth, quickly switching to English. "I heard about your friend, Beth. I'm sorry."

"How did you hear?"

"Jeremy Blake is famous, even here in Paris. There was an article in *Paris Match* about his wife's tragic suicide. Tragic suicide always gets attention in France, especially if it's a rich American." She paused. "But I don't mean to sound flip. I remember Auntie Beth. She used to bring great presents to us kids when she visited. She was a lot of fun, and she brought a lot of excitement when she came."

"That was Beth."

"You must be pretty upset. She was one of your best friends. It's so awful when someone commits suicide. . . ."

"Actually, I don't think it was suicide and neither does her son, Dante. I'm going to New York tomorrow to see if I can figure out what happened."

"Does Dad know about this?"

"Not entirely. I told him I need some time alone, to process everything. I've got a week in an Airbnb, and he's going to come next weekend so we can have a little vacation together."

"So you're going to have a bachelorette week, a whole week to yourself in the big city?" Elizabeth sounded amused and somewhat impressed.

"Well, yeah. I guess I am."

"You go, girl! Go straight to Bloomingdale's. Splurge on something wonderful. Promise?"

"We'll see." It was the best Lucy could do. She was already feeling guilty about taking off by herself. And then there was the expense. Sure she'd managed to do it as cheaply as she could, but it was still money that could be used for something else, like new tires for Bill's truck.

"*Bon voyage!*" urged Elizabeth, ending the call.

On Saturday morning, when Lucy squeezed herself into a tight plane seat again, on the flight from Cleveland to New York, she remembered a time when airplane travel was actually a pleasant adventure. Her mother and father used to dress up for a flight, in their best go-to-meeting clothes, and were treated to all sorts of special perks, like hot meals and even freebies like cigarettes and chewing gum. While she didn't relish the thought of flying in a plane filled with cigarette smoke, she wouldn't have minded a bit of breakfast, since she hadn't eaten since last night's dinner. It was now ten a.m. and she'd been on the move since three a.m., when she left home for the drive to Portland to catch the six a.m. flight to Cleveland. And it was truly unfortunate that the large man sitting next to her was spilling out of his seat into hers and reeked of cologne.

Even so, she was excited about the adventure that awaited her in New York. It was rare for her to travel by herself, or even be by herself, and she was relishing the opportunity to sample a different lifestyle. She was a small-town wife and mother and as much as she loved her family and her town, she had to admit that sometimes she found it all a bit confining. She'd grown up in New York City and missed that sense of being in the center of things, the place where things were really happening.

But sitting there on the plane, trying to make herself as comfortable as possible, she wasn't quite sure how she was actually going to investigate Beth's death. She wasn't a cop, she wasn't a private eye, and she had no credentials or official standing whatsoever. All she had were the investigative skills she'd picked up as a reporter for the *Penny-saver*, which amounted to little more than an ability to get people talking and then carefully listening to what they said. But while asking questions and listening to the answers was an important skill, it was also true that she had an advantage in Tinker's Cove because people there knew her and her work and were often flattered by a request for an interview and pleased to read about themselves in the *Pennysaver*.

She knew she wanted to begin with Jeremy Blake, who she considered to be the prime suspect, but she doubted very much that a high-powered, successful billionaire would bother to give her the time of day, much less allow her to question him about his wife's death. Her only hope was to present herself as Beth's friend, reaching out to him as a fellow mourner, grieving her death. How exactly she was going to do this was the problem.

She was roused from her thoughts by the captain's announcement to prepare for landing. Then, once the plane was on the ground, she had to cope with the barely civilized scrum that debarking had become, followed by a long wait in the taxi line. Finally approaching the city on the Triborough Bridge, she was once again enraptured by the familiar sight of the New York skyline. There they were, the Chrysler Building and the Empire State Building, greeting her like old friends. And casting her glance southward, she spotted the shining new Freedom Tower that replaced the twin towers of the World Trade Center, destroyed on 9/11. Like most New Yorkers, she knew someone who'd died that day, and gave a thought to a boy she remembered from her church youth group who'd been aboard the plane that hit the Pentagon.

But then the taxi was slowing for the crawl

across midtown, and finally stopped in front of a tall, white apartment building on the West Side, near Lincoln Center. Somewhat warily she opened the door to the studio that was to be her home for the next week, but was relieved to find it clean and pleasant. She stowed her suitcase next to the futon covered in blue denim that served as both sofa and bed and sat down, determined to make good on her promise to call Dante as soon as she arrived.

"It's Lucy. I'm here, in New York," she announced, encountering his voice mail and leaving a message. "Just checking in with you," she continued, hoping he was too busy to answer her call and not floating face down in the East River. "Give me a call when you get a chance. Love you."

Still uneasy from her failure to contact Dante, Lucy explored her little apartment. It was basically one room, with windows along one wall that looked out onto an alley and a similar white brick building. There was a fake wood wall unit containing recent best sellers and a TV, a rather battered coffee table set on a tribal sort of rug, and a couple of armchairs covered with tan slipcovers. The kitchenette was arranged along one wall and divided from the living area by a small island with a couple of stools. She found a basic set of dishware in the wall cabinet, cutlery in a drawer, and a few pots in a cabinet beneath the small counter. Opening the refrigerator, she discovered a bottle of wine had been left for her to enjoy.

It was late for lunch but still rather early for a drink, so she decided to go out and buy some supplies from the bodega she'd noticed on the corner. Acting on impulse, and feeling a bit guilty about the extravagance, she chose a bouquet of assorted blooms, adding it to the basic groceries she needed. She also bought the day's *New York Times*, which was thick with news, opinion, and weekend happenings.

It was the happenings that interested her, while she ate a hearty ham on rye sandwich. There was so much to do: museum exhibitions, gallery openings, concerts, plays, movies, and restaurants. Special events were also planned in various parks, including, she noted with interest, a ribbon-cutting and award presentation at a newly restored gazebo in Central Park. The honoree, who had funded the restoration, was Jeremy Blake.

Checking her watch, she realized the event was in progress, and only a few blocks away. Abandoning her half-finished sandwich, she grabbed her purse and was out the door, hoofing it along Sixty-Seventh Street to Central Park. She reached the gazebo, a rustic wood structure perched on a hill overlooking the lake, just as the ceremony was ending. Jeremy Blake, clad in a blue blazer and gray pants, and sporting a jaunty bow tie, was accepting a silver bowl and acknowledging the scattered applause of a small crowd of people. Lucy joined the crowd just as Blake began to speak.

"This restoration has been a dream of mine, because it brings Central Park one step closer to restoring Frederick Law Olmsted's original plan for a space open to all that would be a sanctuary from the stress and clamor of city life. I am honored to be able to help support the Central Park Conservancy's important work and want to en-

courage everyone to join me. Thank you so much
for this award, which I have to say should really
have gone to my late wife, Beth Blake. She was the
one who urged me to undertake this restoration."
Here he stopped and looked upward toward the
sky, raising the bowl, and with his voice breaking,
said, "Bethie, this one's for you."

The crowd erupted in applause and Blake was
quickly surrounded by people offering congratula-
tions. Lucy saw an opportunity and joined them,
smiling and waiting for a chance to speak to him.
Much to her surprise, he recognized her and
greeted her with a hug. "Lucy, thanks for coming."

"My pleasure. I'm so glad you mentioned Beth."
She glanced up at the gazebo's intricate construction, crafted of twisty wooden boughs retaining
their bark. "This is just the sort of thing Beth
loved."

"Yeah," he nodded. "People are already booking
it for weddings."

"It's a beautiful spot."

"And there's no charge. Can you believe that?
Most places would charge an arm and a leg. Try
booking a wedding at the Met or the library or the
Brooklyn Museum."

Ever the businessman, thought Lucy. "And this
is much nicer, too, with the view of the lake and
all." Lucy knew that this was probably the only
chance she'd get to talk to Jeremy, but there were
a lot of other people who wanted to talk to him,
too, and she couldn't monopolize him. "You know,
I wish I'd had a chance to talk to you at the funeral
service."

He looked at her, seemingly surprised, then came to a quick decision. "Can you stick around? Wait for me to finish up here and then we could go for a drink or something? The Cardiff is just across the way."

"Sure," she said, slipping away and perching on one of the benches that lined the gazebo. Watching as Jeremy chatted with his admirers, she became aware of his social skill. He seemed to give each person his undivided attention, saying exactly the right thing, and then handing them off without giving the impression that that was what he was doing. They all left with smiles on their faces, still basking in his reflected glow. It was as if he were the sun, radiating light and warmth.

She only hoped that when it was her turn, when she was alone with him, that she wouldn't make a complete fool of herself.

# Chapter Eight

When the last of Jeremy's lingering admirer's finally left, he approached her with an apologetic smile. "I'm sorry to keep you waiting."

Lucy stood up, wishing she was wearing something dressier than the comfy jeans and striped fisherman's jersey she'd worn for the flight. The jeans were faded from wear and many spin cycles, but she reminded herself that some high-end retailers were selling torn, and even muddy jeans, for hundreds of dollars. The mud was fake but intended to make it seem as if the well-heeled person wearing them had actually been working, digging ditches or some other strenuous job, a concept which Lucy found somewhat ridiculous but clung to, attempting to convince herself that her casual outfit would be acceptable in the classy Cardiff Hotel.

Tossing her head back and standing up as straight

as she could, she gave him a big smile. "No problem. I've enjoyed sitting here and people watching."

"That's right," said Jeremy, as they walked down the path that led out of the park, "you're a writer."

"Not really. I'm just a reporter for a small town weekly."

"A reporter! I'll have to watch what I say."

"Right. Or you'll be exposed to the *Pennysaver*'s dozens of subscribers in Tinker's Cove, most of whom use the paper to line birdcages or wash windows."

He smiled, taking her arm as the light changed and they began to cross the street. "Wash windows?"

"A little housewifely trick," explained Lucy. "Newspaper is much better for washing windows than paper towels. There's something about the ink that makes the windows shine."

"I'll tell my housekeeper," said Jeremy, and Lucy was reminded that he occupied a loftier perch in the social hierarchy than she did.

This truth was confirmed as they approached the hotel and the doorman greeted Jeremy with a big smile. "Nice to see you, Mr. Blake." He opened the door for them with a flourish and Lucy suspected she could have been wearing nothing at all, or could have had a pet python draped over her shoulders—it didn't matter because she was with Jeremy Blake.

Entering the bar, which was paneled with dark mahogany and dimly lit by crystal sconces, they were offered a prime table in a secluded corner.

"The usual, Mr. Blake?" asked the waiter, speaking with a French accent.

"That will be fine, Pierre." He turned to Lucy. "What will you have? I can recommend the Blue Sapphire martini. They do them very well here."

"A glass of chardonnay would be fine."

"Then I think the Rivers-Marie," said Jeremy.

"Excellent choice, Mr. Blake." Pierre departed and Lucy settled back in the plush banquette seat, noticing the little bouquet of fresh flowers on the table, the gentle tinkle of piano music, and the other well-dressed, well-behaved customers. She should have felt out of place, but instead decided that she could definitely get used to this pampered lifestyle.

Money certainly smoothed out life's rough spots, she thought, watching Jeremy take his seat. He wasn't the best-looking man, she realized, comparing him to Bill, who was naturally handsome in a rugged way. Jeremy, however, despite a double chin and developing paunch, had the advantage of expert tailoring and barbering and the confidence that went with a billion-dollar portfolio.

"So what brings you to the big city?" asked Jeremy.

"I'm a New York girl, you know. I grew up in the city, and when I was here last week for Beth's funeral, I realized how much I miss it. I decided to take a break and have a little vacation here."

"Beth used to tell me that she envied your life in Maine."

"I guess it's true that the grass is always greener, that we always want what we don't have."

The waiter delivered their drinks and they clinked

glasses. "Cheers," said Jeremy, proceeding to gulp down half his martini in one big swallow.

"I can't quite believe that Beth really envied me, with my highly mortgaged old house and my secondhand car." Lucy took a sip of wine, realizing it was definitely a cut above the stuff she usually drank, and paused, savoring the complex flavors before swallowing. Then she continued, choosing her words carefully. "She had everything people dream of, including a penthouse. Do you have any idea what went wrong?"

Jeremy shook his head. "I don't. I wish I did. Maybe then I could have done something to prevent what happened."

Lucy was quick to offer the sympathy and reassurance he expected. "That's natural after a suicide, but you shouldn't blame yourself."

"I wish I could believe you." Jeremy had finished his martini and was signaling the waiter for another. "How long have you known Beth?"

"Since kindergarten," said Lucy, remembering once again the little girl who had welcomed her. "But, well, you know how she was. She went her own way, and sometimes I didn't hear from her for long stretches of time. But then she'd pop up again, and we would just pick up where we left off."

"Amazing," said Jeremy. His second drink had arrived and Lucy had the sense that he was losing interest in her.

"I've often wondered, how did you and Beth meet?" she asked.

"It was at a benefit gala for the Red Cross. She

was one of the planners, one of the gals who make these things happen."

"Like a chairperson?"

"No. She was working for some outfit, some party planner."

"Was it love at first sight?"

"For me, yeah, but not for her. Beth wasn't eager to marry again. She was gun-shy after three tries. She'd been on her own for a long while and liked it that way." He looked down at his fresh drink, as if it were a crystal ball holding all the answers. "Maybe she was right—the marriage didn't work out. We were in the process of divorcing when she . . ." He broke off, staring glumly across the room.

Lucy thought of Dante's claim that Beth was demanding a huge divorce settlement in exchange for silence about some shady business deals. She wondered who this guy sitting across the table from her really was. Was he truly grieving the loss of the woman he loved, or was he relieved to be rid of an expensive problem? Was he an honest dealer or a crook? That heavy jaw, those bristly brows and sweep of jet black hair didn't offer any clues, and she wasn't getting anywhere with this polite chitchat. She decided to press him and was about to ask him if the police considered him a suspect when he glanced at his watch and then stood up.

"I'm so sorry, but I have to go. I have an appointment."

"Of course," said Lucy politely. "It's been a pleasure. Thank you."

"You're very welcome." He was looking toward the exit and anxious to be on his way. "Do stay and finish your drink, have another if you want. I have an account here." He pulled a twenty from a money clip and laid it on the table; Lucy set the complimentary dish of salted nuts on it, acknowledging it was for the waiter. "Well, uh, have a nice day," he said, throwing the words in her direction as he hurried out of the bar.

Lucy remained, waiting a moment or two, then followed him. She was just in time to see him greet a very tall, very curvaceous blond wearing a white, sleeveless dress so tight that it seemed she must have been sewed into it, and a pair of pointy-toed five-inch heels. Lucy slipped behind a handy potted palm and watched as the gilded couple seemed to glide across the carpeted lobby to the elevators, where they waited. The elevator was slow and Jeremy impatient. He slipped his hand around her waist, and when the doors slid open, cupped her derriere and gently pushed her inside, stepping beneath the glowing arrow that indicated the elevator was going up.

The doors closed and they disappeared from view. Lucy proceeded on to the ladies' room, wondering what exactly one wore under such a tight dress, and decided the answer was probably nothing. Nothing at all.

She took her time in the well-appointed ladies' room, admiring the painted paneling and gleaming sinks with gold taps. The soap smelled like almonds and the towels were cloth, neatly folded and stacked on porcelain trays. A mirrored makeup counter was just inside the door, offering a selection of expensive scents, and Lucy combed her hair, applied some fresh lipstick, and treated herself to a squirt of Chanel No. 5. She remembered hearing somewhere that it was all that Marilyn Monroe claimed to wear to bed and wondered what was going on upstairs; she was smiling to herself as she stepped out into the lobby.

"Lucy! Lucy Stone! What are you doing here?"

Startled, she stopped in her tracks and turned to see her friend Sam, along with her husband, Brad. The two were dressed formally, he in a suit and she in heels and a cocktail dress, and Sam was leaning rather heavily on her husband's arm for support.

"I'm in the city for a week," Lucy replied. "What about you?"

"Wedding! Little Suzie all grown up!" declared Sam, slurring her words.

"Our friends' daughter," explained Brad. "Suzanne Fogarty."

"Married ver' well," added Sam. "Inveshment banker. Li'l Suzie's gonna live in London."

"There was an open bar." Brad caught Sam as she stumbled. "I think we better find some coffee for Sam. There's a Starbucks around the corner."

Lucy nodded and took Sam's free arm, and together they led her out of the hotel and into the coffee bar. She sat with Sam at a table while Brad ordered a Trenta iced coffee for his wife and a couple of bottled waters for himself and Lucy.

Sam was feeling no pain and offering a commentary on the wedding in a loud voice. "Pershonally, I don' like those strapless dreshes, no' for a bride. She was in whiy, 'coursh, but no'foolin' an'body sinche she's prac'ly forty. If shesh a day."

"Here you go, sweetie," said Brad, bringing the cup of iced coffee to her lips. "Drink up."

He shook his head ruefully while Sam slurped noisily. "It's really not her fault. She rarely drinks and the waiter kept topping off her wineglass, running up the bar tab."

"'Lishus sea bass," volunteered Sam, pushing away the coffee. "But those purple dresshes, yuck."

"It's a nice surprise, running into you," said Brad. "We thought you'd gone back to Tinker's Cove."

"I did, but I came back. I just arrived this morning."

"Where are you staying?"

"I got an Airbnb, a studio. It's not far from here, on the other side of the park."

"Whish ya coulda shtayed wif ush. Contractor sho shlow."

Brad raised the cup to his wife's lips again and she sucked up more of the cold liquid. "Does coffee work?" he asked Lucy. "I've got to get her home somehow."

"I think so. Give it time."

"Thaw I saw Jerrr'my." Sam had slipped down in her chair and seemed to be nodding off.

"You did. I had a drink with him. There was a ceremony in the park, thanking him for restoring a gazebo."

"Saw a gurrrl . . ." Brad was quick to offer the cup once again but Sam pushed it away. "Probly call gurrrl." Sam nodded seriously. "Woulda cost him in divorsh."

"Please, Sam," protested Brad, looking nervously

around the Starbucks where a good number of people had settled in for the afternoon. Some were pecking away on laptops or swiping smartphones, others were reading newpapers or the occasional book, and some were engaged in conversations. A couple of loners kept glancing at them, unable to resist observing an amusing spectacle. "We're in public."

"Is that true?" Lucy asked Brad, keeping her voice low. "Is he known as a philanderer? Is that why they were getting divorced?"

"I can't really talk about it. Client confidentiality."

"Your client is dead."

"True, but her husband is very much alive. . . ."

"Frishky fellow," volunteered Sam, giggling. "Ever'body knowsh."

"And very litigious. He's got swarms of lawyers, influential connections, and deep pockets. All of which could make my life miserable."

"He seemed pretty upset when I was with him. I got the feeling that he really loved Beth, but then I saw him at the elevator with . . ." She leaned in and whispered, "Was that really a working girl?"

Brad nodded. "Most likely."

"She didn't look . . . Well, not like I'd expect a girl like that to look." Lucy wasn't sure what she thought a New York call girl looked like, but Jeremy Blake's companion had a polished appearance that seemed at odds with her profession. Maybe she was thinking of the flashy clothes and ripped plastic boots Julia Roberts wore in the movie *Pretty Woman*.

Brad smiled. "A lot of these girls are college students or millennials saddled with student debt, sick of trying to eke out a living as interns or working at Starbucks."

Lucy thought of her daughters, Sara and Zoe, who she'd insisted go to Winchester College, which offered discounted tuition to townies and was an easy commute, allowing them to live at home. She certainly wouldn't want them prostituting themselves to get an education; no degree was worth that.

"There's no shame these days," added Brad. "They make good money and they make good connections. Intimate connections with powerful, influential men."

"Goodness me," said Lucy, shocked to her core.

Sam was snoring, sunk down in the comfy armchair. Brad wouldn't be going anywhere soon.

"Dante said his mother was upset about Blake's shady real estate deals, but maybe it was really the other women. At bottom Beth was a very loyal person; she would've expected loyalty from her husband."

"They were separated, had been for a couple of years. I don't think even Beth would have expected him to remain loyal to a marriage that was merely a legal technicality. They weren't living together anymore."

Lucy thought of Beth living alone in that luxurious aerie above the city, and couldn't accept the idea that she'd voluntarily stepped off her balcony into thin air. "When was the last time you saw her? What was her mood? Did you think she was considering suicide?"

Brad leveled his gaze and looked at her, a serious expression on his face. "You're having a hard time with this, aren't you? Sam is, too. She can't believe Beth killed herself, and she's always coming up with theories. Maybe it was an accident, maybe she was reaching too far, deadheading a climbing vine or something. Maybe it was a robbery gone wrong." He paused, glancing at his slumbering wife. "What it all comes down to is that she thinks she could have saved her, if she'd only known."

"That's exactly how I feel," admitted Lucy. "I need to know what happened."

"And that's why you came to New York? To investigate?"

"To find out as much as I can in a week," said Lucy. "Pretty hopeless, hunh?"

Brad smiled. "Yeah. And dangerous."

Lucy stared at him. "So you do think there was foul play?"

"No." His voice was firm. "Not at all. But the case is closed. It's officially suicide and, trust me, nobody wants to see it reopened. Just let it alone. For your own safety. Don't tangle with Jeremy Blake."

"Is that your professional opinion, as a lawyer?" asked Lucy, in a teasing tone.

Sam snorted, and outside the window they saw a cab pulling up and discharging a passenger. "Grab that cab for me, Lucy. I've got to get Sleeping Beauty home."

Lucy popped up, grabbed her bag, and ran out the door, waving at the cabbie, who was just pulling away. He stopped and she leaned in the window. "Thanks, my friend is coming."

Then Brad appeared, supporting a very groggy Sam. Lucy opened the door, Sam collapsed on the seat, and Brad lifted her legs into the cab. "Remember what I said: don't mess with Blake," he said, before running around to the other side and hopping in beside his wife. Lucy watched as he gave the cabbie his address and then raised his hand in a small wave. Lucy waved back as the cab pulled away.

Her phone rang and she was relieved to see that Dante was returning her call. "Hi. How's it going?" she asked, retreating to the front wall of the hotel where she was out of the stream of busy pedestrian traffic.

"Better, much better."

"That's good to hear. I've been worried about you."

"No need to worry." He paused. "I'm really sorry about that call. I was just a little down and had one too many. But things are really okay. I've got a new gig, in San Francisco actually. I've never been, so I'm pretty excited about it. I leave at the end of June."

"That's wonderful. You'll love the West Coast."

"That's what I hear. So don't worry about me. I'm moving on."

"Well, I'm here for the week, so maybe we can get together. . . ."

"Sure." Dante sounded hesitant. "I'll have to check my schedule and get back to you."

Lucy smiled tolerantly, used to her daughters' social manipulations and their reluctance to commit to an engagement in case something better came along. "Fine. You've got my number."

"Righto. Talk to you soon." He paused. "Oh, and I really want to thank you for, well, being there. It made a big difference."

Lucy smiled. "Ciao. And take care."

# Chapter Nine

Lucy stood on the sidewalk for a moment, wondering if Dante was really doing as well as he claimed and watching the endless traffic jam that seemed to be a fact of life in the city. For a moment she missed Tinker's Cove, with its single traffic light and plenty of parking. Only in Maine, she thought, would the town's single most attractive spot, the harbor, be designated as a parking lot.

She wasn't in Maine now, and she wasn't at all sure what to do with the rest of her afternoon. She had come to the city to investigate and, while she'd already managed to interview her prime suspect, she had to admit she hadn't gotten much out of him. Not that she'd expected him to blurt out a heartfelt confession, she thought, as she started walking toward the stop for the crosstown bus, but she did feel as if she'd wasted an opportunity that would not come her way again.

Of course, it wasn't what people said as much as

what they did that counted, at least that's what her mother always told her. "Beauty is as beauty does" was what her mother actually used to say, and she'd meant it as a reproof when teenage Lucy fretted about a pimple or moaned about her impossible hair. That being said, there was an underlying truth to the adage, which, when applied to Jeremy Blake, seemed to indicate a lack of character.

Where was his human decency? she asked herself, as she approached the cluster of people waiting on the sidewalk for the crosstown bus. Sure, Beth had been his soon-to-be ex-wife, but she was someone he had professed to love and had once vowed to honor and protect, but now he seemed indifferent to her death. Even hardened New Yorkers were horrified by Beth's gruesome end, and her friends were deeply shaken, coping with guilt as well as grief. But not Jeremy, once her nearest and dearest, who was happily bopping around the city collecting awards and consorting with call girls.

*Maybe I've got this wrong*, thought Lucy, checking the sign with the bus schedule and comparing it to her watch, concluding the bus should be pulling up to the stop but was nowhere in sight. And judging from the number of people who were waiting, the last bus hadn't come, either.

"Weekend. They always run late on the weekend," advised a friendly, older woman dressed in sensible shoes and a neat pantsuit.

"Thanks," said Lucy, concluding she might as well walk. It was a pleasant spring day and she could use the exercise. Walking always helped her think, and she had plenty to think about after her meeting with Jeremy.

Picking up her earlier train of thought, she wondered if Jeremy's seeming indifference to Beth's death was really a cover-up for his true feelings. Maybe he was absolutely devastated and was choosing to drown his sorrows in martinis and sex. That woman in the white dress would certainly be distracting, if only for a while.

By now Lucy had reached Fifth Avenue, where an entrance to Central Park was on the opposite side of the street. She never would have considered walking through the park alone when she was a girl; back then it was considered far too dangerous. But today, the leafy green of the park beckoned and everybody said the city was much safer. People flocked to the park, rollerblading and jogging or simply sitting on the benches that lined the paths.

When the light changed she crossed and went in, joining the throng making their way through a cluster of vendors selling ice cream, balloons, T-shirts, and hot dogs. There was a scent of freshly mown grass in the air, and a light breeze rustled the leaves as Lucy walked along, fascinated by all the different people. There were young, athletic types zipping along on skates and bikes, moms pushing strollers, elderly women walking small, fluffy dogs, and very fit young men with shaved heads walking large pit bulls. She saw veiled Muslim women, bearded and turbaned Sikhs, Orthodox Jews in hats and long black coats, and lots of kids of all ages. All that movement, and the brightly colored clothes, was somewhat dazzling and reminded her of the impressionist paintings, vibrating with light and color, that hung in the Met.

She knew the way, had taken this path to Wollman Rink for ice skating and hot cocoa with friends many times as a girl, and back then they'd always held hands and screamed as loud as they could when they ran through the dark pedestrian underpass that went under the busy road connecting Fifth Avenue to Central Park West. Her steps slowed as she approached the shadowy underpass and she wished that her old school friends were with her today. Looking around, she realized the crowd had disappeared and she was almost alone, except for a couple of shady-looking guys. There was a simple explanation, she realized. The rink was closed this time of year and most people had stuck to the north-south path that paralleled Fifth Avenue rather than venturing into the depths of the park.

The guys, two bearded men in hooded sweatshirts, were walking slowly, smoking and speaking in some language she didn't understand. They were foreigners, immigrants or visitors, she didn't know which, but she certainly didn't want to be alone with them in that dank, dark space where they could easily confront her and snatch her purse. Or *even worse*, she thought, remembering her mother's dire warnings.

What to do? She considered taking the path that led to the road above and trying to hail a cab, but figured that would be absolutely pointless since all the cabs would be occupied, carrying passengers to the West Side. She could try to find another route, heading south to Fifty-Ninth Street, but that would take her miles out of her way and she was already beginning to feel tired. There was nothing for it but to make the dash through the underpass, so she took a deep breath and grabbed a firm hold of her purse and marched on, screaming silently. When she emerged into the sunshine the two men were standing to the side of the bridge, as if waiting for someone. For her?

"Good afternoon," said one, looking concerned. "Are you okay?"

"We thought you might be ill," suggested the other, in a crisp British accent.

"I'm fine, thank you," said Lucy, smiling and keeping her distance as she continued on her way. Maybe they were really Good Samaritans, maybe they were attempting to lure her close enough to do her harm. That was the trouble in the city, she thought. Everyone was a stranger and you never knew who you could trust.

It was a relief to step inside her little studio apartment, where she carefully locked the door behind her before collapsing on the futon with a big glass of water. There were lots of kilim pillows on the corduroy spread and she arranged them so she could raise her swollen feet above her head and reached for her phone, wanting nothing more at that moment than to hear Bill's voice, but either one of the girls would be fine, too. What she got was her own recorded voice, advising her to leave a message. She did, reporting that she'd arrived safely and missed everybody, and then she asked for a return call and ended with love to all.

She had some text messages so she checked them, finding mostly ads, which she deleted, and one from Ted. Probably not good news, she guessed, reluctantly opening it. As she expected, he was peeved and it was all her fault. Following the interview, the Bickfords had had second thoughts about her upcoming story portraying their marriage and had asked him to kill it. When he'd objected, they'd asked to read it in advance of publication, which he'd agree to against his better judgment.

Against established policy, too, thought Lucy.

Of course they'd hated it and pressed him not to print it, but when he flatly refused they demanded free ad space, which he agreed to do but realized afterward was probably the motivation for the whole thing. Thanks to her, he'd been taken.

*Thanks to your own foolish self,* thought Lucy. She tucked a pillow under her head and looked around the little apartment, all hers for a week. City life wasn't so bad, she thought, trying to decide which of the Lean Cuisine dinners she'd picked up at the bodega to have for supper. She opened the tiny freezer and studied her options, deciding that none of them were very appealing. She considered going out again to the bodega to find something more appetizing, but the thought of stuffing her swollen feet into her running shoes convinced her to settle for the chicken with noodles. The bottle of wine in the fridge caught her eye when she grabbed a package of salad, and she decided to pour herself a glass.

After polishing off her low-cal meal she indulged in a second glass of wine, which turned out to be a respectable sauvignon blanc, and turned on the TV. The owner of the apartment subscribed to premium cable and she was dazzled by the huge number of options, not to mention the rare opportunity of choosing exactly what she wanted to watch. At home, TV viewing was dominated by Bill's sports and the girls' reality TV. So tonight she opted for a Scandinavian crime series everyone raved about that she'd been dying to see, intending to binge watch the whole six episodes. She only made it through two, however, before she began to feel sleepy and made up her bed on the futon.

It was recalling the frightening camera shot from under the bed in episode two, the viewpoint of the creepy guy who'd been hiding there, waiting to attack the unsuspecting young woman who was kicking off her bunny slippers, that kept her awake. Of course she'd checked beneath the futon, finding only dust bunnies and an ancient *New Yorker* magazine, but that didn't seem to help. Neither did the voices of passersby, the constant sirens, roaring motorcycles, and slammed car doors, all of which kept her on edge. Lying there in the darkness, she fretted about Elizabeth, far away in Paris where terrorists might attack at any moment. Then there was little Patrick, off in Alaska, where polar bears roamed the streets and untamed wilderness was only steps away from his backyard. Sara and Zoe were on her mind, too, since they seemed set on careers, which was fine with her so long as they also settled down with nice husbands who'd keep them safe and provide her with more grandchildren. She knew this was ridiculously old-fashioned of her, and selfish as well, but that was how she felt, deep down, and she was frustrated by her daughters' lack of interest in finding suitable mates.

She finally did drift off for a few hours, but woke bright and early at her usual six o'clock. There was no reason to get up so early, so she rolled over and tried to go back to sleep, but her internal clock had decided it was time to be up and doing. Deciding to go out and explore the neighborhood, keeping an eye out for a shoe store where she could return later in the day to buy comfortable sandals, she got up.

It was a cool morning that promised to be clear, and the trees dotting the sidewalk still had the springtime look of freshly opened leaves. She had the sidewalk to herself as she walked along, but found she really didn't have the energy for a long walk, especially since her feet were still somewhat swollen. When she discovered the bodega was already open, with the morning papers stacked on an outside bench made from a plank set on two grubby plastic milk cases, she grabbed a thick *New York Times* Sunday edition and went inside to pay for it. Coffee was brewing, so she bought a large cup and a huge bagel as well, and went back to the apartment intending to treat herself to a lazy morning.

Lucy had more than a passing interest in the *Times*; as a reporter herself she was interested in learning as much as she could from the paper that was regarded by many as the gold standard of journalism. She especially admired the obituaries, because they often offered unusual insights about famous people, and also recounted the lives of interesting but lesser known individuals. When she finished the first section, with the news of the day, she turned to the business section, which she knew usually had an interesting couple of pages covering New York real estate and lifestyles. She never got that far, however, because the front page had a story about Jeremy Blake.

According to the story, which was bylined E. L. Haley, the state attorney general was calling off an investigation of alleged condo fraud by Jeremy Blake. The story included allegations that Blake's company had pressured occupants of rent-stabilized apartments to move so the units could be converted to condos, and had also delayed turning over the management of condominium buildings to the unit owners, thus continuing to collect bloated HOA fees. The AG had given no explanation for the decision, which had outraged some of the condo owners who were quoted in the article. Jeremy Blake himself could not be reached for comment, which amused Lucy.

The reporter's e-mail address was printed at the end of the article, so Lucy sent a brief e-mail requesting a meeting. She figured a *New York Times* reporter was probably much too busy to bother with a housewife and part-time, small-town reporter from Maine, but figured it was worth a try. Then she turned to the Arts & Leisure section, looking for something to do that afternoon, and found a notice listing an art show in Soho featuring works by Tito Wilkins, Beth's second husband.

Aware that Soho was a bit of a trip, and would require the use of her feet, Lucy did some research on her laptop and found a nearby shoe store that opened at eleven a.m. on Sundays. She was there when the door opened, and after commiserating with her over her tired feet, the proprietor sold her a pair of butter-soft sandals with guaranteed arch support. They cost a fortune, but Lucy wasn't about to quibble.

The new sandals were fantastic, like little foamy clouds beneath her feet, practically carrying her up the subway stairs into the heart of Soho. She wasn't familiar with the area, which had become gentrified in recent years, but expected to find a quiet, artistic neighborhood with quaint, narrow streets and unusual shops and galleries. The streets were indeed narrow, dating from the early settlement of lower Manhattan, but they were thronged with masses of people who had apparently come from all over the world to shop at high-end designer boutiques like DKNY, Tommy Hilfiger, and Stella McCartney, as well as the numerous vendors selling cheap knock-off scarves and sunglasses from tables on the sidewalk.

Lucy was carried along by the crowd, not exactly sure where she was or where she would find the gallery. She passed a L'Occitane shop selling fancy toiletries and paused, considering going into the crowded store, but someone bumped into her and she figured she'd better keep moving. Passing a tiny French bakery, she realized it was connected to a bistro called Balthazar and she darted inside, hoping to find shelter from the buffeting crowd and maybe a ham sandwich.

Those dreams were dashed when the maître d' informed her there would be a three-hour wait, and indeed the place was packed with people. No

wonder, she thought. It was a bit of Paris right here
in New York and she wished she could stay and be
served by the waiters in their black jackets and
long white aprons. She did spot a sign for TOI-
LETTES and descended to the basement level, just
as one did in Paris. The ladies' room was clean and
attended by a small, wizened woman in a black
dress, so after washing her hands Lucy gave her a
couple of dollars and asked for directions to the
gallery.

The directions were spot-on accurate and Lucy
soon found the XYZ Gallery, which was located
one floor up in a spacious white-walled loft with
large windows overlooking the river of humanity
streaming below. An attractive young woman
dressed in a black dress with a clunky, artistic, silver necklace was seated at a desk by the door, but
merely acknowledged Lucy with a small nod.

Continuing into the exhibit space, Lucy saw a
number of large paintings featuring vibrant, bright
colors, in an abstract Jackson Pollack style. But
after putting on her reading glasses and taking a
closer look, she realized what she had taken for abstract shapes and dots were instead body parts and
blood. Axes, nooses, guns, and all sorts of knives
were worked into the designs, along with bullets
and bombs. The pictures were all disturbing, but
one with a baby impaled on a bayonet sent her
reeling onto a well-placed bench.

This was not what she expected from a man
whom Beth had chosen to marry, not at all. Beth
had a child when she married Tito Wilkins. Whatever could she have been thinking, exposing little
Dante to art like this? Even worse, exposing him to

a man who created such disturbing images. What sort of person was Tito? What kind of mind thinks of stuff like this? she wondered, glancing around.

The work didn't seem to be very popular, as she was the only one in the gallery, apart from the gallerina. It certainly wasn't anything you'd want to put on your wall, unless you were a sadist or psychotic killer. She supposed it was meant to be a commentary on the violence of modern life, but Lucy felt it was difficult enough to read the newspaper every morning without having to look at graphic depictions of explosions and decapitations. Maybe Tito had changed since his marriage to Beth, thought Lucy, remembering Beth's accounts of him as an exciting and liberating partner. Maybe he'd become bitter, or overwhelmed by hopelessness, unable to distance himself from the never-ending reports of senseless mass shootings and terrorist attacks.

Shaking her head, she approached the gallerina, who reluctantly put down the smartphone that seemed glued to her hand. "I'd like to contact the artist. I knew him years ago when he was married to a good friend, but I lost track of him when they divorced. Can you give me a phone number? I'd really like to get in touch with him."

"I'm sorry but that's not possible. The artist himself asked us to protect his privacy, and when you consider the nature of his work, it's probably for the best." She picked up a packet of papers stapled at the top. "This is his bio, if you're interested."

"Thank you," said Lucy. "Have you met him? What is he like these days?"

"He's really old, very polite, quite reclusive. He was only at the opening for about fifteen minutes, long enough to pose for a photo and shake a few hands."

"Does his work sell?" asked Lucy.

"Oh, gosh yes. A big rock star was in the other day, and he's considering several for a new house he just bought in Rhinebeck."

"Interesting," said Lucy, preparing to go. "Perhaps you could pass along a message to Tito, from me?" She scribbled her phone number and name on the corner of the top sheet of the bio and ripped it off. "I'd really appreciate it."

"I send him an e-mail every day. He wants to know when someone is interested in buying a painting. I don't suppose it would do any harm to mention your interest."

"No harm, only good," said Lucy.

Lucy didn't really have any hope that Tito would contact her, and she wasn't actually sure if she wanted him to. He might be able to offer some insight into Beth's death. He might even have been her killer, come to think of it. Those images were really disturbing and unsettling, and Lucy feared they possibly represented a deranged personality, perhaps even prone to violence.

Beth really knew how to pick 'em, she thought, ticking off the whacko phony religious leader Gabe, the fraudster Jeremy, and now the crazy, violent artist. The chiropractor, husband number three, seemed the most normal of the bunch, but that marriage hadn't lasted either.

Stepping out onto the busy sidewalk again, Lucy decided to head home. She was tired, and she still had the Book Review, Travel, and Sunday Style sections of the *Times* to read. The subway station was nearby, on the corner, and she descended, hoping for an uncrowded train with plenty of seats. Maybe even one of those benches on the platform would be free and she could sit and rest while waiting.

Once she got through the turnstile, however, and found the platform, she discovered something was amiss. A cluster of people had gathered at one end of the subterranean tunnel and were anxiously looking around, as if waiting for help to arrive. Further along on the platform, she saw several girls in brightly colored, form-fitting track suits yelling insults at each other and pushing and shoving. Then one, the largest, grabbed one of the girls by the hair and dragged her down onto the filthy concrete, pummeling her.

*Someone should stop this*, thought Lucy, terrified that one or more of the girls would end up on the train track. She knew she couldn't do it; she was much too small. She looked to the other passengers, counting a couple of families with kids, older women, and one young man whose arm was in a cast, and decided there was no help to be gotten there. Making a quick decision, she dashed up the stairs to the mezzanine containing the turnstiles, ticket machines, and an information booth with an attendant. She pushed her way through the exit, losing her fare, and banged on the thick, protective Plexiglas window to get the man's attention. When he looked up from his copy of the *Daily News* she reported the fight, getting a shrug. The attendant did pick up the phone, however, and Lucy hoped, but wasn't convinced, he was calling the transit police.

There was nothing more she could do, she decided, and she certainly wasn't going back to the platform. She'd have to pay another fare, for one thing, and she wasn't about to subject herself to real violence, not after seeing all that painted violence. She climbed the steps to the street and positioned herself on the corner, arm raised to hail a taxi.

# Chapter Ten

Sunshine was streaming through the slatted shutters and striping the wall when Lucy woke on Monday morning, feeling refreshed after a good night's sleep. Maybe she was feeling more comfortable in her temporary digs, maybe it was all the exercise she'd gotten the day before, or maybe it was the fact that she'd had a nice phone call with Sara just before bedtime. Everything was fine at home, she'd learned, except for the fact that they all missed her.

When Lucy popped around the corner to the bodega to get coffee and a fresh bagel, she realized it was a day in a million with a clear blue sky, temperature in the sixties, and a light, fresh breeze. Determined to take advantage of such a fine day, she decided to venture up north to the Bronx and the New York Botanical Garden. She seemed to recall that the garden wasn't far from Beth's chiropractor husband Colin Fine's office, and that hunch was confirmed as she studied a street map while chewing on her warm, buttered bagel. She called his office while walking to the subway and was able to get an early afternoon appointment, which she'd decided was the best way to approach the doctor. She hadn't made up her mind whether he'd remember her as Beth's friend, and even if he did there was no guarantee he'd want to meet with her to hash over old times. There was also the fact that she considered him an unlikely, but still possible suspect in Beth's death, so choosing the office setting seemed the safest option.

But she put all that out of her mind after buying her ticket at the gate and entering the botanical garden, where she wandered through the beautiful grounds, admiring the various blooms and ending up in the rose garden, which was just entering its prime period. The varieties were all labeled and she marveled at each one, often wondering about the names and who exactly were people like Rita Levi-Montalcini and Charles de Mills and why these particular roses were named after them. She was waiting at the tram stop when she saw a little golf cart carrying a bride, complete with long white dress and veil, stop by the rose garden. There the bride, groom, photographer, and assistant all got off and prepared to take formal portraits. Lucy watched this little drama, delighted, until the tram arrived and brought her back to the entrance, where she treated herself to lunch in the café and bought a bar of rose-scented soap in the gift shop. Then, renewed with fresh optimism, she walked the seven blocks to Dr. Fine's office.

Lucy had never been to a chiropractor, but she

discovered that Dr. Fine's office was pretty much like every medical office she'd ever visited, with a middle-aged female receptionist who demanded her insurance card and ID in a strong, Brooklyn-accented voice, then gave her a clipboard with a long questionnaire to fill out. The waiting room was crowded and Lucy checked out the other patients before choosing a seat. They were a mixed lot of men and women, some seemingly quite prosperous while others looked as if they were on the other end of the economic scale. Lucy didn't want to be judgmental or snobbish, but some of those people appeared to need a good wash. She finally seated herself on one of the few empty leatherette armchairs, next to a casually dressed man in sweatpants who was reading the *Wall Street Journal,* and began to fill in the form. It was quite a thorough inquisition, beginning with name and address, which caused her to pause before putting down the address of the Airbnb. Then she went on to tackle questions about her next of kin, age, and sex, but also her age at the onset of menstruation, obstetrical details such as number and outcome of pregnancies, and even her parents' causes of death.

She had plenty of time to think about her answers, as the earlier patients were called to the examining room one by one. Some of them didn't seem to stay very long, while others were gone for quite some time. She tried to determine from their expressions whether or not their treatments had been successful, but couldn't tell. Some coughed up quite a lot of money for their treatments, usually in cash, which she thought was odd. In her experience, medical offices usually billed for the portion of the bill that wasn't covered by insurance or a copay.

Then her name was called and she was ushered to an examining room where she was given a gown and told to take off everything except her underpants. She complied and then, as usual, she waited for a good ten minutes until the doctor appeared, studying the chart of the human spine that hung on the wall. Dr. Fine was now much older than the young groom she remembered, who had sported long sideburns and pale blue tux. Now he was carrying an extra twenty pounds and was balding. He didn't look up when he entered, but stood inside the doorway, reading through her questionnaire.

"What brings you here today?" he asked, in a puzzled tone. "You seem quite healthy, um, Mrs. Stone."

Lucy studied the doctor, with his rumpled chinos and white lab coat, his double chin and potbelly, his comfortably worn shoes, and decided he didn't seem to be much of a threat. She might as well drop any pretense of being a patient and admit why she was there.

"I'm quite well, thank you. I came to talk to you about my friend and your ex-wife, Beth Gerard. Perhaps you remember me? I'm Lucy Stone. Beth and I were best friends."

Their eyes met and she saw a glimmer of recognition in his. "Ah, yes. Lucy." He paused, considering his words. "You know what happened to Beth?"

"I do. That's why I wanted to talk to you. I really can't accept the idea that she committed suicide. I'm looking for answers."

"Well, the police investigated and concluded it was suicide. The case is closed."

"I'm aware of that, but I can't help wondering about it. Do you have any insight into why she might want to kill herself? Or if there was anyone who might have wanted to kill her?"

"Oh, my goodness, no. We didn't stay in touch after the divorce; we went our separate ways. It was more than twenty years ago, you know. I'm remarried, quite happily. And of course Beth remarried, too. But I will say this, in my experience she was quite unstable, and it was impossible to live with her. One day she was on top of the world, singing and dancing, and the next she wouldn't get out of bed because everything was so hopeless. I tried to get help for her but she was very resistant. In the end, I simply couldn't take it."

Lucy found his attitude rather callous, especially since Beth had a child when she married Colin Fine. "You had a stepson, Dante. Weren't you concerned about him?"

"A very odd child, indeed. I can't say I ever felt fatherly toward him, and he clearly resented me. He wanted his mother to himself."

"That's not unusual, is it?"

Dr. Fine sighed. "Looking back, I suppose I could have tried harder. I was pretty young, you know, just out of university and beginning my practice. I guess I saw getting married as something you did when you grew up, like it made me an instant adult. Now I realize I still had a lot of growing up to do." He looked at her and furrowed his brow. "Would you mind standing up?"

Next thing Lucy knew he was telling her to

bend forward, sideways and backward, then asked her to stand and raise one leg at a time. Next she walked a line painted on the floor, feeling a bit like a suspected drunk driver, followed by the request that she loosen the back of her gown so he could observe her spine while she walked in place. She found the whole thing somewhat amusing, until she was asked to lie down on the examining table so he could palpate her spine. She realized she really didn't want this man to touch her but wasn't quite sure why. Besides, she reminded herself that, since she was probably going to pay for the exam, she might as well get some benefit from it. She had her doubts about chiropractic, but all those people in the waiting room were presumably getting some good from Dr. Fine's treatments. Somewhat reluctantly, she climbed onto the table and lay face down, as instructed.

Next thing she knew the doctor was running his hands up and down her back. He then pressed down hard on her shoulders, which forced the air out of her lungs. She was primarily concerned with getting some air back in when she felt his hands on her lower back, where they seemed to stay for quite a while. Adding to her discomfort was the odd little *hmmmm* noise he made as he stroked her bottom. She was about to protest when the hands were suddenly removed.

"It's as I thought," he finally said, "you have a subluxation."

"I feel just fine," said Lucy, quickly sitting up with her legs dangling off the table and refastening the ties on her gown.

"You're probably just used to the discomfort. I

see this all the time. People come in and say 'Oh, Dr. Colin, I had no idea what feeling healthy is really like. I've been feeling twenty years younger since my adjustment.' Now, if you'll just sit on this stool and allow me to make an adjustment. . . ."

"Really, there's no need. . . ."

"Nonsense. I'm the doctor."

Something in his tone convinced Lucy that the only way she was going to get out of this examining room, short of screaming bloody murder, was to let Dr. Colin do this adjustment, whatever it was. So she sat on the stool and allowed him to take a series of measurements using various devices.

"It's exactly as I thought," he said, standing behind her and massaging her shoulders. "Now, I should explain that a subluxation is an alteration of the contiguous structures in the spine that can cause a neural disturbance. You will feel an immediate improvement after this adjustment, but it's likely you will need to return regularly for further adjustments. Now, I want you to relax and breathe deeply," he intoned, running his hands up and down her sides, brushing her breasts before suddenly grabbing her shoulders and yanking sharply upwards, causing her to yelp.

"Very good," he said, "the adjustment was successful."

"Uh, good," said Lucy, rising rather gingerly to her feet and discovering, much to her relief, that everything still worked.

"Now, you may experience some soreness tonight and tomorrow, but I can give you a prescription, guaranteed to make you feel like a million bucks."

"No, thanks," said Lucy, who was a firm believer in nothing stronger than an occasional aspirin.

"Are you sure?" He leaned into her face, causing her to step back. "These are perfectly safe, nonaddictive, and my patients swear by them."

"I'm sure." Lucy looked at her watch. "I must go. I have a, um, meeting. . . ."

"I understand." He held up his hands in a gesture of surrender. "But if you change your mind, just call the office. Anytime, day or night, and I can call in a prescription to your pharmacy. And I would like to see you again for another adjustment in four weeks."

"I'll consider it," said Lucy, desperate to get away from the doctor but aware she was still dressed in nothing but her underpants and the exam gown.

"You can make an appointment with my receptionist," he continued, leaning against the closed door. "And I would advise you to reconsider the prescription," he added, producing a pad from his pocket and tearing off a preprinted script. "Just add your name at the top," he advised, pressing the slip on gray-blue paper into her hand. Then he grabbed her hand with both of his and held on, stroking it. He stepped close and brought his mouth to her ear, brushing it with his lips as he whispered, "I only want to make you feel good." Lucy flinched and pulled away, which caused him to chuckle before finally releasing her and leaving the examining room.

She crumpled the prescription into a ball and tossed it on the floor, ripped off the gown, and began to put on her bra with trembling hands, struggling with the tangled straps. *Calm down*, she told herself. *You're overreacting.* The exam was certainly creepy and uncomfortable, but she doubted it qualified as sexual assault. *Or did it?* she wondered, pulling her top over her head. She didn't bother to comb her hair but grabbed her purse and reached for the doorknob, pausing to take a last look to make sure she didn't leave anything behind in her hasty exit. Spotting the prescription on the floor, she considered picking it up and throwing it in the trash basket, then decided to leave it and marched down the hall and through the waiting room to the door. She had her hand on the knob when the receptionist called her name.

"How do you plan to pay, Mrs. Stone?"

Lucy turned and answered sharply, "Just send the bill. You have my address."

"I'm sorry, but payment is due at the time of treatment." She held up a sheet of paper and waved it. "Right here, you signed the agreement."

"All right," said Lucy, pulling out her wallet as she crossed the waiting room to the receptionist's counter. "How much is the copay?"

"Two hundred and forty dollars for today's initial appointment."

Lucy's jaw dropped. "What did you say?"

"It's right here," said the receptionist, sliding the bill across the counter and indicating the total with a scarlet-tipped fingernail.

"What about my health insurance?"

"You have a deductible that you haven't met; after you meet the deductible your plan covers eighty percent."

"I see," said Lucy, realizing resistance was futile

and giving the woman her charge card. Just like death and taxes, health insurance wasn't something you could fight.

"Would you like to make another appointment? It's best to book now as the doctor's schedule fills up quickly."

"No thank you," said Lucy, turning and finally making her exit. "Not over my dead body," she muttered, stepping out into the fresh air and breathing deeply.

Lucy had to admit she felt somewhat different as she walked to the subway, which in this part of the city was actually elevated above the street on a steel superstructure. She wasn't convinced she felt better, just looser and kind of jelly-like, and she found climbing the steps to the train platform rather tiring. She was standing up there in a sunny spot, waiting for the train, when her cell phone beeped, announcing a text. Much to her surprise, it was from E. L. Haley, suggesting an early Tuesday morning meeting. Lucy was sending off her response when the train rattled into the station.

Since the train would be above ground for a while, before descending to the dead zone below ground, Lucy decided to call Bill, and to her surprise he answered.

"Finally!" she exclaimed. "I've been trying to reach you for days."

"I left my phone in the truck and then it was dead. I got your messages this morning, but I've been busy all day. Sylvia hired me to remodel the storefront of her bridal shop, wants it done in time for Orange Blossom Bridal's Silver Anniversary Weekend."

"Since when is it Orange Blossom Bridal's Silver Anniversary Weekend?" asked Lucy.

"Since the banners arrived on Friday; Sylvia made a few changes to the original order. Some of the participating businesses aren't happy, since they agreed to pay for the banners, and you can imagine how busy poor Corney is, trying to smooth a lot of ruffled feathers."

Lucy could imagine only too well. "Why on earth did you agree to Sylvia's remodel? You know what she's like."

"I do indeed, but she's handed this project off to Warren and I get along fine with him. It's not a big deal, either. She just wants some old-fashioned gingerbread trim added to the facade, along with some flower boxes. Piece of cake."

"Famous last words."

"Probably, but worst case scenario I should be done by Thursday, ready to head for New York on Friday. I'm driving, so don't expect me before late afternoon."

"How come you're driving?"

"I don't want the hassle of flying, and I figured driving would probably be just as fast if you add up the time it takes to drive to the airport, sit there for a couple of hours, and then you know there'd probably be some sort of delay."

"I'll be waiting for you, with a nice, hot dinner. . . ."

"How about a nice, hot you?"

"That too," said Lucy, smiling. "Any news from the kids?"

"Nope. Sara and Zoe are studying for final exams. Elizabeth sent a selfie with Hugh Jackman. He's making a movie in Paris and staying at the Cavendish."

"Wow."

"And no news from Alaska, which I take to mean everything's okay."

"Sounds good," said Lucy, as the lights blacked out momentarily and the train was swallowed up by the dark tunnel. "I love you," she added, as the phone went dead.

She spent the remainder of the train ride replaying her conversation with Dr. Colin, wondering what Beth had seen in him. Looking back, Lucy had to admit he'd been a good-looking guy in his youth, but even then she had found him unappealing. She hadn't spent much time with him, but she remembered feeling a sense of relief when the newlyweds went on their way after dropping in for an unexpected visit to see Lucy and Bill's new house in Maine. Back then, she'd put that sense of discomfort down to the fact that the house was in terrible shape, a real handyman's special, and she was embarrassed by its ramshackle condition. But after today's unpleasant examination she wondered if even back then she'd sensed something a bit off about the doctor. Dante had remembered Dr. Colin as a germophobe who had fits if he forgot to remove his shoes when he came into the house, and today the doctor himself had as much as admitted he hadn't really cared for his young stepson.

When Lucy got off the train, she resolved to keep an open mind about the chiropractor. She didn't like him—she'd never liked him—but that didn't mean he'd pushed his ex-wife off a balcony to her death. As he'd reminded her, they'd been apart for decades and he was unlikely to have a motive.

Emerging onto the street, Lucy noticed a going-out-of-business sale in a boutique on Lexington Avenue, so she decided to check it out. She wanted to find some little presents for the girls, and for her Thursday morning breakfast friends. An hour or so later she emerged with a large shopping bag filled with infinity scarves, cute change purses, and a black T-shirt with a large, glittery, neon-green Statue of Liberty she planned to give to Sue. It was a risk. She wasn't sure Sue would actually wear it, but they would all get a good laugh out of it.

The crosstown bus dropped Lucy in front of a Vietnamese restaurant that had a sign in the window advertising *bánh mì* sandwiches. Lucy had never had one, but had heard from Pam that they were to die for, so she decided to take a chance on one for supper. Back in the studio apartment she found she'd made a good choice as she bit into the crusty French bread and discovered a delicious combination of flavors: roast pork, pickled carrots, and luscious pâté, perfectly complemented by the last of the wine.

After washing up her single plate and wineglass, Lucy settled in to DVR the episodes of *Call the Midwife* that she'd missed. She hardly ever got to watch the show at home, since Bill and the girls absolutely detested it. She didn't mind the messy obstetrical details they found so offensive, and always cried happy tears when the babies finally arrived and were wrapped in towels and put in their mother's arms. Unlike last night's gruesome crime drama, she was confident that these heart-warming stories would guarantee a peaceful night's sleep. But first, she was going to indulge in a lovely, long, rose-scented bath.

There was no one knocking on the bathroom door, urging her to hurry up, and there was an endless supply of hot water, which wasn't the case at home where the aged water heater didn't quite keep up with demand, so Lucy enjoyed a leisurely soak. She even managed to complete the crossword puzzle in the day's *New York Times*, which she'd picked up on her way home.

She was drying herself off when she heard a noise that sent shivers up her spine. Probably just the chill of getting out of the tub, she told herself, when she heard a familiar creak. She'd heard that noise before, every time she got up from the futon and stepped on a loose board. The bathroom door was ajar, so she wrapped the towel tightly around herself and peeked out, spotting a dark figure leaning over the suitcase she'd left open on the floor. A burglar!

She quietly closed the bathroom door and locked it, then scrabbled through the jeans she'd dropped on the floor, searching the pockets for her cell phone. She punched in 9-1-1 with trembling fingers, and reported the intruder and her address, keeping her voice as low as she could. Then she quickly pulled on her jeans before sliding down the bathroom door and sitting with her back pressed against it, her hands wrapped around her knees while she waited for help to arrive. She only had her bra and the towel to cover her chest because

she'd stripped off her top in the living room and
had carefully folded it and replaced it in the suitcase.

Help took its time to arrive, and it was nearly an
hour later when she heard loud banging on her
door and a voice announcing, "Police! Open up!"

Clutching the towel, she unlocked the bathroom
door, checked that the studio was empty, and dashed
for the hall door. Two uniformed patrolmen came in
and Lucy wished she was wearing something more
than a towel, but they were more interested in
checking the windows and closet than in her state
of undress. "So you saw an individual?" asked one.

"He was right there," she said, pointing to her
suitcase.

"Did you recognize him?"

"No. He was just a dark shape." She paused. "It
might even have been a woman. The minute I realized someone was there I shut the bathroom
door, locked it, and called for help."

"Is anything missing? Jewelry?" he asked, while
his partner busied himself studying the door to
the unit.

Somewhat awkwardly, Lucy knelt down and examined the neat piles of clothing, the shoes tucked
in the sides, and the mesh pocket where she stowed
her underwear. Nothing was disturbed. "I didn't
bring any jewelry," she said. "Everything's here."

"What about your purse?"

Lucy checked her wallet, finding cash and
credit cards undisturbed.

"It doesn't seem like the lock on the door's
been tampered with, not that it's much of a lock,"
said the partner. "Did you lock it?"

Lucy tried to remember. At home she wasn't in the habit of locking her door, and tonight she'd been eager to eat her *bánh mì* sandwich, which had given off a tempting aroma despite the paper wrapping. "I'm not sure," she admitted.

"So you're from out of town?" asked the cop.

"I'm here for a week, from Maine. This is an Airbnb. I've got it until Sunday."

"Well, I've got to get some information, for my report," he said. "If you want to put on something. . . ."

"Uh, right." Lucy grabbed a shirt and scurried into the bathroom, where she hastily pulled it on and ran a quick comb through her hair. Returning to the studio, she produced her driver's license, signed her name, and listened to a brief lecture about the importance of securely locking doors and windows. Then the cops left and she carefully shut the door after them, making sure to twist the knob on the dead bolt, which closed with a reassuring snap.

Wishing she hadn't finished the wine, she sat down on the futon, trying to make sense of what had just occurred. What was the matter with her? Why hadn't she locked the door? She knew better—she'd grown up in the city wearing a house key on a long chain around her neck. Her mother would never have left her door unlocked, not even when she was losing her mind to Alzheimer's. It had become an obsession with her, even in the memory care unit where she lived out her final days.

For a moment she even wondered if there actually had been an intruder. Had she imagined the whole thing? No, she decided, someone had definitely been there. There was no mistaking the fear she'd felt, the absolute shock of seeing someone who shouldn't be there.

She yawned, exhausted by the day's activity combined with the loss of adrenaline, which left her shaky and empty. She got up and began stripping the kilim pillows off the futon and tossing them on an armchair. Then, double-checking that the lock was fastened, she went into the bathroom and changed into her nightgown. She felt very small and vulnerable as she slipped under the covers, pulling them up tight to her chin.

She was safe, perfectly safe, she told herself. Whatever had happened, there'd been no harm. She was okay and tomorrow was going to be a fine new day. She turned out the light and shut her eyes, preparing to sleep. Drowsiness soon crept over her, but her sleep wasn't peaceful and she woke, terrified, an hour or so later. It had only been a dream, she told herself, but this time the intruder hadn't gone away. He'd confronted her, grabbed her, and dragged her to the railing, where he'd thrown her off the balcony into thin air. It was only a dream, she told herself, and the studio was on a low floor and didn't even have a balcony. It was Beth who had a balcony.

# Chapter Eleven

It took Lucy a long time to get back to sleep and she ended up drinking a glass of milk and reading for over an hour before she finally felt drowsy enough to turn out the light. Even then her mind was restless, fretting about locks and tuition bills and polar bears, and the sky was lightening by the time she finally did get back to sleep. When she woke, she couldn't believe the time: it was nearly eight o'clock.

She was supposed to meet E. L. Haley, the *New York Times* reporter, at nine. She quickly threw on some clothes, grabbed her purse, and ran out the door, then ran back to check that she really had locked the door. Then she was dashing along the sidewalk, wishing for coffee, and realizing that she could get a go-cup at the bodega. No wonder New Yorkers were always carrying cups of coffee; they were probably all running late.

The Starbucks where they'd agreed to meet was

handy to the subway exit, but when Lucy arrived at the stroke of nine she didn't see anyone there who looked like a reporter. She was standing in the doorway, a puzzled expression on her face, when a young woman whom Lucy had taken for a college student approached her. "Lucy?" she asked.

"Are you E. L. Haley?" she asked, in a skeptical tone of voice.

"I am."

"Sorry. I really expected somebody, uh, older."

"And male?"

"Well, yeah," admitted Lucy, as they got in line at the counter.

"People just don't take a girl named Emmy Lou seriously."

"I suppose not," said Lucy, with a chuckle. "So what do I call you?"

"Ellie's fine."

Lucy stepped up and ordered a pastry along with her coffee, then asked Ellie what she would like, offering to buy it.

"No, no. Company policy."

When they were seated at a small table, Lucy took a bite of pastry and wondered where to begin. She was slightly intimidated. This tiny woman, really just a girl with long hair, oversized glasses, and a backpack, was a reporter for the *New York Times*! That was quite an achievement, especially for one so young. "How did you get a job with the *Times*?" she blurted out, immediately wishing she could take the words back.

Ellie laughed. "Hard work, all A's in college—no, really, it was just a lucky break. A story I wrote for a little neighborhood weekly, the *Riverdale Press*, went viral and they were looking for some younger people to enliven"—here she paused and made little quotation marks with her fingers—"the *Times'* rather staid reputation." She took a sip of coffee. "It all worked out, and I've been there almost ten years now."

"You don't look that old."

"It's my cross to bear." Ellie shrugged. "So why did you want to talk to me? Something about the story in the Sunday paper?"

"Yes. Beth Gerard, Jeremy Blake's estranged wife when she died, was my best friend, ever since kindergarten. She fell to her death off a balcony on the twenty-second floor and the cops say it was suicide and they've closed the case, but I can't accept that. I've been trying to find out what really happened, and when I saw your story about Jeremy Blake, I thought you might have some information."

"I'm not surprised that they've closed the case. Nobody wants to tangle with Jeremy Blake. He's got legions of lawyers on retainer and doesn't hesitate to use them."

"You tangled with him," said Lucy, picking up the Danish and taking a bite.

"That story was thoroughly vetted by the *Times'* legal department, believe me, and quite a bit was cut."

Lucy swallowed. "Anything to do with Beth?"

"Actually, yes. She was the source who tipped off the AG. She was going to be a prime witness against him, and when she died, so did the case."

Lucy dropped her Danish on the paper plate. "That means he had a motive, a big motive, much bigger than not wanting to pay alimony."

"A major fine, for sure, and possibly even a jail sentence," said Ellie.

"With all this, I can't believe the cops aren't going after him."

"They probably want to, but don't have enough evidence for a case. It's not like they have a witness who saw him push her off that balcony." Ellie paused and took a swallow of coffee, then set her cup down carefully. "Chances are, if he wanted her dead, he wouldn't have done the deed himself. He would have hired a pro, and those guys don't leave any evidence."

"I met him, you know," said Lucy, picking up her Danish again. "He really seemed to be an okay guy. He got an award from the Central Park Conservancy for restoring a gazebo." She took a bite, savoring the buttery, cheesy goodness.

"The two aren't mutually exclusive, you know."

Lucy popped the last bit of pastry into her mouth and chewed thoughtfully. "A funny thing happened," she began, after swallowing. "Last night I found an intruder in my apartment. I thought he was a burglar, but do you think he could have been working for Blake?"

Ellie, who had been taking a swallow of coffee, choked. "What?"

"I was in the bathroom, drying off, and heard a noise. I peeked out and saw this figure—I think it was a guy but I'm not really sure 'cause it was dark—rifling through my suitcase. I locked the bathroom door and called the cops, and by the time they came he was gone."

"Was anything missing?"

"No, which is weird when you think about it. Maybe he was looking to see if I'd found any evidence against Blake."

"He didn't try to attack you?"

"No. I don't think he realized that I'd seen him, and he had plenty of time. It was at least an hour before the cops came."

"Figures," said Ellie.

"I think they thought I was a nervous Nellie and dreamed the whole thing up. They almost had me convinced I'd imagined it."

Ellie caught her gaze and kept it. "Listen to me, Lucy. I don't think you imagined it. I think you might really be in danger. If Jeremy Blake killed his wife to squelch a fraud case, he won't hesitate to knock you off, not if he thinks you have evidence that he was behind her death."

"But I don't have any evidence," said Lucy, not liking the direction the conversation was taking, "only hunches."

"Trust me on this: Jeremy Blake is not a man who takes chances. If he has even a mild suspicion that you're a danger, he won't think twice about getting rid of you."

"Like I said, there was nothing there. I haven't been keeping notes or recordings. I've just been talking to her son and her exes, and I haven't come up with anything incriminating." She paused and sighed. "To tell the truth, I really think I'm mostly just trying to convince myself that she did in fact take her own life."

Ellie nodded and gave her a sympathetic smile. "I understand. Suicide is really hard to accept."

"I'm getting closer to accepting it," said Lucy.

"Good." Ellie rose to go, slinging her messenger bag over her shoulder and picking up her go-cup. "But don't forget what I said. Be careful, okay? I don't want to be writing your obit."

"Thanks for everything."

"You're welcome. Bye."

After Ellie left, Lucy lingered over her coffee, wondering if she'd had a closer call than she realized. To be honest, she hadn't really given the frightening incident much thought, preferring to put it out of her mind. She'd been terrified at first, when she glimpsed the intruder, but that emotion had turned to frustration and impatience during that long, chilly wait for help to arrive. The fact that the cops hadn't taken her seriously had made her doubt herself, but now, after talking to Ellie, she was beginning to trust her instincts. Maybe she really was on to something, even if she wasn't sure what that something was.

Her phone started sounding off in the preset tune that she hadn't bothered to change, and a lot of people in the Starbucks started checking their own phones. She didn't recognize the number, which turned out to belong to Tito Wilkins.

"I remember you," he said, in a gravelly voice. "You were Beth's friend. Whenever you came to visit you'd wash the dishes."

"I was just trying to be helpful," said Lucy, feeling rather embarrassed.

"I know. You were like a little Girl Scout, doing your good deed for the day." He paused. "I suppose you know that Beth is dead. They say it was suicide."

"That's why I'm here. I'm trying to understand what happened."

"Me too."

Lucy found this admission encouraging. "I'd love to talk to you. They say two heads are better than one."

"You'd have to come here," he said, presenting a challenge. "I hardly ever go out."

"Where is here?" asked Lucy.

"Red Hook." He paused before adding in a patronizing tone, "It's in Brooklyn." He spoke slowly and clearly as he gave her the address.

"I'm on my way," she said, before she could change her mind.

"There's no rush. Like I said, I hardly ever go out. I'll be here."

Before leaving the Starbucks, Lucy consulted her smartphone and obtained directions to Tito's studio. She discovered it was going to take more than an hour to get there, thanks to service delays and repairs, and that she would have a long bus ride after getting off the C train at Jay Street–MetroTech.

Lucy discovered that due to ongoing maintenance there were indeed plenty of stops and starts in the tunnels between stations, and she had ample time to think about what she wanted to say to Tito. She'd found him distant and difficult in the past, when he was younger, and now he seemed to have morphed into a rather cranky old man. She was still bothered by the violent images in his paintings, and wondered what drove him to create such ugly artwork. The more she thought about it, the more she was tempted to get off the train and go back to Manhattan, perhaps stopping at a hardware store she'd passed that had a window display of burglar-proof locks. It could be her gift to her Airbnb landlord.

That desire to flee grew stronger when she climbed out of the station and found herself in a busy, crowded street full of people who knew where they going and were in a hurry to get there. She didn't immediately see the bus stop and finally asked an older woman where she could catch the B57, which turned out to be a couple of blocks away. The bus came promptly, much to her relief, and she joined the handful of passengers, mostly older women with shopping bags. She asked the driver to let her off at the nearest stop to Tito's address, and she was the only rider remaining when he finally announced they'd reached Lorraine Street.

Back on foot, she sensed she was near the harbor; the light was somehow lighter and the air smelled fresher. She consulted the map again, folding it into a small square so she wouldn't be viewed as an easy mark, an out-of-towner with a thick wallet. Not that there was anybody to fear, she realized, making her way along the empty streets, past modest one- and two-story wooden structures. Some were houses, some were old storefronts that had been converted into living spaces or workshops, and some were old garages, like the one Tito occupied. It had been painted gray many years ago, but now the paint was peeling. The garage door was closed, but there was a scarred plywood entrance door beside it with the house number painted in beautiful calligraphic figures. She took a deep breath and knocked.

Tito took a long time to answer the door, and Lucy soon knew why. After he opened it he turned and walked away from her, leading the way on stiff, arthritic legs. Lucy closed the door behind herself and followed, watching his slow, obviously painful progress into the space where he worked and lived. A large canvas was propped against the back of the garage door, and was covered with paint only halfway up.

Tito noticed her studying it and snorted. "That's how I work. I paint up as far as I can reach, then I flip it over and work from the bottom up. Critics say there's no up or down to my work, that it represents the universality of my view. Assholes."

"It's good to see you," said Lucy, surprised by the intensity of her feeling. Her fears had been unfounded. The scary young artist with the huge Afro had become a crippled old man with ashen skin and a patchy fuzz of gray hair.

"Want a beer?" he asked, making his way to an ancient refrigerator with a rounded top.

"Sure," said Lucy, who was very thirsty after her long trip.

He indicated a sagging sofa covered with numerous blankets, quilts, and even a sleeping bag, and Lucy sat down. Tito gave her a can of Pabst, then slowly lowered himself into a tall, stiff-backed armchair and popped the tab on his beer. He took a long drink. "So you want to talk about Beth?"

"Were you in touch with her recently?"

He nodded slowly. "Actually, I was. She was married to this rich guy and she got him to buy some paintings." He shrugged. "I don't know what he did with them, but I don't think he hung them over his sofa. I sure don't think he was the sort of guy to go for my stuff."

"How was Beth? What was she like?"

Tito took another long drink. He sighed. "Beautiful. She was beautiful. She brought sunshine with her. She was rosy. She was kind. She could've rubbed it in, like she was rich now and I'm still a struggling artist, but she didn't. She took my work seriously, and she'd done her research. I quoted a real high price, knowing she was loaded, and she argued me down, paid what the gallery charges." He nodded his head in approval.

"But she could have given you more. Wasn't she being cheap?"

"No. That would have been charity. She was letting me know that my work was truly valuable and she respected me."

Lucy drank some beer, enjoying the refreshing cold, sour taste in her mouth. Finally, she asked, "Do you think she killed herself?"

Tito shrugged. "I don't know. Could be. She was too good for this stinking world. She called me after that Sandy Hook school shooting, all those little ones killed. She said she didn't want to live in a world where something like that could happen. Me, either, I told her. I said, why don't we go down to the bay here, hold hands, and jump in? We'll go together. She just laughed, said she'd think about it."

"Dante thinks she was murdered," said Lucy.

"Does he?" He considered this for a moment, staring down at his paint-spattered shoes. "Could be. Why not? Why should she be different?" he asked, brushing away a tear. "People get killed all the time. They get mowed down by trucks, planes explode, they're massacred in theaters and night-clubs and restaurants."

"I saw your show in Soho," said Lucy. "I thought you were a deranged personality, full of violence and hate. I almost didn't come today."

"I paint what I see," he said. "There's evil every-where. I wish I could paint daisies and bunnies, but that's a lie. Just look at the newspaper." He pointed to a copy of the *Daily News* that was lying on the floor. DUMPSTER SLAYER SOUGHT was the headline. "He kills women and leaves their bodies in dumpsters, like they're garbage." Tito got up and limped over to his unfinished painting. "I put it here," he said, tapping a tiny blue shape. "The dumpster."

"There really are daisies and bunnies," said Lucy.

"Not around here," said Tito, and Lucy had to agree she hadn't seen a single daisy or bunny in Red Hook.

"Well, I guess I better be going. I've got a long trip back on the bus and subway."

"There's a ferry, you know. From the IKEA store."

"Where's that?"

"Go straight a couple of blocks. It's right on the bay. You can see the Statue of Liberty from there, too." He snorted. "Another big lie: 'Give me your tired, your hungry . . .' Now they want to build a wall. We used to say 'Tear down that wall.' Now we want to build one." He narrowed his eyes and stud-ied the painting. "Here she is: Lady Liberty." He tapped a tiny, crumpled verdigris figure. "She's not standing. She's broken."

Lucy felt terribly sad and was afraid she was going to start crying; anymore of this and she'd be jumping into the harbor. She got up. "Thanks for seeing me," she said, embracing Tito in a hug. "Take care."

"You too," he said, limping to the door and opening it a crack, peeking out before opening it all the way for her. "It's a dangerous world out there."

# Chapter Twelve

The neighborhood didn't seem especially dangerous to Lucy as she approached the waterfront, where she found a busy supermarket, a quaint crab shack restaurant, and a giant IKEA store. She walked past the entrance to the superstore and through the parking lot to the pier, where a line of people had already formed and were watching the ferry chug across the East River. It was one of those spots in New York that took your breath away, offering a stunning panoramic view of lower Manhattan, the Statue of Liberty, the Verrazano Bridge, and Governors Island. If you turned and looked up the river, you saw the hulking shape of the Brooklyn Bridge.

Lucy gazed, struck by the fact that few of the other riders were taking in the view, but were instead busy keeping track of their purchases, their children, and even a small dog that yapped furiously at anyone who stepped too close to his

owner. The little ferry docked, discharged its passengers, and Lucy joined the surge of people
eager to board.

Moments later the little boat began its return
trip to South Street Seaport, and Lucy found herself enjoying this short trip across the water. The
afternoon sun glinted off the windows of the tall
skyscrapers, including the new Freedom Tower,
which dominated the skyline. A few helicopters
hovered overhead, a huge orange Staten Island
Ferry was briefly glimpsed before buildings blocked
the view, and then, entirely too soon for Lucy, the
ferry docked. She found herself on a dark, sooty
street beneath the FDR Drive, where she could
hear the hum of the overhead traffic. Crossing the
street, she stepped into sunlight and followed a
cobblestoned street to the heart of the seaport
shopping district. Continuing on up the hill toward
the beckoning Freedom Tower, she discovered a
brand new, strikingly modernistic Fulton Street subway station constructed of glass and steel. Somewhat surprised by this example of modernity, she
was reassured when she discovered the escalator
wasn't working and the subterranean platforms
were every bit as filthy and smelly as they'd always
been.

The platform was also packed with people, as
rush hour was beginning and many of the people
who worked in the financial district were heading
home. Her train was already standing room only
when it screeched to a stop, but the people on the
platform pushed their way in, squeezing together
so the doors, which bucked a bit at the pressure,
could finally close.

Lucy tried not to think of the bodies pressed against hers, deciding that there was a certain advantage in such close contact because it eliminated any possibility of having one's pockets picked or purse snatched. They were packed together so tightly that it was impossible to move one's arms; even the slight expansion of one's chest that breathing required was problematic. These stoic New Yorkers seemed used to the situation and focused on avoiding eye contact.

Lucy eased her discomfort by practicing a bit of mental translocation, imaging herself stopped at the single traffic light in Tinker's Cove, alone in her air-conditioned SUV. It was a lovely thought and got her to Grand Central, where she shuttled over to Times Square and caught a crowded, but not jam-packed 1 train to Sixty-Sixth Street.

Ascending to the street, she found herself at Lincoln Center, where she admired the classic modern architecture of the theaters and considered buying a ticket to a concert or dance performance. She'd never been to the opera—maybe this was her chance. She paused for a moment, in front of a sign promoting current performances, but the advertised ticket prices were high and nothing on offer appealed. She was tired and hungry, and all she really wanted to do was get home, take off her shoes, and eat something.

She stopped at the bodega to pick up something for supper, settling on a frozen diet TV dinner. When she brought her purchases to the counter, the clerk smiled at her.

"You're new in the neighborhood?" he asked, in a heavily accented voice. He had very black hair, neatly combed, and his skin was mocha colored; Lucy thought he might be Pakistani or Indian but wasn't sure.

"I'm just here for a week, from Maine. I grew up in the city, though, up in the Bronx."

"You have come home?"

"I guess you could call it that. It's funny, the city changes, but not that much. I can still find my way around."

"This is a good neighborhood—people are nice."

"Business is good?"

"No complaints." He scanned the TV dinner, then clucked disapprovingly. "You could do better. I have some soup, my mother makes it. Much more, um, nourishing, is that the word?"

"Is it good tasting?" asked Lucy with a smile.

"Delicious," he said. "Do you like curry?"

Lucy wasn't sure she did but didn't want to be rude. "Okay, but I'll take the dinner, too."

Noticing a sandwich board announcing a wine tasting in front of the liquor store next door, Lucy decided to pick up a bottle of wine to accompany her dinner.

Finally back in her apartment with the chain on the door securely fastened, Lucy emptied the container of soup into a pot and set it on the stove to heat up, then opened the wine and poured herself a glass, adding a few ice cubes to chill it. Then she sat down in the armchair, slipped off her shoes and propped her feet on the coffee table, and used the remote to turn on the TV to catch the evening news.

She'd finished her glass of wine when she became aware of a heavenly aroma: the curry soup. She set herself a place at the all-purpose table that served as dining table and desk, renewed her glass of wine, and ladled up a generous bowlful of soup, rich with chunks of chicken and lots of rice. It was delicious and she savored every spoonful, trying to figure out what the ingredients were and whether she could reproduce it back home in Tinker's Cove. Probably not, she decided, doubtful that Marzetti's IGA stocked the necessary, no doubt exotic, spices.

Dinner done, she washed up the pot and her dishes, fixed herself a cup of instant decaf, and settled down for an evening of TV viewing. She flipped through the channels, but didn't find anything she wanted to watch. It was still light outside, and she felt restless, so she decided to go for a stroll and further explore the neighborhood.

This time, instead of going right toward Broadway, she turned left intending to catch a glimpse of the Hudson River. The clerk at the bodega was right; it was a nice neighborhood. Lucy's walk took her past neatly maintained apartment buildings with clipped hedges and planters filled with seasonal flowers. Rounding a corner, Lucy passed a gray stone church that was encircled by an ornamental black metal fence. The gate stood open, as did the red-painted doors with ornate black strap hinges. Lucy was intrigued; the church reminded her of St. Andrew's, though on a much grander scale, and she paused to read the sandwich board that was propped on the stone stairs. FREE CON-

CERT it announced, in somewhat shaky script, advertising an evening of chamber music performed by the DeLillo String Quartet.

Lucy had never heard of the DeLillo quartet, but she had a suspicion that, since Lincoln Center was nearby, the musicians might well be members of the symphony orchestra. She wasn't really one for classical music—her car radio was set to an oldies station—but she figured a live performance would beat anything the TV might offer.

She went inside the church, which had beautiful woodwork and stained glass windows, and joined the handful of people sitting in the pews. By the time the quartet took their places on the raised dais in front of the altar, the audience had grown, and the center sections were pretty much filled. The musicians, two men and two women, were highly accomplished and the audience was appreciative, filling the sanctuary with loud applause. Lucy hadn't expected to recognize the music, but much to her surprise, a lot of the selections were familiar from movies and even TV shows.

As she sat there in the sacred space, she let the music flow over her, and found it comforting. The notes seemed to carry away the tensions of the day as well as the confusion and sadness she felt following Beth's death. The city could be ugly and even threatening, but there was beauty here, too. She thought of Tito, consumed with dark thoughts and overwhelmed by random acts of violence, and wished he were here, soothed as she was by beauty and peace. Maybe this was the answer, she thought. Maybe people simply needed to take time to pause and reflect, allowing themselves to gain respite and perspective.

All too soon the music ended and the audience was invited to meet the performers and partake of refreshments in the Macmillan Fellowship Hall, just through the door on the right. Lucy was feeling a bit peckish. The soup hadn't actually been all that filling, and she decided to see what was on offer. She joined the line of well-dressed, pleasantly courteous concertgoers and found herself in a large room where several smiling women were ladling out lemonade and encouraging people to help themselves to bakery cookies. Lucy was happy to oblige, and took her refreshments to one of the small café tables that dotted the room.

Moments later a pleasant, round-faced woman in wire-rimmed eyeglasses approached and asked if she could join her. Lucy agreed, and Terry, as she introduced herself, took the other chair, setting her cup of lemonade on the table.

"Do you come to these concerts often?" asked Lucy.

"Oh, yes. They have them every week and I always try to come. The performers are from the symphony, you know. Last week they had an organist—she was really something. The instrument in this church is quite famous. It was sacred music, of course."

Lucy took a bite of butter cookie and studied Terry, noticing her long hair, which she had twisted into a ponytail and pinned up with a barrette. She was wearing a simple cotton blouse, white with blue flowers, and a rather long, loosely gathered blue skirt. It was the sort of outfit she'd seen many women wearing in the city, comfortable in the warmer weather. Terry had prepared for the cool of the evening with a sweater tucked into a roomy tote bag.

"It's nice to have someone to talk to," said Lucy. "I'm just here for a week, on my own, and I'm not used to being by myself so much."

"Where are you from?"

"A little town in Maine." Lucy finished the butter cookie and moved on to a mini black and white cake.

"I just love Maine," said Terry, in an enthusiastic voice. "It's so beautiful. Do you have family there?"

"Oh, yes. A husband and four kids. Two are grown and flown, but we still have two daughters at home."

"Do you work?"

"Part time, for a local weekly newspaper."

Only two cookies were left, and Lucy offered one to Terry, but she shook her head no, preferring to continue the conversation. "You're a journalist! That must be so interesting."

"I guess it is," said Lucy, thinking of the daily grind in an enhanced light. "How about you? Do you work?"

"Not outside the home," said Terry, "but that keeps me pretty busy. And I do a lot of volunteer work. There's a great need in the city, you know. We have a lot of homeless people, and working poor—people whose paychecks don't last the week."

"It's the same in Maine," said Lucy, leaving the cookies and taking a sip of lemonade. "Our town's been hard hit by this opioid crisis."

"Really? In Maine? That surprises me. You'd think people would be high on all that natural beauty."

"It may be beautiful, but beautiful doesn't pay the mortgage or put food on the table. Our local food pantry has seen steadily increasing numbers, in spite of the improving economy."

"It isn't improving for everyone," said Terry. "I wonder . . . This is perhaps too personal, but are you a woman of faith?"

"Well, I guess I am, *faith* being the operative word. I'm not what you'd call a *believer*, but I do confess to a certain amount of faith. Remnants from my childhood and Sunday School. I can rattle off the Apostles' Creed from memory, but I'm not convinced it's completely true. . . ." Here she paused and smiled before adding, "Especially the part about 'born of the virgin Mary.'"

"Well, I find great comfort in my faith," said Terry, ignoring Lucy's heretical comment and fingering the simple gold cross she wore on a chain around her neck. "Faith is the beginning, that's what my minister says. It's like a tiny little mustard seed, and if its cared for, you know, watered and fertilized, it will grow into a wonderful, sturdy plant that enhances our lives, just like mustard enhances a hot dog."

Lucy was unable to resist teasing Terry. "I put pickle relish on my hot dogs," said Lucy. "Never mustard."

"Well, while you're here, if you're feeling lonely again, you'd be very welcome at my church. . . ."

"Not this church?"

"No, no. I go around the corner. We have Bible study every night, and you'd be very welcome. And we have cookies, too," she added, with a nod at Lucy's plate. "I just happen to have a pamphlet," she said, producing a folded piece of paper from her tote bag and placing it on the table. "I do hope you come. I think we're on the same wavelength, you and me."

Lucy wasn't at all convinced of that but wasn't going to contradict the woman. She stood up, thanked Terry for the pamphlet, and tucked it in her purse, which she swung over her shoulder. "It's been nice talking to you," she added. Lucy continued on her way to the exit, pausing to congratulate one of the musicians, who was also leaving. She turned, thinking perhaps she ought to thank the church ladies who provided refreshments, and saw Terry surreptitiously wrapping the two cookies she'd left on her plate in a napkin and tucking them into her tote bag.

It wasn't that odd a thing to do, she thought. Lots of people packed up leftovers to take home for later. But from the guilty look on Terry's face, you would have thought she was committing grand theft. Or maybe one of the seven deadly sins.

When Lucy stepped outside, night had fallen and the streetlamps were lit. There were still plenty of people about, some busy running errands and others simply out for an evening walk. She saw older couples walking sedately, arm in arm, and imagined they were returning home from dinner at one of the many little neighborhood restaurants. She had been struck by the numerous bistros tucked in among the shops, and wondered how they could all stay in business. Back home in Tinker's Cove, diners could choose from very expensive dinners at the Queen Vic Inn and the newly opened Cali Kitchen, moderately priced mass-produced fare at Lobster Lickin', which catered to tourists, and greasy pub fare at the roadhouse, which always had several motorcycles parked outside. There was also Jake's Donuts, but that was only open for breakfast and lunch.

Of course, folks in Tinker's Cove tended to eat at home, often enjoying freshly caught fish and veggies straight from their gardens. New Yorkers, on the other hand, seemed to eat out a lot, which she guessed was because their apartments tended to be small, with tiny kitchens. The kitchen in her studio apartment was fine for making toast or zapping something in the microwave, but wasn't equipped for serious cooking. If she wanted to eat with a lot of friends, or had a hankering for roast turkey with stuffing, she would have to eat at a restaurant.

Rounding the corner from the busy avenue, which was the neighborhood's commercial center, she turned onto one of the more residential numbered streets. There were no big apartment buildings here, but instead rows of old brownstones, survivors from an earlier time. They had been built as one-family houses, complete with servant's quarters, but now most had been converted into apartments.

As she walked along, she became fascinated with the glimpses of domesticity she caught through the windows. The basement levels, which had once contained kitchen and laundry facilities, were now desirable "garden level" apartments, because they had access to the little patches of garden behind each brownstone. Some people had closed their shutters and curtains, but others left their windows unobstructed and, to Lucy, the scenes seemed like little stages or dioramas illustrating modern life.

In some she saw toys scattered on colorful ethnic rugs, bicycles hung from hooks on the wall or ceiling, and enormous numbers of shoes in all sizes that had been removed at the doors and left there. City people apparently believed that street dirt should be left at the door, which she thought was probably good policy. Raising her eyes to the first, or parlor floors, which were entered from an exterior flight of stairs, she mostly saw ceilings. The ceilings oftentimes had fancy moldings and ornate plaster rosettes from which light fixtures and even elaborate chandeliers hung. Other apartments had been stripped of the Victorian trim, and mobiles and sleek overhead lights hung from the smooth plaster. She also caught glimpses of the top shelves of bookcases, often loaded with decorative bins and baskets filled, she guessed, with Christmas decorations and off-season clothes. There was also lots of artwork, ranging from museum posters to family photos to valuable oils in gilded frames. Lucy found it all absolutely fascinating, and noted with some amusement that she wasn't the only one peering into strangers' windows. Though sometimes they weren't strangers; she also encountered people chatting through open windows with friends. Others stood outside the locked front doors, pushing buzzers for entry, or using their cell phones to invite friends to come down.

Then she was around another corner and back

at her Airbnb, which was beginning to feel like home. Almost. As soon as she stepped inside her door she made sure to turn the dead bolt and latch the chain, thinking as she did so that they didn't even have such things on their doors in Tinker's Cove. There they had doorknobs that locked with a turn of a button, but could be easily jimmied with a credit card. That was rarely necessary, however, since nobody locked their doors unless by accident or if they were going away for an extended period. Then there was the problem of finding the key, which most people dealt with by hiding a spare in a somewhat secure place, like under a potted plant, behind a shutter, or on top of the door casing. Places where no thief would ever think to look.

Once safe and secure in her studio, Lucy set her purse on the table and poured herself a glass of water in the kitchenette area. Returning to the table, she began unpacking the papers she'd accumulated during the day. There was the Starbucks receipt, a crumpled *Metro* newspaper, and a number of flyers thrust on her by people who she guessed were paid to do just that. She smiled at one promising "Extra-special Eastern Massage, Satisfaction Guaranteed" before ripping it into shreds.

Checking her bag and making sure she'd gotten it all, she found the flyer that Terry had insisted on giving her. Somewhat belatedly, Lucy realized Terry had been proselytizing and had targeted her as a likely convert to whatever church it was that she attended. Curious, she opened the folded piece of paper and was startled to recognize the person pictured inside. It was Gabriel Thomas, Beth's first husband, who was still evangelizing, if that's what you called it. Lucy had always seen him as a huckster, who used religion to ensnare vulnerable people, encouraging them to donate cash and labor for his benefit. She thought he would have run afoul of the authorities long ago, charged at the very least with fraud, but it seemed he was still in business. Now it wasn't the Angel Brigade that he was running, but the Guardians of the Faith, and Lucy suspected there had been quite a few others in between.

# Chapter Thirteen

Lucy was wakened out of a deep sleep by her phone, playing that insistent little tune. Shreds of a dream lingered in her mind, confusing her with the need to care for several small children who were in danger while somehow dealing with the charming black-mustached man she'd just kissed, or maybe wanted to kiss, and it took her a few moments to clear her head. It was Bill, calling at a quarter to seven.

"Were you sleeping?" he asked.

"Uh-hunh."

"I'm sorry. . . ."

"It's okay. I should be up."

"Are you having a good time?"

"Yeah. I visited the botanical garden on Monday and went to a concert yesterday," she said, offering an edited version of her activity. "I guess that's why I slept in."

"You're turning into a real city girl." He sounded both amused and slightly disapproving.

Lucy figured swift remedial action was required. "Nah. I miss Tinker's Cove. I miss you! I can't wait for the weekend."

"Well, that's just the thing. I don't think I'll be able to make it after all."

"Oh, no! Why not?" She was surprised to discover how much she had been looking forward to spending the weekend with Bill and was intensely disappointed.

"You can guess: it's Sylvia. This simple little remodel has turned into something like building the Taj Mahal. Nothing is right, everything has to be done over, and over. I'm at my wit's end. I'd toss in the towel and tell her to get lost, but I'm in so deep on materials and time I can't afford to. Though I'm not convinced I'll actually ever see a penny."

"We'll sue, take her to small claims court."

"I have a feeling there's a long line ahead of us."

"Oh, well. Chalk it up to experience. It's not like I didn't—"

"Stop! I know. I know. Next time I'll listen to you."

"That'll be a first," said Lucy, changing the subject and asking about the girls. Finally satisfied that everything was okay at home, and after getting Bill to promise to reconsider the weekend, she said good-bye and made herself a pot of coffee in the ridiculous little coffee press she found in the kitchenette.

When the dinky gadget finally produced something like coffee, she filled a mug and sat, drinking it and thinking that maybe she was the one who should throw in the towel and head home. She certainly hadn't made much progress so far on her investigation, and she wasn't sure she ever would. Of the three exes she'd interviewed, she hadn't come up with any solid leads at all. There was still Gabriel Thomas, but she didn't really consider him to be in the running, since that relationship had ended so long ago and she'd learned from Dante that Beth hadn't had any contact with him since leaving the sect.

She was seriously beginning to wonder if the cops were right, and Beth really had killed herself. People did commit suicide, leaving others to wonder why they took such a desperate act. The human mind was so impenetrable—her dream was just one example. What had that been about? There had been such strong emotions, a terrific sense of urgency, doubts, and even embarrassment about the kiss, and it was all nothing but a figment of her imagination. Maybe a replay of a movie or book? Maybe it was all symbolic, referring to something else entirely, like anxiety about Patrick?

And if her mind could play tricks on her, why couldn't Beth's mind have done the same thing? But to a larger degree? And why not, since Beth had never been as tied to reality or as grounded as Lucy was? She'd always been impulsive and flighty, sometimes even unstable.

Lucy got up to refill her coffee mug, and discovered the remaining coffee in the press was only lukewarm. She decided to drink it anyway, and was considering looking into changing her ticket and heading back home, when her phone rang again. This time it was Sam Blackwell, full of apologies for neglecting her and inviting her to lunch. "I've got something you'll be interested in," she said, suggesting they meet at a favorite spot near her office.

Lucy decided to skip breakfast, opting instead for a hearty lunch with Sam, and treated herself to a leisurely shower, followed by plenty of body lotion and a thorough session with the blow dryer, instead of her usual slapdash approach. She dressed carefully, choosing a pair of beige slacks and a loose boho top, along with her new comfy sandals. Even so, it was only a little past nine when she was done and she had three hours to kill before meeting Sam.

She decided to head out anyway, figuring the city had plenty to offer, beginning with the open plaza at Lincoln Center. She wasn't disappointed, finding a citywide youth orchestra playing an outdoor concert by the fountain, and joined the audience of proud parents and grandparents. When the music ended, she wandered into the branch of the New York Public Library at the center, which contained a large music collection. She didn't have a card and couldn't take any books or records out, but there was an area where she could listen to recordings. There she found a display of early blues albums and she chose one by Bessie Smith, enjoying the grainy recording with plenty of sexy double entendres and trumpet *wah-wahs.*

She was smiling to herself when she left, planning to walk the mile or so down Broadway that would take her to the forties, where Sam's office was located. She enjoyed checking out the store windows and the other pedestrians, mostly retired people now that rush hour was over. As she walked she wondered if she and Bill would ever return to the city, like the empty nesters she'd been reading about in news stories about social trends. It didn't seem likely, she concluded, doubting that Bill would ever leave his beloved Maine.

As for herself, she could see the allure of the city once all the kids had fledged and left the nest. There was lots to do, and many events were free, like the concert she'd attended last night. And public transportation meant you didn't have to drive, which she supposed could become a problem as one grew older. She had almost convinced herself that returning to the city was a possibility when she noticed some sort of scuffle taking place in front of a dry cleaners.

An older man was waving his cane angrily at a kid who was running off down the street, and a number of people had circled a very heavy, gray-haired woman who was lying on the sidewalk. A young woman was on her knees beside her, offering her water from a plastic bottle.

"Did she fall?" Lucy asked. "Has anyone called nine-one-one?"

"They say they're coming," offered a tiny old lady, with a shrug.

"She didn't fall. She was knocked down by that kid when he grabbed her purse," declared the man with the cane.

"She held on. You should never do that. Just let 'em take it," advised an Asian woman who was holding tightly to a little boy's hand.

"That's right," added a stout woman dressed in a bright pink track suit. "I only take the cash that I need for the day in my bag. I keep my subway pass and credit cards close to me, if you know what I mean." She patted her large bosom by way of demonstration.

Lucy heard a siren in the distance and figured help was on the way. Since she wasn't a witness to the purse snatching and the woman was in good hands, she decided to continue her walk, wondering why the articles about retirees returning to the city didn't mention street crime. Nothing like that happened in Tinker's Cove, and there were weeks when Ted joked they'd have to make up some news, but maybe that wasn't such a bad thing.

She still had some time to kill when she reached Sam's office building, so she bought a newspaper and sat herself down in an outdoor plaza where there were chairs and tables, trees and greenery, and even a fountain. These open gathering spaces were now required by the city for new developments, and Lucy thought they were a very good idea.

Sam spotted her there when she left the building. "You're here!"

"I am," said Lucy, folding the paper and getting up to hug her friend. "It's great to see you."

"Same here," said Sam, as they began walking to the restaurant. "I would have called you sooner but I've been swamped with work. It's one crisis after another. It's discouraging. No matter how hard we work, the opposition works harder. Now they're even trying to limit access to contraceptives, saying men shouldn't have to pay for them through taxes or health insurance premiums because they don't get pregnant." She shook her head. "I guess they think women conceive all by themselves or something. I really don't understand it. Why do so many men hate women?"

"I saw some guy snatch an old lady's purse this morning on my way here."

"Disgusting, and all too common," said Sam, pulling open the door to the restaurant. "Enough of that. This is my favorite place. It's sort of cafeteria style, but the food is great. You can even have a glass of wine. None for me, of course. I've got to go back to saving the world's downtrodden women."

"I'll stick to iced tea," said Lucy, scanning the menu and choosing ham and brie with arugula on a mini baguette. She was given a glass for her drink and a metal holder with the number seventeen on it, with the explanation that a server would bring her sandwich to her.

She and Sam were soon seated at a cozy table, beneath a roughly plastered wall dotted with French faience plates. "So what have you got that's so interesting?" asked Lucy, as they sipped their drinks and waited for their sandwiches.

"It's this," said Sam, producing a plastic sandwich bag containing a graying scrap of paper covered with Beth's handwriting. "It came in the mail and as soon as I realized what it was, I put it in the bag. I think you're supposed to do that to preserve fingerprints. I hardly touched it and they can compare mine, anyway."

"Good thinking," said Lucy, studying the paper. It wasn't large, perhaps two by four inches, and fit easily into the little bag. The handwriting was undoubtedly Beth's, and could be easily read.

*Forgive me. I can't go on like this. It's better this way.*

"A suicide note?"

"Maybe. Maybe just a breakup note," said Sam.

"Who sent it?"

"I have no idea. There was no return address."

"The postmark?"

"The main New York post office, 10001."

"It's funny colored paper."

"It looks old to me, like somebody held on to it."

"One of her exes," said Lucy, as an aproned server arrived with their sandwiches.

"There was more to it. It's been torn," said Sam, pulling the toothpick out of her sandwich and taking a bite.

Lucy tore open the little bag of chips that came with her sandwich. "Probably personal information that would reveal the sender's identity."

Sam swallowed. "Why would you keep something like this?"

"As an insurance policy, to prove to investigators that Beth was considering taking her own life, just in case she did actually do it." Lucy took a bite of chip and chewed. "Or in case you killed her and wanted to make it look like suicide."

"My thoughts exactly," said Sam. "But who?"

"It seems to predate her relationship with Jeremy Blake, right?" Lucy took a bite of her chewy sandwich, finding it absolutely delicious.

"Yeah. So that means Gabe Thomas, Tito Wilkins, or Colin Fine, right?"

"I still think it must've been Jeremy. I haven't

got any proof, but he just seems right for it, especially since she was ratting on him to the attorney general about his shady dealings." Lucy considered the scrap of paper while dealing with another bite of sandwich. "The other three marriages ended so long ago, it's like ancient history. Who would nurture a grievance for more than twenty years?.

"Somebody who really hated her. It's not so unusual, believe me. I see it all the time." Sam nodded sadly and raised an eyebrow. "It's called revenge, and a lot of people like it cold."

"I did think Tito was a possibility," admitted Lucy, "especially after I saw how violent his art is. But when I trekked out to Red Hook . . ."

Sam sputtered and pressed a paper napkin to her mouth. "You went all the way to Red Hook? In Brooklyn?"

"I did. It was quite a trip, but I was glad I went. Tito's become a wise old gentleman. He's terribly concerned about violence and climate change, which is why his art is so disturbing. He's trying to raise awareness."

"That doesn't mean he didn't push Beth off her balcony."

"No, I'm sure he didn't. He's quite frail, for one thing. And I don't think Colin the Chiropractor did, either. He's remarried and has a very profitable practice. I have the bill to show for it."

"You saw Colin?"

"I not only saw him, I received what he called an adjustment. It's done wonders. My subluxation is gone and I'm back in proper alignment."

"Oh, I could tell," teased Sam. "I was just waiting for the right moment to say how well aligned you seem to be."

"I have to admit I found him kind of creepy and he wasn't above copping a free feel during the exam. . . ."

Sam's reaction was immediate. "Lucy! Did you confront him? Are you going to file a complaint?"

"No way. I'm not even sure it wasn't a legitimate part of the exam."

"Well, I think you should pursue it, but I certainly understand your reluctance."

Lucy once again picked up the plastic bag containing the scrap of paper, thinking there was something familiar about the paper. Then she thought of the flyer Terry had given her when she invited her to visit the Guardians of the Faith. "Funny," she finally said, "maybe the Lord does work in mysterious ways."

"What do you mean?" asked Sam, picking up the second half of her sandwich.

"I really hadn't considered Gabe Thomas. Like I said, it was so long ago and I figured he'd taken his evangelical message to more receptive ground somewhere west of the Hudson, but a funny thing happened last night. I went to this free concert at a church near my apartment, just for something to do, you know. . . ."

"Oh, I'm so sorry," interrupted Sam. "I had to work late or I would have invited you over for dinner, and the night before that Brad had a dinner with an important client and I had to go, too. I feel so guilty. . . ."

"Honestly, don't. I'm a big girl. I've been doing

fine, believe me. I'm enjoying being on my own, like a grown-up."

"If you say so . . ."

"I do. Now, back to this concert. There were cookies afterward and this woman approached me, so we chatted a bit and she told me about her church and how I'd like it, and I said I didn't think so, really, but she gave me a flyer about a Bible study class and . . ."

Sam's eyes lit up. "Father Gabe!"

"His new effort is called the Guardians of the Faith, and get this—the flyer was printed on gray paper."

"I guess we have to go and see what Father Gabe is up to now," said Sam.

"I think we owe it to Beth," said Lucy. "They have classes every night at seven. Does tonight work for you?"

"Sure thing. I'm actually free. The grant proposal went out yesterday, and Brad has a board meeting tonight. I'll come by your place and we'll go together."

"Good. Meanwhile, I'd like to take the note to Detective McGuire."

"Okay by me," said Sam, checking her watch and rising from her seat. "I've got to go. See you tonight."

Lucy stayed at the table, watching her friend leave. She hadn't finished her sandwich, for one thing, and she wanted to consider how to approach Detective McGuire. Her careful plans flew out the window, however, when she found herself sitting opposite him in a small, secure interview room.

"So what's this new evidence?" he asked, in an impatient tone. Today he was dressed in a gray summer suit complete with a necktie and he seemed ill at ease, as if he wanted to change into more comfortable clothing.

"Somebody sent this to my friend Samantha Blackwell. She was one of Beth Blake's friends." Lucy passed over the scrap of paper in its bag. "She put it in the bag in case there were fingerprints on it."

McGuire snorted, and quickly scanned the note while loosening his tie and unbuttoning his collar. "So it's a suicide note. . . ."

"Maybe. But isn't it weird that somebody felt the need to send it? I think that whoever sent it might very well have killed Beth, but wants to make it look like suicide."

"The case is closed. It was suicide."

"But somebody has a guilty conscience," protested Lucy.

"I'm not interested in consciences. Heck, I've got a guilty conscience. I forgot to send my mom a Mother's Day card. I forgot my nephew's allergic to peanuts and bought him a Reese's. We've all got guilty consciences if you ask me."

"Is he okay?"

"My nephew? Sure, he's fine. He didn't eat it, but he made me buy him Swedish Fish."

"Oh, good." Lucy tapped the note, which was lying on the table between them. "Couldn't you just check it for fingerprints? See who turns up?"

"No. I am not going to waste taxpayer's money on foolishness." He stood up and slid the note back across the table. "Thanks for coming by."

"I have something else to tell you," said Lucy. "I spoke to a *Times* reporter who wrote about Jeremy Blake and she told me that Beth was preparing to testify against him in a big fraud case."

McGuire's bristly eyebrows shot up and he leaned across the table, bringing his face close to hers. "Don't tell me you've been conducting a little investigation of your own. Are you crazy or something? Don't you realize that if, and this a very big *if*, somebody did kill Beth Blake, that person wouldn't like you poking around and might decide to get rid of you. And I gotta say, I wouldn't blame him. Or her. We're equal opportunity around here." He paused. "Get out of here, and go back to Podunk, Maine, or wherever you're from. Got it?"

Lucy picked up the little plastic bag containing the scrap of paper and placed it carefully in her purse, then stood up and walked out of the room with as much dignity as she could muster. Who did he think he was, talking to her like that?

# Chapter Fourteen

Sam was right on time, and Lucy buzzed her into the building at a quarter to seven. She took a quick look around the studio while Lucy grabbed her purse and sweater, pronouncing it "absolutely adorable." They continued discussing the owner's decorative choices while walking the eight or nine blocks to the Guardians of the Faith chapel. Lucy was glad for the distraction, still fretting over Detective McGuire's warning.

"You know, I'm thinking of putting shutters in my bedroom, like the ones in your place. I thought they looked awfully nice," said Sam, as they stopped on a corner and waited for the light to change.

Lucy nodded. "They can be tricky to install, especially in an older place like yours, where things have settled a bit and aren't absolutely true." The light changed and they both stepped off the curb into the crosswalk, where Sam was nearly hit by a turning motorist. Lucy yanked her out of the way and glared at the driver, who continued to bully his way through the crosswalk.

"Oh, my! Good thing you saw him, Lucy, or I'd be roadkill."

Lucy kept her arm around her friend as they finally got a chance to cross the street, watching the blinking numbers counting down the seconds until the light changed. It hit zero just as they reached the safety of the opposite curb, and they stood for a moment, waiting to catch their breath.

"That driver was irresponsibile. There was a woman with a baby stroller there, and some old people," said Lucy, properly indignant.

"It happens all the time," said Sam. "I should've been more careful. I wasn't paying attention."

"It wasn't your fault—we had the walk signal." They were strolling along, and Lucy impulsively squeezed Sam's hand. "I'm so glad you're coming with me tonight. I don't know if I'd have the courage to go alone."

"Why not? It's a church, after all, filled with people of faith. What harm could come to you there?"

"Well, you hear things about some of these sects. . . ."

"We have to be open-minded and tolerant of other faiths, Lucy."

Lucy had noticed that the neighborhood was changing, and this block was somewhat shabbier than the one on the other side of the avenue. It was closer to the river and efforts at gentrification hadn't taken hold yet, though there were signs that change was on the way. A couple of storefronts had been remodeled and new businesses had opened, including a coffee shop, nail salon, and even a hardware store, clearly hoping to cater to urban homesteaders.

The Guardians of the Faith storefront chapel had made a few efforts in that direction, too, decided Lucy, as they paused and looked it over. A simple brass cross hung in front of thick white curtains in each of the plate glass windows, and a neat sign over the door bore the sect's name in gold letters on a blue background. The door this evening had been left open, and music could be heard, inviting people to come in.

Sam and Lucy looked at each other, as if silently deciding whether or not to continue, and came to a mutual agreement. They went inside, finding themselves in a tastefully carpeted and wallpapered hallway that reminded Lucy of McHoul's Funeral Home in Tinker's Cove. As at McHoul's, they were warmly greeted, though not by the somberly suited McHoul brothers. The greeters here were two smiling women dressed in traditional white cassocks with rope belts around their waists. They were each given a name tag and invited to go on into the chapel, which was just through a set of open double doors.

This chapel was a far cry from Gabe Thomas's first place, which had featured secondhand folding metal chairs, worn linoleum, and windows covered with butcher's paper. Here, there was red carpet, real pews, and freshly painted cream walls. The space had no real windows, but a skilled muralist had painted trompe l'oeil stained glass windows on the side walls that depicted pleasant scenes from the Bible like the raising of Lazarus, the feast of the loaves and fishes, and the wedding at Cana. Jesus, Lucy noticed, looked an awful lot like Elvis Presley. In the front of the chapel, instead of an altar, there was a stage with drawn curtains. Soft recorded organ music was playing and Lucy guessed it was a New Age reworking of something by Bach, with fragments of familiar tunes here and there.

The service had attracted quite a few attendees, who were scattered about in the pews. They seemed to be mostly women, but there were a few men, too. They were the sort of people you saw riding the subway, people of various races and occupations who worked hard for a living. Lucy and Sam chose a pew in the middle, seating themselves behind an overweight woman who was deeply absorbed in prayer, her head bowed. She was praying aloud, mumbling in a soft voice in a language neither Lucy nor Sam recognized.

Lucy was wishing she'd been given an order of service, which would give her an idea of what to expect, when the lights suddenly went black and there was a collective gasp from the congregation. They sat there, in the dark, as the organ music became more intense. When it reached a crescendo, the curtains on the stage opened, revealing a large video screen containing a depiction of the Pentecost, the occasion upon which the disciples received the Holy Spirit in the form of dancing flames. The music grew even louder, the flames on the screen began to flicker, and the disciples began speaking in tongues, at which time Gabe Thomas made his entrance in a spotlight, wearing a backward collar and robed in scarlet. The video image grew fainter, the spotlight grew brighter, and Gabe Thomas stretched his arms out in the sign of the cross.

Lucy studied him, taking in the carefully coiffed, probably dyed hair and aging but well moisturized skin. His teeth, which Lucy remembered as stained and crooked, were now perfect and very, very white. She spotted beneath the robe a pair of expensive, well-polished tassel loafers on his feet.

"Let us pray," he said, inviting everyone to stand. "Almighty One, God of the Universe, God of All, you have opened the way to eternal life for poor, miserable sinners like ourselves." A guitarist in the background provided a beat, and bluish spotlights colored the chapel.

The woman in front of them shouted "amen" and began to shake and wave her arms above her head. Lucy and Sam shared a glance, equally surprised by this behavior, which they soon discovered was shared by others in the congregation.

"Let us be grateful for this gift, available to all people, whoever or wherever they may be, and obtainable to all who are contrite and repent of their sins. So let us say together: Dear God, have mercy on us, who are burdened by sin and guilt and deserve nothing. Let your bountiful grace and mercy deliver us from evil through our Lord Jesus Christ, who bought our forgiveness with his precious blood. Shower us with forgiveness, grant us weak sinners your amazing grace, purify us, and embrace us in your glory. Keep us in your holy light, now and forever. Amen." The lights began to strobe in various colors, and the guitarist was joined by a keyboardist and a drummer. The music surged as the congregation began joining in, singing along as the words to these rock 'n' roll hymns were cast on the wall above the stage.

The service continued in much the same manner, as rock song prayers were punctuated by readings of fiery Bible passages. And there was not one collection of offerings but the plate was passed three times. Each time, Father Gabe's exhortation, or extortion as Lucy thought of it, became more fervent as he encouraged larger and larger donations. "Lord Jesus himself told his disciples they must give up earthly possessions and follow him. He told them it is easier for a camel, which you know is a rather large animal, to pass through the eye of a needle than it is for a rich man to enter the gates of heaven, so give and give generously, for your soul's sake."

The sermon was more of the same, but with additional warnings of the dreadful, fiery fate that awaited unbelievers. Lucy and Sam recognized it as the same message he had been promoting decades earlier, when he was married to Beth, but the delivery was a lot jazzier and more theatrical. Light and music were used to great effect, emphasizing the message that the only true way to salvation and eternal life was by joining the Guardians of the Faith. If one couldn't manage to join the sect, donating generously was the next best thing.

That message seemed to resonate with the congregation, who not only sang the hymns enthusiastically and prayed ardently, sometimes trembling and speaking in tongues, but dutifully opened their purses again and again, donating bills in ever larger denominations. Those who found their purses empty shook their heads sadly as the white-robed greeters passed the plates; some scrabbled pathetically in purses and pockets for stray coins. Lucy and Sam repeatedly offered up single dollar bills, earning disparaging looks from the ushers.

At last, the lights and music reached a crescendo and everyone was on their feet, waving arms and singing mightily, begging God to come down among them as a holy and purifying flame. Then a crushing silence as the lights were dimmed, and a spotlit Father Gabe offered the final benediction, reminding them that God was with them always, nothing could be hidden from the judge who saw all, and He was the only one who could save them from the eternal fires of hell. It ended with a great clap, as of thunder, and Gabe Thomas disappeared in an explosion of smoke and flame.

The curtains were drawn, the lights went on, and people began to leave, passing through the hallway where those two white-robed ushers gave them a final opportunity to make a last, soul-saving donation.

"Well, what did you think?" demanded Sam, when they stepped outside. It was somewhat surprising to see that the sun hadn't yet set. It was still light, and there were parked cars, plenty of pedestrians, and all the trappings of everyday life. It was hard to tell, but none of the passersby seemed to be worried about the state of their souls.

"He's turned into quite a showman, what with the dental work and new hairdo, but it was pretty much the same old gig," said Lucy, as they walked along. "He really ought to be ashamed of himself, shaking down those people who don't seem to have much to begin with."

"They seemed to get something from him, though," said Sam. "Those people seemed to be genuine believers, like that lady in front of us. She was really into it."

"There must be quite an operation behind the scenes," said Lucy. "That was a pretty slick production, complete with lights and music."

"I agree," said Sam. "I suppose he's got a bunch of followers who've turned everything over to him and work for nothing, hoping to save their souls. That's the usual modus, isn't it?"

"Yeah." Lucy was thoughtful, noticing the sky had turned a lovely shade of violet and the streetlights were coming on. "He puts on quite a show, but he seems kind of weirdly sincere about the whole thing. I have to admit I really was kind of moved, despite my doubts. Do you know what I mean?"

"I'm conflicted, too. I don't think he's a complete hypocrite. I think he really believes in the snake oil he's selling. And like I said, it does seem to help some people."

"Helps them right into the poor house," said Lucy.

"Or into the sect, I guess."

Lucy nodded. "I doubt very much that he's given a thought to Beth in years."

"I wonder what he's really like, beneath the robes and hair and in the clear light of day."

"Me too," said Lucy, as they passed a frozen yogurt shop. "Are you hungry?"

"I didn't have time to eat," confessed Sam.

"I just had some salad. Shall we?"

The two went inside and chose mixed berry sundaes, eating them at a counter in the front window and watching the darkening sky and the passing parade. As she licked her spoon, Lucy thought about what Sam said about not seeing the real man. The Father Gabe they saw tonight was a lot more polished and controlled than the fervent young evangelist Beth had married, caught up in his magnetic, blazing passion and religious fervor. People mellowed as they got older, of course, but Lucy wondered if he'd really changed that much. She remembered how shaken and fragile Beth had seemed after leaving him. Frightened, too.

"I wish we'd had a chance to talk to him," said Lucy, stirring her yogurt.

"I suppose you could call and ask to see him," said Sam.

"But it's a cult," protested Lucy.

"It didn't seem very cultish to me. Even mainstream churches have changed a lot in recent years, you know. My own church has adopted new, more modern liturgy. They even got rid of the pews and they sometimes have electric guitar instead of organ music, all to attract younger people. Of course, we only pass the collection plate once." Sam dug into her frozen yogurt. "I didn't see any evidence of cult stuff tonight, just a gathering of sad and probably lonely people looking for comfort."

"I suppose you're right. Want to come with me to talk to Gabe? Maybe tomorrow?"

Sam swallowed her mouthful of yogurt. "I wish I could, but I've got a jam-packed schedule tomorrow and for the rest of the week." She looked at her watch and stood up. "I better get going. I've got an early morning tomorrow."

"I'll go with you to the subway," said Lucy, picking up her cup of frozen yogurt to take along and eat as they walked. At the entrance to the subway they hugged.

"If I don't see you before you leave for Tinker's Cove, have a safe trip home," said Sam. "And give my love to Bill and the kids."

"Will do," replied Lucy, watching her friend descend the grimy, littered stairs that led down to the station. She then headed back to her apartment, finishing up the last of the frozen yogurt as she went.

Next morning, however, Lucy doubted the wisdom of Sam's suggestion that she arrange a meeting with Father Gabe. Maybe his storefront church had seemed pretty mainstream to Sam, but Lucy suspected it was all gloss and wondered if this former tiger had really changed his stripes. Still in her pajamas, she dug the crumpled flyer Terry had given her out of her purse and read the mission statement on the back.

> *The Guardians of the Faith invite all to join them in worship and fellowship. Father Gabe is always available for counseling and confession. Call 212-543-6257 for an appointment, or drop by at the chapel. You are welcome!*

It all seemed so innocuous that it made her feel ashamed of being so suspicious and distrustful. Time was running out; the week was almost over and she had nothing to show for it. Here it was Thursday and she wasn't any closer to understanding what had happened to Beth than she was when she arrived last Saturday.

So far she'd learned that Jeremy Blake was a shady character, but that was hardly a surprise and certainly didn't mean he was a murderer. As for Tito Wilkins, despite the violent imagery in his art, he'd struck her as a genuinely caring and kind person. Dr. Colin, on the other hand, hadn't struck her as either caring or kind, despite his credentials as a healer, but she didn't see him as a killer, either. The one thing all three exes had in common, she decided, was the way they had all moved on after divorcing Beth. Or maybe in the case of Jeremy Blake, it was the way he claimed to have moved on. She still thought he was the most likely to have killed Beth, since she was willing to testify against him in the fraud case, but Lucy had come to doubt he was overly concerned about it. He was far too arrogant to believe that Beth, or anyone for that matter, could bring him down.

So that left Father Gabe, and she couldn't leave New York and go back to Tinker's Cove without being sure about him, too. In her heart she felt that if she'd only been a better friend to Beth, she might have somehow saved her. She owed it to Beth to find out what had really happened, and maybe Father Gabe could give her some insight.

After she'd eaten breakfast and dressed, she headed back to the mission. The front door was

closed, unlike the night before, but had a welcoming sign inviting any and all to enter. She took a
deep breath and stepped into the carpeted hall,
which was empty. There must have been some sort
of alert system, however, as a sweet-faced woman
appeared almost immediately and greeted her.

"Welcome," she said. "How may we help you?"

Lucy noticed that the woman was wearing a
name tag that identified her as Megan, but that was
the only clue that she was one of the Guardians of
the Faith. She was dressed simply in a striped cotton
knit shirt and navy slacks, and her curly hair was
cropped short in a flattering style.

"I'd like to see Father Gabe. We're old acquain-
tances and a dear friend of mine has passed. . . ."

"Say no more," replied the woman, in a gentle
voice. She took Lucy's hands in hers, her eyes ooz-
ing sympathy. "I'm sure Father Gabe will want to
see you." She gave Lucy's hands a reassuring little
squeeze before dropping them and hurrying down
the hallway, disappearing around a bend. Moments
later she returned and invited Lucy to follow her.

Lucy did and found Father Gabe standing in
the doorway to his office, a welcoming smile on
his face. Lucy couldn't get over how much his appearance had changed and didn't think she would
have recognized him if she hadn't seen him at the
service last night. This morning he was dressed
simply in a black shirt with a backward collar and a
pair of gray slacks; it was the sort of thing Father
Pete, the rector of St. John's Episcopal Church,
wore back home in Tinker's Cove. "Do come in,"
he said, stepping aside.

Lucy entered the carpeted and wood-paneled

office, noticing that it could have belonged to a lawyer or banker, except for the simple gold cross hanging on the wall behind the handsome mahogany desk. That put it more in the McHoul's league. Father Gabe did not seat himself behind that desk, however, but instead chose one of a matching pair of armchairs on the opposite side of the room. Lucy understood that she should take the other, and seated herself. "Thanks for seeing me."

"Megan mentioned that you are grieving for a friend who has passed?" Father Gabe leaned forward, making eye contact. "Would you like to talk about that?"

"Well, yes, that's actually why I came. Perhaps you remember me? I'm Lucy Stone. I was at the service last night with Samantha Blackwell. We were both friends of Beth Gerard, your first wife. . . ."

"So you have come about Beth? Has something happened to Beth?"

Lucy could hardly believe he didn't know, but he sounded completely unaware. "She's dead. She fell off the twenty-second floor of her building. You must have heard. It was in all the papers. She was married to Jeremy Blake, the billionaire real estate developer."

"I don't read the papers," he was quick to say. "They are full of sin and debauchery. I only read the Bible. I will pray for her soul. The Lord forgives all but only if one is truly repentant. I fear our dear Beth may need our intercession." He nodded, as if reflecting. "You know, I thought I recognized Sam. That red hair reminded me, but I couldn't quite place her. And now that you've identified yourself, of course I remember you, Lucy. How have you been?"

"Fine," began Lucy, somewhat amazed at Father Gabe's smooth transition. Why was he so interested in her? "I'm married and live in Maine. I have four grown . . . well, almost all grown children and I work for a little weekly newspaper."

Hearing this, Father Gabe raised an eyebrow. "So you're a journalist? An investigative reporter? A muckraker, digging about in the filth of sinners?"

"Not exactly," said Lucy, smarting at the accusation. "I came to New York because I can't believe that Beth would have taken her own life. It just doesn't make sense to me."

"Ah." Father Gabe had tented his hands, and nodded somberly. "It is indeed difficult. I have counseled many souls grieving the loss of a loved one who committed suicide. We see through a glass darkly. Only the Lord sees what is in our hearts and loves us unreservedly. Would you like to pray with me? For Beth's soul?"

"Thanks, but not right now," said Lucy. "I'd rather that you told me about Beth. Have you seen her recently? Did she come to you for help or comfort? For advice?"

Father Gabe shook his head sadly. "No. Nothing like that." He paused. "It troubles me. I wish she had come. Perhaps I could have helped her." His voice grew somewhat firmer. "Suicide is a sin, you know. I wish I could be confident she asked for forgiveness before she took that final step." He seemed to catch himself. "Or act. Final act."

Lucy was beginning to wonder if Father Gabe

was actually being honest with her. She suspected he knew all about Beth's death; it would have been nearly impossible to avoid hearing about her spectacular fall. And she wouldn't have noticed his use of the word *step* if he hadn't been so quick to correct himself, as if he feared it implied he knew more than he was admitting. She decided to press him, hoping he'd misspeak again.

"I saw Dante," said Lucy. "He was at the funeral service, and we met afterward. I even saw his show, and he's a very talented performer. He gave a very loving tribute to Beth, singing her favorite song."

Father Gabe's expression and demeanor underwent a sudden change, and Lucy thought she might have gone too far. The sympathetic counselor was gone and now his face hardened and his eyes glared. "He's no son of mine," he insisted, practically spitting out the words. "He's a filthy pervert, an abomination to the Lord and his creation. He deserves to burn in hell."

"But you said God loves us all, unreservedly."

"Jesus said if your right hand offends you, you should cut it off. Dante offends me and I have cut him off. What the Lord does, is up to him."

"Fair enough," said Lucy, deciding it was definitely time to go. She'd gotten a clearer picture of Gabe Thomas and, as she suspected, he hadn't really changed all that much. At bottom, he was the same false prophet he'd always been, preying on people's fears and frailties. She stood up. "Well, it's been nice seeing you again, even if it was a sad occasion that brought us together."

The loving pastor had returned. Gabe adopted a kindly expression and took her by the hand. "I can't let you go without a prayer," he said. The office door opened and several people filed in. Lucy recognized the woman who had greeted her, along with two others she didn't know. There were also two young men, muscular youths who were wearing the same white cassocks the ushers had worn the night before.

Lucy was immediately fearful, but they were all smiling at her as they took hands and formed a circle around her and Father Gabe.

"Let us pray," he intoned, and they all bowed their heads. When in Rome, thought Lucy, also bowing. She hoped the prayer wouldn't go on too long, and then she'd make her excuses and leave.

"Heavenly Father, all thanks and praise are yours, creator of all. We stand before you today burning with your spirit's power, and begging forgiveness for our sins. We thank you for the gift of our departed friend Beth, to whom we ask that you will grant eternal rest with you in your heavenly kingdom. We also ask that you offer comfort to all who suffer grief or trouble, especially our friend Lucy. Now send us forth that we may proclaim your redeeming love to the world. Amen."

Lucy joined the others in the amen and, since Father Gabe was leaving the room, prepared to leave herself, but found the group were still linking hands, encircling her. Her bag was on the chair and she moved toward it, intending to retrieve it, but encountered one of the muscular robed youths.

"Lucy, why are you in such a hurry to leave?" he asked, smiling. "Won't you stay with us a while? We can pray for your friend Beth."

"I really can't stay," sputtered Lucy.

"Nothing's so important as friendship," said the woman who had greeted her in the hallway.

"Friendship is special," cooed another. "It's a gift from God."

"And we all want to be your friend, to share God's love," said another.

"You're beautiful, you know," said the greeter, beaming at her.

"We're all beautiful in God's sight," said the other robed youth.

"We're all beautiful," they intoned, in one voice. "You're beautiful. God loves us all. God loves you."

"That's all very well and good and I appreciate your good intentions, but I do have important matters to attend to," said Lucy, in what she hoped was an assertive tone.

"Well and good, well and good, you're well and good and we're well and good," intoned the group, still maintaining the circle with linked hands.

"Praise the Lord," said Lucy, hoping this was the magic phrase that would break the circle and free her. "I'll see you all at the service tonight, but now I must go."

From somewhere in the distance a gong rang, and the group gathered more closely around her. "It's lunchtime! Join us in the breaking of bread."

Lucy had to admit she was hungry, and it didn't seem as if they were going to allow her to leave without feeding her. In a way, these smiling people reminded her of her grandmother, who was always showering her with affection and tempting her with special treats.

"Thank you," said Lucy. "Lunch would be lovely."

They all gathered around her in a happy throng and went together down the hall and into a communal dining room, where Lucy noticed several obviously homeless street people were seated at long tables, eating bowls of soup. The room was simply decorated, but there were checked cloths on the tables and little vases of fresh flowers.

Lucy was offered a seat at an empty table, and the two robed youths joined her, sitting on either side. "I'm Luke and he's Matthew," said the taller one. "We're so glad you've decided to stay."

"Well, just for lunch," said Lucy, fingering the thin paper napkin.

One of the women brought her a bowl of soup and a roll, another set down a cup of tea. "Herb tea," she said, with a smile. "It's delicious."

Lucy didn't really like herb tea; she preferred a simple cup of Lipton. But she had been well brought up and had good manners, and she knew she should at least taste the tea. She raised the cup and took a sip. Finding to her surprise that it was indeed delicious, she smiled gratefully at the woman and drank deeply.

# Chapter Fifteen

The sound of jackhammers woke Lucy, who soon discovered that the noise was in her own head. She must have been drugged or something, she realized as she struggled to become conscious. All she wanted to do was go back to sleep and escape the pounding between her ears, but some survival mechanism, some instinct for self-preservation, impelled her to struggle against the temptation to sink back into unconsciousness. Gathering all her strength, she opened her eyes.

The first thing she saw was the ceiling, which was white and bare, except for a cheap light fixture with a square glass shade. Blinking from the bright light, she turned her head and saw white walls, a wood floor, a plain oak table and chair. Her purse was on the table. She was on a bed, a cot really, with a pillow. A gray thermal blanket covered her. She sat up and saw a small wooden cross had been pinned up on the wall behind her bed. Looking around, she noticed there were no windows, and no light switch, either. There was a closed door.

Suddenly panicked, she stood up and staggered across the room to the door, grabbing the knob. Much to her surprise, the door opened and she peered into an empty hallway; her room was at the end. Seizing the opportunity, she grabbed her purse from the table and left the room, reeling from side to side as she staggered down the hallway, which was lined with doors. A larger door was at the end, which she prayed was the exit.

She opened it a crack and discovered the dining hall, now empty except for a few women who were clearing the tables. She took a deep breath and entered, intending to march right on through and out to the hallway, past the chapel to the mission's entrance. Eyes fixed on the opposite doorway, she steadied herself by grabbing the backs of the chairs as she moved along crabwise. She was almost there when a high-pitched voice called her name. She turned her head slowly, trying to control her dizziness, and made out a fuzzy image she recognized as Terry.

"Oh, hi," Lucy said, lurching toward the next chair and grabbing it.

"You came! I'm so glad," enthused Terry, wrapping her in a big hug. Lucy fell against her, noticing that the other women were now approaching, weaving their way through the long tables.

Lucy's heart was pounding, adrenaline flooding her system, urging her to flee. "Iss been great," said Lucy, who was finding speech difficult but was determined to continue the fiction that she was merely a visitor, "but I gotta leave."

"Oh, no. I was so hoping we could continue our conversation," said Terry, her voice dripping with disappointment. "I so enjoyed talking with you the other night, at the concert. And so happy to know you read the leaflet I gave you and now you're here."

By now the other women had joined them in a loose knot. "Who's your friend, Terry?" asked one.

"Oh, please, introduce us," said another.

"Well, this is Lucy," said Terry, who was holding tight and essentially propping Lucy up. "I met her at a concert the other night and gave her a brochure."

Lucy remained draped over Terry while studying the group and assessing her chances for escape. There were five of them, including Terry, all dressed similarly in blouses and long skirts. Their ages varied—a couple were in their twenties, the others older. She realized with a sinking heart that the odds were not in her favor.

"Let me introduce my friends," said Terry, sounding like someone at a party. "These youngsters are Grace and Charity—isn't that too sweet? And these others are Ruth and Elizabeth," she added, pointing out two women in their forties. Ruth had a worn, tired appearance and Elizabeth had tightly curled hair and a stern expression. "I'm Terry. You know that, but you don't know that it's short for Temperence."

"Nishe to mee' you all," said Lucy, "but I got shome friends waiting for me. . . ."

"But we're you're friends," said Charity. "Can't you stay just a little longer?"

"No really, no," protested Lucy, pulling away from Terry and encountering Grace. Grace, she realized, was rather large and looked as if she had played field hockey at some time in her recent past.

"Don't you like it here?" asked Grace, whose expression reminded Lucy of a bulldog.

"We all like you so much," volunteered Ruth, with a sad sigh. "Don't you like us?"

"Nah queshion of like," said Lucy. "I got an appoin'men'."

"Appointments can be changed. I'll do it for you," said Elizabeth, snatching Lucy's purse and efficiently digging through it until she found her cell phone. She must have been expert in the use of the device, because it only took her a moment or two to check Lucy's calendar and discover her falsehood. "Are you sure? I don't see anything here," she said.

"Tha's mine," said Lucy, but her words seemed to fall on deaf ears.

Elizabeth was shaking her head as she scrolled through the calendar. "No, I thought you might have confused the date, but I don't see any appointments until . . . Oh, here's one in August."

"What good news. Now you can stay with us a bit longer," said Terry.

"Gimme phone," said Lucy.

"Sure. No problem," said Elizabeth. She continued in a firm, no-nonsense tone, "But now it's time for our afternoon service. Won't you join us? It's wonderfully uplifting."

Lucy didn't see any other option, but hoped

that if she went along to the service she might be able to find a way to slip out. "Okay. Just give me my things. . . ."

"No phones or bags are allowed at the afternoon service," said Terry, whispering in Lucy's ear as she grabbed her hand and pulled her along. "You understand. It's for security." She stopped suddenly and pointed to Lucy's wristwatch, then, speaking as if she were confiding a sad truth to her, went on to say, "You know, better safe than sorry. The service is open to the public and we've had problems with some of the homeless. Better leave your watch in the kitchen, with your purse and phone, where it will be safe."

Next thing she knew Lucy was hustled, sans watch, phone, and purse, into the chapel. It was darkened for the service, which Lucy found was easier on her eyes than the brightly lit dining hall. She was seated in one of the front pews, with Terry on one side and the field-hockey player, Grace, on the other. Terry kept smiling at her and insisted on holding her hand, pretending it was a sign of friendship. Lucy's mind was clearing and she hung on to the hope that whatever they'd given her would wear off during the service and she'd be strong enough to seize an opportunity to flee.

That hope was somewhat dashed when brightly colored strobe lights began flashing, accompanied by loud rock music. The music was some sort of hymn, as everyone got to their feet and began singing. Lucy couldn't make out the words, except that *my Lord* was frequently repeated. The music pounded in her ears and shook her body so she could barely stand and she ended up leaning heavily once again on Terry.

When the music ended she sank to the pew, but was yanked upright by Terry and Grace. Father Gabe had appeared, robed in a voluminous red garment that had yellow and orange flames embroidered around the hem. He stood center stage, his arms outstretched and making himself into a cross, and once again the music surged. Lucy was dizzy, the room was reeling around her, but Terry and Grace wouldn't let her sit down. They began swaying from side to side as they sang the next incomprehensible rock hymn.

The service seemed to last forever, alternating between ear-shattering, thumping music accompanied by flashing lights, endless prayers, and thundering oratory from Father Gabe promising endless torment to sinners who refused to repent and persisted in resisting confession and salvation. When it finally ended, Lucy was feeling better physically but was struggling emotionally, terrified by the realization that she was trapped. Like an unwitting housefly, she'd stumbled into a truly sticky situation and it seemed that, like the fly, the more she struggled the worse it got. Her best option, her only option, was to pretend to submit. Maybe then she'd figure out why Father Gabe wanted to keep her. The spider trapped the fly to eat it, but there seemed no simple explanation for the cult's refusal to let her leave. And now, she no longer had any doubt that the Guardians of the Faith was indeed a cult and Father Gabe was its charismatic leader.

When the lights came on, Terry gave Lucy a big hug. "Wasn't that wonderful?" she asked. "Father Gabe is so inspirational, isn't he?"

"Oh, yes."

"You don't still want to leave, do you?" asked Grace, confronting Lucy with slightly bulging eyes.

"Well, I don't want to," said Lucy, choosing her words carefully in the faint hope that they might actually let her go, "but I do have obligations in the city before I leave. I'm only here until Sunday, and I have to go home to my family in Maine."

"They can wait, can't they? Your first obligation is to the Lord your God, isn't it?" persisted Grace, with the stubborn attention of a dog gnawing a bone. "It's a question of your salvation, your immortal soul."

"I hadn't thought of it like that," said Lucy, losing hope.

"Here you can serve the Lord," added Terry.

"You'll find such happiness, here with us," said Grace.

"You will stay a little longer, won't you?" pressed Terry.

Lucy didn't see that she had a choice. "Well, if you insist."

"We do," said Grace. "Now, I suppose you're hungry? You didn't touch your soup."

"Well, rather," admitted Lucy.

"Good. Because we're going to have a wonderful meal together tonight," said Terry. "But first, we have to work to earn our daily bread. You don't mind, do you? Just some housekeeping. We all pitch in."

Terry made it sound like they would be doing a little light dusting, but Lucy discovered the reality was quite different. She was brought back to the dining hall, where there were a half dozen people busy lifting and moving the tables and chairs to one side of the room, where they piled them up. Seeing the newcomers, the workers paused and formed a loose line, heads bowed.

"We have a new member joining us today," said Grace, who seemed to have a position of authority. "This is Lucy."

"Welcome, Lucy, hello, Lucy." Heads still bowed, the workers spoke in unison. Lucy noticed that these people were not well dressed, like Terry and Grace, and appeared to be thin and undernourished.

"Umm, let's have Hagar and Zeke, please," Grace said.

Two of the workers stepped forward. Hagar was barely out of her teens, and her lank hair fell over her eyes. She was wearing black leggings and a man's flannel shirt with the sleeves rolled up. Her arms were very white, and Lucy could see the blue veins beneath her skin. Zeke was tall and bearded, pushing forty, and was wearing a ripped T-shirt and worn jeans.

"Hagar and Zeke are two of our most devoted, hardworking members," said Grace.

The compliment seemed to fall on deaf ears as Hagar and Zeke showed no reaction whatever, but kept their heads bowed.

"They will show you what to do, Lucy. And remember, hands to work and hearts to God." She raised her hands in blessing. "God bless you in your labor." Then her voice hardened. "Back to work, everyone."

The work, as Lucy discovered, was to clear one side of the large dining hall so the floor could be cleaned on their knees with scrub brushes, and dried with old towels. Then the furniture was replaced and the floor on the other side of the room was scrubbed. When that side was dry, all the tables and chairs were replaced.

As she worked along with Zeke and Hagar, Lucy tried to initiate some sort of conversation, but neither one would speak to her. It was very odd, she thought, becoming aware that all the workers were silent. This was nothing like the work parties Lucy had participated in back in Tinker's Cove, setting up for a craft fair or bake sale, where everyone chatted and laughed together. This was like being in some sort of prison camp, although Lucy didn't see any guards keeping watch on them.

"Well, that's done then," said Lucy, when the job was finished.

Hagar's eyes grew wide, and she gave her head an almost imperceptible little shake, warning Lucy.

Sure enough, the stern woman named Elizabeth had returned and they all formed a line again, heads bowed. Lucy was feeling rebellious, and dared to look Elizabeth in the eye.

"Lucy, please step forward."

This was completely crazy, thought Lucy, taking that forward step. She felt like she did a zillion years ago, when she got caught checking out a classmate's answers on a multiplication test, looking for the answer to seven times eight.

"Perhaps I didn't make myself clear, but here we work in silence. Work is worship and an opportunity for sustained prayer. Do you understand?"

Lucy nodded.

"You may return to your place."

Lucy stepped back, joining the line.

"I will now inspect your work." Elizabeth walked around the perimeter of the room, checking that the tables and chairs were in the correct position. Then she dropped to her knees in one of the corners and scratched at the floor with a finger. Rising, she returned to face the workers waiting for her verdict.

"I am well pleased," she said, bestowing the group with a lukewarm smile. "You may go to the chapel to give thanks for serving the Lord so well."

The group filed out of the dining hall and through the corridor to the chapel. Lucy kept her head bowed, but managed to catch a glimpse of the entrance, hoping to make a dash for it. Unfortunately, it was guarded by Matthew and Luke, those two large, muscular youths in white robes. Fighting back tears, she took a seat along with the other workers in one of the pews, and offered a silent prayer. "Please, Lord, help me get out of here."

After a while, and many repetitions of her prayer, a bell sounded and the group rose to return to the dining hall, which was fragrant with the scent of beef stew. Lucy was starving, after working so hard, and eagerly joined the line in front of a cafeteria style serving window. As the group shuffled along, she saw people carrying plates loaded with meat and vegetables to the tables, where they sat down. They didn't begin to eat, but sat with heads bowed, probably waiting for everyone to be served and grace to be said. Servers moved among them, filling glasses with water.

By the time Lucy and the others in the work party got to the window, they were told that there was very little stew left. The workers were given large scoops of rice and a small spoonful of meaty stew, but by the time it was Lucy's turn there was only rice, and not much of that. She was given the pot scrapings, which amounted to only a few dibs and dabs of burnt rice.

Somewhat incredulous, she carried her mostly empty plate to the last vacant seat and sat down. Head bowed, she waited, looking enviously at the well-filled plates of the other diners. Terry appeared behind her, carrying a pitcher of water, but she only filled Lucy's glass halfway. "You're so fortunate, we envy you," said Terry. "Fasting will rid your body of vice and corruption. Praise be."

Father Gabe did not appear at the meal. Elizabeth rose and gave the blessing, which was mercifully brief. The meal was eaten in silence, and Lucy chewed slowly, making the most of her meager meal. While she ate she tried to decide whether the kitchen had really run out of food or if it had been purposely denied to her as some form of punishment. The pot had indeed been empty, but there were plenty of other pots and they might have contained food.

After chasing the last clump of charred rice around her plate, and swallowing the bit of water remaining in her glass, Lucy waited to see what came next. She figured she would probably be assigned to cleanup after the meal, but instead was taken downstairs to the cellar by Matthew. There she was introduced to Philip, who was a chubby fellow in a white robe.

Philip had an easy smile and a twinkle in his eye, reminding Lucy of Friar Tuck, so she was hopeful that this job would be an improvement. Perhaps she would have to stuff envelopes, or apply stamps, or something like that. Instead, Philip pointed out a big pile of boxes that he said had just been delivered and told her to move them to a counter where they could be unpacked. Lucy didn't think this job would be much of a problem as she considered herself to be quite strong from working in the garden and doing housework. She obediently grabbed one of the boxes, only to discover it was very heavy. Much heavier than the big bags of dog chow she hauled home to feed the dog, heavier even than the bags of mulch she spread on her flower beds, or the cat litter she kept in the car in winter in case she got stuck on an icy road.

She managed to move the box, but it took all her strength and left her weak and panting. "Uh, Philip, do you have a dolly or something I could use? These boxes are really very heavy."

"Sorry," he said, eyes on a computer screen. "Hands to work, hearts to God."

"Well, this work is going to give me a heart attack," said Lucy.

He turned and faced her, the twinkle in his eye definitely gone. "If that's the Lord's will, so it will be."

She bent to her task, grabbing another box from the stack, placing it on the floor so she could slide it across the floor. That got an instant, angry response from Philip.

"Is this the way you treat the word of the Lord?" he demanded.

"Is that what's in the boxes? Bibles?"

"Yours is not to reason why, or to ask questions," he snapped. "Yours is but to do or die."

Lucy felt a wave of hysteria rising in her chest; this was ridiculous. "That's not from the Bible, you know. You're paraphrasing "The Charge of the Light Brigade." It's by Tennyson."

"Ah, who do you think you are?" demanded Philip, picking up a yardstick and slapping it against his hand in a threatening way. "You're a worm, a lowly sinner, and we are striving to save your soul. So get to work."

Lucy got the message: work or be beaten. She bent to pick up the box, but now it was on the floor and that much harder to lift. She struggled with it, trying to jimmy one side up so she could slide her hands under it, but the box was unmoveable. Out of breath from exertion, she looked at Philip, wordlessly expressing her difficulty, but he was every bit as stubborn as the box. She tried again, this time succeeding in lifting the carton a few inches off the floor, but it slipped out of her hands and dropped with a thud. By now, she was quite light-headed. She tried to stand, but everything went black and down she went.

When she came to she was back in the room with the cot. Scrambling to her feet, she felt dizzy, but fought to stay upright. She reeled across the room, grabbing the chair to steady herself, and made it to the door. She reached for the knob but it refused to turn. This time, the door was locked.

# Chapter Sixteen

Lucy's first impulse was to yell and bang on the door with her fists, demanding to be released, but something made her hesitate. For one thing, she was alone, which hadn't been the case so far, and her head was clearing. She was hungry and thirsty, to be sure, but the dizziness was subsiding and she figured that whatever they were drugging her with was wearing off. She decided to use this time—which might be brief, since she suspected that she was probably being observed—to do some thinking.

Just in case there was a peephole or even CCTV recording her every move, she figured she'd give the watchers a little show. Pretending to still be confused and dizzy, she staggered across the little room and made a show of collapsing onto the bed and passing out. The trick, she realized, was to stay awake while pretending to be asleep. She flipped over to face the wall, and that way was able to keep her eyes open.

Her mind was slow and sluggish as she tried to figure out how long she'd been held captive. She'd arrived at the storefront church on mid-morning on Thursday, had met with Father Gabe, and attended a service followed by a meal. That probably brought her to early afternoon, when she'd passed out, probably from something in the supposedly healthful herb tea. She had no idea how long she'd been unconscious, and since all the windows in the mission's interior were blocked, she had no idea whether it was day or night. Adding up the various periods of work and the prayer services she'd been obliged to attend, her best guess was that it was probably now Thursday night or even Friday morning.

If only Bill hadn't changed his plans, she thought, as tears stung her eyes. If he were coming for the weekend, as they originally planned, he would find the Airbnb apartment empty and would sound the alarm, instituting a search for his missing wife. But thanks to Sylvia, that wouldn't be happening. Still, determined to remain positive, she clung to the hope that he would probably call, and when she didn't answer might also become concerned. Or, probably more likely, figure that her phone had run out of power, or that she'd turned it off in a theater or someplace and forgotten to reactivate it, which she sometimes did.

Reluctantly concluding that she couldn't rely on a white knight to rescue her, Lucy knew she had to get herself out of this situation. Rebellion and resistance would get her exactly nowhere—

that seemed clear. Her only hope was to pretend that she was a genuine convert to the cult's crazy beliefs. If she seemed eager to pray and confess her sins, if she worked willingly and obeyed all the commands, maybe then she'd at least get a square meal. It would take some real acting on her part if she were to convince her guards, but maybe then they would relax their watchfulness and she'd be able to find a way to escape.

The thing that puzzled her was why the cult wanted to keep her. In her mind she replayed her meeting with Father Gabe, wondering what she'd said that caused him to decide she was a danger to him or to the cult. She remembered that he'd been very interested when she'd said she worked for a newspaper, and she wondered if he thought she was some sort of muckraking journalist intending to expose him. That was one possibility. Another was that he had been involved in some way with Beth's death, and didn't want her to continue her investigation. Or maybe this was simply the way the Guardians of the Faith operated. Maybe they lured people in with their pretended friendliness and warmth and then used a variety of techniques to control them and eventually bind them to the cult. She remembered reading a book about Patty Hearst and the techniques the Symbionese Liberation Army used to turn the sheltered heiress into a gun-toting bank robber. It was a chilling thought and she was determined not to let that happen to her. She had to find a way out of the cult.

But now, her first priority was to get out of this room. She was hungry and thirsty, and more importantly, she really had to pee. Really. So she rolled over on her back, as if waking, rubbed her eyes, and stretched. Playing the part she was assuming to the max, she sat on the side of the bed and bowed her head, softly reciting the Lord's Prayer. Then she got up, staggered a bit for effect, and went to the door. This time the door opened, and she was met in the hallway by the chubby, tired-looking woman named Ruth.

Ruth gave her a warm hug. "How are you feeling?"

"Much better," said Lucy. "I prayed for strength, so that with God's help I can be a better worker."

"Wonderful." She gave Lucy a big hug. "It's amazing what we can do with the Lord's help. I'm sure you'll find that to be true."

"I feel stronger already," said Lucy. She lowered her voice. "I do have an urgent need to use the toilet, however."

"Of course. Follow me." Ruth led the way to an unmarked door, which when opened revealed a toilet and small sink. Lucy smiled gratefully and stepped inside, pulling the door shut behind her. It didn't close all the way, however, as Ruth insisted on leaving it slightly ajar. "Just in case you need help. Why just last week one of our new converts passed out and fell right off the seat. It was a good thing I was there to help her."

Lucy had no difficulty imagining such a scenario; she felt a bit woozy herself and put it down to hunger, or even drugs. After relieving herself she washed her hands and face and was able to scoop up some water and drink it, which helped her feel better. Thus refreshed, she followed Ruth to the chapel, for yet another prayer service.

This time, when the worshipers were asked to confess their sins, Lucy stepped forward. Head bowed in a posture of penitence, she admitted to being weak and lazy. "I know that I've been stubborn and have resisted the group's efforts to help me become a better person, and I ask for forgiveness. I hope with God's help, and with the help of our Lord Jesus Christ, and also the Holy Spirit, but most especially with the group's help, I shall succeed."

Father Gabe stepped forward and placed his hands on her head. "Bless you, Lucy. We welcome you, we embrace you, we will support you in your journey."

She was immediately surrounded by the women who had originally welcomed her so warmly: Elizabeth, Charity, Grace, Ruth, and Terry. They joined a circle around her and sang a hymn of thanksgiving, then led her back to a pew where they sat with her. Then, once again, the service became a light show, with flashing strobes and thumping rock music. Lucy felt quite light-headed when it finally ended and they shuffled off to the dining hall, where she hoped and prayed she would receive more than a dab of rice and a quarter cup of water.

This time she was not at the end of the line, but the group of women shepherded her right to the front, where she was given a big scoop of brown rice with a couple of fried eggs and a cup of tea. She watched carefully as her cup was filled, fearing it might be doctored with drugs as before, and was reassured when she saw that the others also received tea from the same pot. They were quite a jolly group as they seated themselves together at the table, and Lucy had the strange feeling that she'd been admitted to the popular girl's table in the high school lunchroom. The meal was eaten in silence, but there were lots of smiles and winks among the women. As before, she was assigned to cleanup after the meal, and this time Terry was in charge of the work party.

Lucy waited with the other workers as the dining hall emptied and the cult members went off to their various jobs. She recognized Hagar and Zeke, as well as some of the others, who were clearly of a lower status in the cult than the women she'd been sitting with. She was trying to work all this out, wondering why these people were consigned to menial jobs like cleaning, and was unsure if she was still considered one of them and would have to scrub the floor on her knees.

It was her old friend Terry who provided the answer when, instead of ordering Lucy to begin shifting the tables, gave her a spray bottle of cleaner and a rag. "You and I will clean the tables, then the others will move them to one side and clean the floor."

"Praise be," said Lucy, getting right to work and polishing the Formica table until it shone.

"I see you're beginning to understand the value of work as a form of prayer," said Terry.

"Hands to work and heart to God," said Lucy.

"It must be a real struggle for you, though," said Terry, who was working beside her, spraying the next table with cleaner. "You have family in Maine, don't you?"

"I do," said Lucy. "And I pray that with God's help we'll meet again."

"Perhaps you'd like to see them sooner rather than later," said Terry, in a whisper.

"Whatever God wills." Lucy wasn't about to give up her act, and feared that Terry was merely testing her.

"When I first came here, I thought Father Gabe was a modern-day prophet, a true man of God, but now I'm having doubts."

"We all have doubts from time to time," said Lucy. "You should pray for strength to overcome your doubts."

"I have prayed, but I've seen some things that disturb me." Terry sounded genuinely troubled and Lucy wasn't sure how to react, or whether she could really trust her.

"What things?" she asked.

"Well, Father Gabe has special, private prayer meetings with certain members." Terry paused. "They're always young girls, and very pretty."

*Not exactly a surprise,* thought Lucy, figuring that seducing attractive young converts was pretty much the sort of thing charismatic cult leaders did.

"I'm sure he's just bringing them closer to God," said Lucy. "Who are we to judge Father Gabe?"

"I'm sure you're right, Lucy." Terry left her and went across the room to supervise the group that was washing the floor.

Lucy had finished polishing the tables and moved on to the chairs, giving them a once-over with the rag. When Terry returned, she praised Lucy for her initiative and willingness to undertake the chore. "You know, I'll be going out tonight to spread the good news about the Guardians. There's a poetry reading in that bookstore on Broadway. Would you like to come with me?"

Lucy's heart skipped a beat; this could be the chance she was waiting for. She had to answer very carefully. "Do you think I'm ready?" she asked.

"Well, it would be up to Father Gabe to decide, but I think he's quite impressed by the progress you've made. Shall I ask him if you can accompany me?"

"I will be happy to do whatever he decides," said Lucy.

Terry stepped closer and this time her voice was urgent, even desperate. "You could help me. We could get away. We could escape together."

Lucy wanted to believe Terry; she wanted to believe Terry's offer was genuine. But something held her back from committing herself. "What will be, will be," she said, and Terry squeezed her hand.

After Terry inspected the dining hall and declared it satisfactory, Lucy wondered what her next assignment would be and if she would be included in the work party that included Zeke and Hagar. She was still curious about these people, who were obviously the cult's worker bees. She thought that they might be resentful about their treatment and perhaps willing to give her information, or even stage some sort of rebellion. But as it turned out, she was the first on Terry's list and was merely told to go with Grace, who had suddenly materialized out of thin air.

Lucy suspected there was some sort of surveillance and communication system in the storefront mission that allowed for doors to magically unlock and for people to suddenly appear. It was a powerful control technique that allowed some people to know what was happening while others were kept in a state of ignorance and surprise, a situation which Lucy was experiencing firsthand. Here she was, completely at the mercy of Grace, who was bringing her who knows where. She had no idea what to expect, and it was only too easy to imagine horrible possibilities.

Grace was smiling when she stopped in front of yet another unmarked door, and Lucy understood that the numerous doors and twisting passageways were in effect a maze that created confusion and made it impossible to find a way out. When the door opened, revealing a dressing room with showers, Lucy wasn't entirely reassured. Grace showed her to a locker and produced a blouse and skirt similar to the one she was wearing, along with a cotton bra and pair of panties in the roomy style her grandmother used to wear, and a pair of navy blue sneakers. Lucy was then shown to a curtained cubicle, which provided a modicum of privacy, where she stripped and then stepped into the adjacent shower stall. There were no knobs, just a showerhead, from which warm water magically began to flow. A few minutes later it stopped, and she opened the curtain and found a towel hanging on a handy hook.

Just that little fact unnerved her. Was the towel there when she stepped into the shower? Or did someone put it there while she was showering?

Grace? Someone else? Or had it been there all along and she hadn't noticed? Was she imagining the whole thing?

"Do hurry," urged Grace, who was waiting for her outside the cubicle. "Father Gabe is waiting for you."

Lucy's heart skipped a beat and fell into her stomach—at least that's what it felt like. She was suddenly terrified, consumed with dread. She knew only too well that Father Gabe held ultimate power in this little world he'd created and she was completely at his mercy. Anything could happen. She could be killed, diced up, and served as mystery meat for lunch. She could be drugged and raped. Or simply raped.

"Lucy, do be quick. We can't keep him waiting."

Struggling to control her fear, Lucy toweled off and put on the clothes. The bra was much too large and useless, the underpants too small. The skirt, a navy blue dirndl, and the simple white blouse were okay, but the sneakers were a bit tight. Finally dressed, she stepped outside the cubicle, feeling like a lamb about to be led to the slaughter.

"Let me just give your hair a little combing," said Grace. Lucy was about to protest that she could do it herself, but realized there were no mirrors in the dressing room.

"Thanks," she said, bowing her head and allowing Grace to part and arrange her damp hair with clumsy hands. The woman was surely no stylist and Lucy couldn't imagine the combing was much of an improvement.

"There, you look very nice," said Grace. "Follow me."

Lucy followed her keeper down the hall to another closed door, which when opened revealed a small private chapel, where the walls were covered with red velvet curtains. There, Father Gabe was kneeling at a prie-dieu beneath a large, uplit crucifix. He remained there for a few minutes, then rose and approached Lucy. Grace stepped back, and Father Gabe enclosed Lucy in a big hug.

The first thing Lucy noticed was that he smelled great, kind of fresh, like limes. She found herself wishing she could stay there, in that warm, safe embrace, forever. She knew better, knew he was playing on her emotions, but when it ended she felt quite abandoned. Father Gabe offered reassurance by squeezing her hands and smiling at her.

"I'm so glad you've joined us."

"Thanks for having me," said Lucy.

"I have a special gift for you, and only you," said Father Gabe.

*Oh, no, here it comes*, thought Lucy, swallowing hard.

"A new name."

"Oh," was all she could manage to say.

"From now on, you will be Leah."

Grace stepped forward, holding a bowl of water, and Father Gabe began the series of questions familiar to Lucy from baptisms in the Tinker's Cove Community Church. "Do you believe in God the Father?" he asked.

Lucy was about to answer when a high, shrill scream pierced the air. "You stay here," he ordered, and dashed out of the chapel, into the hallway.

Lucy turned, dodged Grace's effort to block her, and ran after him. Reaching the door of the chapel, she stopped, blocked by her chubby buddy, Philip. Looking past him, she saw Matthew and Luke restraining a young girl who Lucy judged to be about fifteen, who was struggling to free herself. There were several other girls, all about the same age, standing in a group behind them, looking anxious and confused.

"Lucy, help me," said Grace, taking her by the hand and approaching the girls. "Let's all go into the chapel for a minute," she suggested, stretching out her arms and herding the group along.

Lucy did as she was asked and joined the group, leading them past the still struggling girl and on into the chapel. As soon as they were through the door, Grace closed it. From the other side they heard another sharp scream, a thud, and then silence.

"Where's the food?" demanded one of the girls, the tallest. "They said there'd be chicken."

"And a movie, with popcorn," added another.

From their rather dirty clothes and hair, and the ratty backpacks and tattered plastic grocery bags the girls were carrying, Lucy guessed they were street kids. Cult members had apparently rounded them up, luring them with the promise of food and fun. The reality, she guessed, was most likely rather different. She remembered Terry whispering to her about Father Gabe's private prayer meetings with young girls and guessed that these street kids had been brought to the cult for his personal pleasure. Or perhaps they would be trafficked to other locations, where they would be held captive and used as sex slaves.

"All in good time," said Grace, as the door opened and Matthew and Luke entered the chapel.

"That's right, chicken's this way," said Luke.

"Go along, girls," urged Grace.

Lucy wanted to tell them to run, to flee, it was all a lie, but they were already leaving the chapel, mouths watering at the thought of the juicy chicken meal awaiting them.

"That Tiffany's a jerk," one said, as she left the chapel.

"Yeah," agreed another, as the door closed behind them.

Now Lucy was alone with Grace in the chapel.

"I'm sorry about that," said Grace, smoothing the front of her skirt. "Father Gabe is so kind to these youngsters. I can't imagine what upset that girl. They are often less grateful than one might expect, considering all the blessings they receive from him."

"It's the way of the world," said Lucy, with a rueful sigh. "Do you think he'll come back and finish my baptism?"

"I'm sure he will." Grace fell to her knees. "Won't you join me in prayer, while we wait?"

Lucy knelt and bowed her head. She prayed, silently repeating the words that had become her mantra. "Get me out of here, get me out of here."

The chapel door opened, but it wasn't Father Gabe who was returning to complete her baptism. It was Luke and Matthew, who she'd come to realize were the cult's enforcers. They approached her and she began to rise, looking for some escape and finding none. They stepped beside her, one on each side, and grabbed her arms. She tried to shake them off, but couldn't free herself. She was dragged to one side of the chapel and one of the curtains that shrouded the walls was yanked aside, revealing a door. The door opened and she was shoved inside a dark space where she could not see but clearly heard the click of the lock.

# Chapter Seventeen

Lucy's first reaction on finding herself in complete darkness was paralysis; she was absolutely terrified. Soon, however, that fear turned to anger—how dare they do this to her—and she decided she had to take control of her situation. She had to figure out where she was, and if there was a way out. The door was locked—she knew that—but she groped around until she found the knob. She didn't expect it to turn but she tried anyway, twisting as hard as she could. The door didn't give, so she proceeded to explore the space, pressing her hands against the wall and feeling her way as she moved along. She didn't have far to go before she reached a corner, then encountered a bunch of sticks, actually mops propped in a bucket. She was in a cleaning closet, a fact that was reaffirmed when she encountered shelves on the back wall filled with plastic bottles. Another corner brought her to the side wall of her prison, which she judged was about four feet square. She hadn't felt a wall switch and she waved her arms above her head, hoping to find a dangling string like the one that controlled the light in her pantry at home, but didn't find it.

She sat down on the floor, which felt gritty, and tried very hard to believe there were no spiders in the closet with her. She hadn't encountered any webs, but that didn't mean spiders weren't lurking in the corners, waiting to bite. Suddenly furious with herself, she hauled herself to her feet and checked out the shelves, hoping to find a hammer or screwdriver, or even a squeegee, anything she could use to pop the lock or break the door. All she found were sponges and rags, along with the bottles of cleaner.

If she'd paid attention in chemistry class, she told herself, perhaps she would know how to use the cleaning products to rig an explosion that would free her. Of course, in the dark, it was hard to know exactly what chemicals the closet contained. She did know that if chlorine bleach and ammonia were combined, they produced a poisonous gas. Better leave the cleaning products alone.

Sinking back to the floor, she knocked against the bucket of mops and remembered a worn out sponge mop that stood in a corner of her cellar, awaiting a fresh sponge. There was a metal panel that held the sponge insert and Lucy figured that if she could find a similar mop she might be able to use the panel to free herself. She scrabbled around in the bucket, examining the mop heads with her fingers, and discovered they were all plastic. A big advance, she supposed, since they wouldn't rust, but useless for her purpose.

If only she had some leverage, she thought, leaning against the door and propping her feet up against the back wall. Oh, gee, she did, she discovered, feeling the panel in the door give a bit. Excited, she explored the door with her fingers and learned it was an old-fashioned one with two panels. Those panels were made of thin wood, she knew, because she had similar doors at home in Tinker's Cove, and her son Toby had once broken one by kicking it when he was practicing soccer skills with a hacky sack.

Swinging herself around, she began kicking at the door panel with her feet and discovered it was much tougher than she'd expected. Much sturdier, apparently, than that door at home. And repeatedly kicking an immovable object, she soon learned, was extremely tiring. She decided to give it a rest for a few minutes and closed her eyes.

Sometime later, she had no idea how long, she was startled awake by a loud noise. Sirens, lots of sirens! At last, they'd come to rescue her! Even with the muffling effect of the thick draperies that covered the chapel walls, she could hear sounds indicating a police raid. First were the sirens, then banging and occasional screams. Listening intently with her ear pressed against the door, she imagined the chaotic scene taking place in the storefront mission. Cult members were running, trying to escape the pursuing cops. Furniture was knocked over, doors slammed, fisticuffs were exchanged between struggling cult members and the cops who were trying to restrain them. She knew she had to help them find her, so she began banging on the door and yelling as loudly as she could.

"I'm in here, in here!" she screamed. "Behind the curtains, pull the curtains!"

But no matter how loudly she yelled, nobody came to rescue her. And soon, the noises outside grew fainter, and eventually ceased entirely. The raid was over and she hadn't been found.

Maybe, she realized with a sinking heart, they hadn't even been looking for her. Maybe somebody saw the street kids entering the mission and called the cops. Maybe those heavy boxes she'd been shoving around in the cellar didn't contain Bibles after all. Maybe they contained contraband. Illegal drugs, gold, guns, it could be almost anything.

She sank to the floor once again, fighting the impulse to cry. Here she was, locked up like some medieval maiden who'd shamed her family, or some poor soul caught in the clutches of a sick serial murderer. A poem by Edgar Allan Poe came to mind, or was it a short story?

Enough of this, she decided. Feeling sorry for herself wasn't going to get her out of this closet. It was time to buckle down and push, with all her might, against that door. So she did, pressing her feet against the wall and pushing as hard as she could with her back. When that didn't work she flipped around and tried it the other way, with her back against the wall and her feet against the panel.

That seemed to work better, as she felt the panel begin to give. Encouraged, she started to kick at it, and heard the welcome sound of splintering wood. It was only a crack, she discovered, feeling it with her fingers, but it was a beginning. Aiming her kicks as best she could, she whacked and whacked at the crack, damning the stupid sneakers Grace had forced her to wear and wishing she had her sturdy orthotic sandals instead. Or even better, a pair of sturdy Maine duck boots.

Take this, Grace! *Wham!* Take this, Terry! Take this Gabe! *Wham, wham! Wham, wham wham!* Suddenly the panel gave, and Lucy was able to crawl out through the opening. Still on her knees, she yanked the curtain open, encountering more darkness. A thud, something falling, indicated she wasn't alone. Someone else was in the dark chapel. She froze in place, holding her breath.

"Damn," that someone said. "There must be a light switch here somewhere!"

The voice was familiar.

"Bill?" It flew out before she could catch herself. What if it wasn't Bill, what if it was one of the cult members?

"Lucy?"

"Oh, Bill!" She ran, stumbling, through the dark chapel toward the sound of his voice and slammed into something warm and strong. He wrapped his arms around her, holding her as if he would never let go. Never, ever let go.

Lucy clung to Bill like a *Titanic* survivor hanging on to a bit of flotsam for dear life as they made their way out of the chapel into the dimly lighted hallway. There they paused and she gazed at the face she'd feared she would never see again. "I can't believe you found me."

"I didn't. I was searching for you, but I never

would have found you in that dark room. You smashed into me."

"I was in a closet. I had to break the door. The police were here. I heard them, but they didn't find me."

"They're still here," said Bill. "They've set up some sort of headquarters outside, in a mobile unit. They're planning a room-by-room search, so they would've found you eventually."

"Probably after I starved to death . . ."

"You'd die of thirst first," said Bill.

"Are you saying I'm fat?" demanded Lucy.

"No, no. It's a fact. People die of thirst before they die of hunger. You can go longer without food than you can without water."

"Well, I sure could use a drink, but maybe something stronger than water."

"C'mon." He led the way, retracing his steps through the confusing passages until they emerged into the dining hall, where the tables and chairs had been tossed every which way, and where a couple of white-suited technicians were combing every surface, searching for evidence. Then Bill and Lucy stepped into the carpeted hallway, walked right past the chapel doors, and out into the street.

Lucy closed her eyes against the bright daylight and collapsed against Bill, overcome with an onslaught of emotions. She was free . . . she was with her husband . . . she was thankful . . . she was saved.

Next thing she knew, a uniformed police officer was wrapping her in one of those aluminum foil blankets and an EMT was giving her a bottle of water and telling her to sip slowly. Then a gurney was rolled up and she was seated on it, covered with a blanket, and told that she would be taken to the hospital for a checkup but Detective McGuire wanted to speak to her first.

"I don't think I need—" she protested.

Bill pressed a finger to her mouth, silencing her, and shook his head. "No heroics."

"Listen to your husband," advised Detective McGuire, joining them. "You've been through a traumatic experience and you'll probably need treatment. PTSD is real. Don't try to minimize what you're going through."

"Okay." Lucy took a sip of water.

"Do you feel up to answering some questions?"

"Yes. I want to talk about it." But first, she thought, there was something she needed to know. "What day is it?"

"Saturday. It's now two p.m., Saturday afternoon."

"I was there since Thursday morning. I had a meeting with Father Gabe on Thursday morning."

"More than forty-eight hours," said Bill.

Lucy fingered the water bottle, a puzzled expression on her face. "Was this raid all because of me?"

"I couldn't find you when I got to the city on Friday, so I went to the police," said Bill.

Lucy was confused. "But you weren't going to come, because of Sylvia."

"I told Sylvia to get lost. I wasn't going to miss our weekend together, not for that"—he paused, carefully choosing his words before continuing—"uh, well, rhymes with *witch*. But when I couldn't find you I called your friend Sam and she told me about your plan to question Gabe about Beth's death. Brad called Detective McGuire to make an official missing person report."

"Your disappearance was all we needed for probable cause," said McGuire. "We've had lots of complaints from neighbors in recent months, quite a few missing persons, stuff like that, but we never had a solid lead. Believe me, we've wanted to get into that cult for a long time. We've suspected they were into human trafficking, drugs, money laundering, you name it."

Lucy shivered and pulled the blanket up to her chin. "What about Beth? Did Gabe kill her?"

"We'll be looking into that, too. He's in custody and he's going to have to answer a lot of questions."

"What about the others?" asked Lucy. "Some were accomplices, but others were just victims, like me."

"We've got a team of psychiatrists and social workers and criminologists. They'll sort it all out. It's going to be a big case. We'll need a statement from you, but there's plenty of time for that." He gave her blanket-covered leg a cursory pat and nodded to the EMTs, and she was lifted up and into the ambulance. Bill clambered in and perched next to her and off they went.

"You actually told Sylvia to get lost?" asked Lucy, seeing her husband with fresh eyes.

"Yeah, but this isn't turning out to be the romantic weekend I thought it would be."

"It seems pretty darn romantic to me," said Lucy, taking his hand. "You're my knight on a white charger."

At the ER Lucy was examined and found to be slightly dehydrated but otherwise healthy. A psychiatrist also examined her and determined she was mentally sound despite her ordeal, prescribed a mild antianxiety medication, and urged her to seek further help if she began to experience symptoms such as panic attacks or suicidal thoughts.

Lucy's thoughts, when she was finally released sometime later that evening, were focused on getting a square meal and enjoying a cuddle with her husband. But when they stopped at a little French restaurant near the apartment, Lucy found she couldn't decide what to order. Bill chose for her, requesting the steak and frites he thought she'd enjoy, but when the plate was set in front of her Lucy found she couldn't eat it. And when they got back to the apartment, all she wanted to do was sleep.

Next morning, Lucy and Bill got a late start because Lucy insisted on cleaning the apartment, leaving it as she found it. When they finally did get going they found a parking ticket on the car, and Lucy began to cry.

"It's okay, Lucy," Bill said. "It's just a ticket. No problem."

"I'm so sorry," she said, blubbering.

Bill plucked the ticket out from beneath the windshield wiper and carefully folded it and placed it in his wallet before climbing in behind the wheel. Lucy was already seated, worrying that the car wouldn't start. It did, and then she began worrying about getting in an accident, or hitting a pedestrian, or driving off the RFK Bridge.

"I gotta tell you, Lucy, I was pretty scared when I got to the Airbnb and you weren't there, and you weren't answering your phone. I couldn't imagine what had happened."

"When did you get there?" asked Lucy, who was trying to get days and times straight.

"Around five, like we planned. I didn't work Friday, so I could drive down." He paused. "Believe me, that was one long night."

"How'd you think to call Sam?"

"Well, I called the police first, but they told me they couldn't do anything for twenty-four hours. That's when I called Sam; she was the only person I could think of. She said she'd gone with you to a service at the Guardians' chapel and she got her husband to call Detective McGuire. When Brad got on the line McGuire seemed to take it all a lot more seriously. And then it turned out somebody had called saying they saw those street kids being lured into the chapel, and it all kinda fell into place."

Bill was whizzing along the West Side Highway, beneath the George Washington Bridge, where he pointed out the little red lighthouse. Lucy had always looked for the lighthouse, ever since her mother had read the book to her as a young girl, but today she didn't even try to catch a glimpse.

"The worst part," said Bill, continuing on to the Cross Bronx Expressway, "was when you weren't found among the cult members. One woman, a tough cookie if ever there was one, insisted that you were never there. She insisted she'd never seen you, but one of the others said she might've seen you. That was enough for me and I began tearing the place apart. I honestly don't know if I would have found you, though, if you hadn't broken out of that closet." He was quiet, concentrating on getting through the tolls on the RFK Bridge. Once through, and safely onto I-95, he picked up his conversation.

"You were really brave, Lucy. I don't know how you managed to do it." His voice grew thick. "Was it terrible? Did they, did he . . . ?"

"What? Rape me?"

"Yeah."

"No. Nothing like that. It was mostly mind games. At first they were all nice and full of compliments. They didn't want me to leave—I was so wonderful and they liked me so much. I knew it was phony but it sort of had an effect. I guess I rationalized the whole thing to myself by thinking that if I was in the cult I'd have a better chance of figuring out if Gabe killed Beth. Then, they must've drugged me. I woke up in this room like a nun's cell or something. I was afraid I was locked in, but the door opened. Then there were these exhausting church services and they made me work, really hard work, and I passed out again. Then when I woke up the door was locked, but I started to figure things out and decided to pretend I was converted. I thought that was the only way I'd get any chance of escaping. It seemed to work. One woman invited me to go out to a bookstore and evangelize with her, but I'm not sure that really would have happened. I was afraid she was testing me and going to turn me in." She sighed. "It was really weird. It got so I couldn't trust my own instincts."

"Well, you're safe now," said Bill. "It's all over and done."

"Right," said Lucy, but she knew it wasn't.

# Chapter Eighteen

Lucy slept for most of the drive back to Tinker's Cove, waking intermittently to check on the progress of their journey. They stopped a couple of times at highway rest areas, and Lucy found she was afraid to go into the ladies' rooms. She tried to make herself as inconspicuous as possible, sidling into the tiled rooms where the women's voices, the flushing toilets, and the *whoosh* of the hand dryers echoed off the walls. She rushed through her business, barely rinsing her fingers at the sink before hurrying out, fearful she would be seized by kidnappers.

Then there was the long walk through the food court, past all those strangers. She didn't know them. What if some of the cult members had escaped the raid and were lying in wait for her? Terrified, she ran outside and dashed through the parking lot, nearly getting hit by a kid driving a pickup truck. "Watch where you're going, lady," he yelled, after he'd slammed on the brakes.

Rattled, she ran off, searching wildly for Bill, whom she had agreed to meet at the car. There were so many SUVs just like theirs in the parking lot. She ran from one to another, looking frantically for one with a Maine plate, unsure where they'd left theirs. It was hot, and the sun was bouncing off the cars. Tears began building in her eyes, and her breath became ragged and uneven. What if Bill didn't wait? What if he figured she was taking too long and drove off? What if he'd been faking it all these years and didn't really love her?

Then he was right there, standing in front of her, a concerned expression on his face. "Are you all right?"

"I—I just got confused," she said, as he wrapped his arm around her shoulder and led her to the car.

Evening was falling by the time they reached Tinker's Cove. It was still light, but people had turned on the lights in their houses, which gave a welcoming glow. Their house was dark, however, when they pulled into the driveway, and Lucy was hesitant about getting out of the car and going inside.

"Are you sure everything's all right? Why aren't the lights on?"

"The girls must be out. It's Sunday night. They're probably enjoying the last bit of the weekend."

"Don't they want to see me?"

"They don't know what happened, Lucy. I didn't

have time to tell them. They think everything went according to plan and we had a weekend escape."

Hearing that, Lucy began to laugh. "Escape. That's what it was. A close escape."

"Yeah." Bill took her hand and helped her out of the car, then held her tight as they went up the porch steps and into the kitchen. He flipped on the light switch, and Libby, the Lab, rose slowly from her doggie bed, stretched, and greeted Lucy with a wagging tail.

That welcome would usually have gotten Libby a cursory pat on the head, but this evening Lucy sank to her knees and embraced the dog, burying her face in the dog's coat and breathing in her doggie smell.

On Monday morning Lucy took Bill's advice and called in sick, saying she'd caught some sort of bug in the city.

"A little too much fun?" asked Ted, in a teasing voice.

Lucy was suddenly overwhelmed with guilt. "No, I'll come in if you want."

"It's okay, Lucy. We'll manage without you. Take it easy."

She managed to blurt out a quick "thanks" and ended the call before bursting into tears.

"Everything okay, Mom?" asked Zoe, who was making her way very carefully down the steep back stairway with a plastic basket full of dirty laundry. She was wearing her lavender and white striped Queen Vic waitress uniform.

Lucy was quick with an excuse. "Sorry, I'm just a little emotional, that's all. Hormones, I guess."

"I'm late for work. Do you think you could throw this stuff in the washer for me?" She set the basket down on the kitchen table. "I've got the early shift, breakfasts and lunches. Lucky Sara—she got dinners when the tips are much bigger."

"I can do your wash. I'm staying home today anyway."

Zoe's eyebrows rose in surprise. "Are you sick?"

"Um, just kind of tired after my trip. I thought I'd take it easy. I've got laundry, too."

"Thanks, Mom."

Zoe flew out the door and Lucy picked up the basket, intending to carry it down to the cellar where the washer and dryer were located. She looked at the door, a two-panel door similar to the one from the closet she'd been trapped in, and dropped the basket. She sat down at the table.

"Mom! Mom! Are you okay?"

It was Sara, shaking her shoulders. "Wha . . . ? Yeah. I'm fine."

"You were just sitting there, kind of staring blankly at the cellar door."

"Just tired I guess."

Sara wasn't convinced. "Are you sure? Maybe you're having some kind of stroke or something. Should I call nine-one-one?"

"No, no. Nothing like that." Lucy shook her head and stood up. "See. I'm fine. Now, what would you like for breakfast?"

"Uh, Mom, it's almost lunchtime."

Lucy checked the kitchen clock, which read a quarter past eleven. "I wonder where the time went."

A horn honked, signaling that Sara's ride had arrived. "See you tonight."

"Right," said Lucy, watching as Sara grabbed her bag and hurried out, letting the screen door slam behind her.

The sudden noise made Lucy jump. Determined to get on with her day, Lucy picked up the laundry basket and carried it across the kitchen to the cellar door. Propping the basket on her hip, in a motion she'd made thousands of times, she pulled the door open and flipped the light switch. But instead of descending the stairs, she paused, looking down at the dusty flight of wooden steps. Even with the light on, it was dark and shadowy down there and she knew there were spiders in the corners. What if the door closed behind her and she couldn't get back out?

She closed the door, set the laundry basket on the floor in front of it, and sat back down at the kitchen table. That's where Bill found her when he came home at one for a late lunch.

"Lucy, you're not dressed," he said. "What's up?"

"You're home already?"

"It's after one and I'm starving. What've you got for me?"

"Past one?"

"Never mind, I'll fix it," said Bill. He opened the refrigerator door and began pulling out bread and sandwich fixings. "What would you like? Ham and cheese? Turkey? There's rye and whole wheat. Lettuce and tomato."

"Anything's fine," said Lucy.

Bill got busy spreading mayo and piling up the

sandwiches, adding a handful of potato chips on the side. He set the plates on the table and added a couple of cans of iced tea, then sat down opposite Lucy. He took a big bite of his sandwich and chewed, observing her.

"It's good, Lucy, if I say so myself. Black Forest ham, swiss cheese, tomato. Give it a try."

"Okay." Lucy picked up a chip and nibbled it.

"What's the laundry doing there?" asked Bill.

"I must've forgot it," said Lucy, eyeing the basket guiltily.

Bill chewed thoughtfully. "I'll help you. We'll do it together," he finally said.

"That'd be great," said Lucy, picking up her sandwich and taking a small bite.

After they'd finished eating, Bill cleared the table and loaded the dishwasher. Then he took the laundry downstairs and got the washer started. That chore done, he coaxed Lucy upstairs and helped her get dressed. After installing her on the family room sofa with a magazine, he told her not to worry about dinner; he'd bring home a pizza.

Lucy was still there, the opened but unread magazine on her lap, when Rachel and Miss Tilley unexpectedly arrived, *yoo-hoo*ing as they let themselves in. Miss Tilley, now retired from her job as town librarian, was one of the first people Lucy had gotten to know when she and Bill arrived in Tinker's Cove. Even so, she wouldn't presume to address her by her given name, Julia. Only her oldest and dearest friends dared do that, and they were a sadly diminished group as age took its toll. Rachel was Miss Tilley's part-time caregiver and companion.

"Bill called," said Rachel, "and asked us to drop by." She helped Miss Tilley seat herself in the rocker, then perched on the sofa by Lucy's feet. "He told us about your trip to New York and the cult."

"We picked up the *New York Times* and the *Daily News* for you," said Miss Tilley, producing the papers from her Broadbrooks Free Library tote bag.

"It's quite a story," said Rachel. "Do you want to read about it?"

Lucy nodded mutely, her eyes brimming with tears. "I'll recap it for you," said Miss Tilley. Rachel took Lucy's hands in hers, and Lucy held on, preparing to face her demons.

"It's a front page story in both papers," began Miss Tilley. She held up the tabloid *Daily News*, which featured a blown-up photo of Father Gabe that filled the entire front page. The headline, superimposed over his scowling face, announced in giant type: FAKE PROPHET PREYED ON YOUNG GIRLS. The *Times* was rather more restrained. The story ran in a single column on the top left of the front page, and the headline announced: AFTER WATCHING CULT FOR YEARS, POLICE FINALLY STAGE RAID. Somewhat smaller type provided an amplification: LEADER ALLEGED TO ENGAGE IN HUMAN TRAFFICKING.

Miss Tilley read the first few paragraphs of the *Times* story, which named Gabriel Thomas as the "'longtime leader of the Guardians of the Faith, which began decades earlier as the Angel Brigade in a Bronx storefront. Through the years the cult grew in numbers and began to engage in questionable activities, which police suspected but never had enough evidence to enable them to act. A report of a missing Maine woman filed by her husband and supporting evidence provided by prominent New York attorney Bradford Blackwell gave police the opportunity they had long sought. A Saturday raid on the cult's headquarters, now located on West Sixty-Ninth Street, has yielded evidence of a wide-ranging criminal enterprise that includes activities such as kidnapping, human trafficking, money laundering, illegal drugs, slavery, and prostitution.' "

Miss Tilley continued: " 'Sources indicate that police are also investigating Gabriel Thomas's possible involvement in the death of his first wife, Beth Blake, née Gerard. Blake, who subsequently married real estate developer Jeremy Blake, plunged to her death from a penthouse balcony earlier in the month. Originally considered a suicide, the case is now reopened in light of new evidence discovered at the cult's headquarters.' "

"It's all because of you, Lucy," said Rachel, giving her hands a squeeze. "You have to keep that thought. Think of the girls who will be safe now."

"You're a strong woman, Lucy." Miss Tilley passed her a tissue. "Now it's time to be up and doing. The longer you sit here feeling sorry for yourself, the harder it will be."

Rachel rolled her eyes. "I know you've been through a lot, Lucy. You have a lot to process. I can recommend a wonderful therapist. . . ."

Lucy shook her head no. "I'll be okay. Miss T is right. I have to concentrate on the positive. I'm safe. It's over and done." She swung her legs off the couch and stood up. "Can I get you some tea or something?"

"Sounds good," said Rachel, jumping to her feet. "I'll help."

In the end, it was mostly Rachel who filled the kettle and made the tea and piled cookies on a plate, but Lucy did drink her tea and ate a couple of cookies. When they left, Rachel pressed a slip of paper in her hand that contained the name and phone number of the therapist. Lucy stood in the doorway, watching them go, then dropped the paper into the trash. She'd survived the cult; the worst was over. For Pete's sake, she'd only been held captive for forty-eight hours and she hadn't been tortured or anything. Miss Tilley was right, it was definitely time to be up and doing. She hadn't been brought up to be a wilting flower and she knew exactly what her late mother would have told her. Those frequently repeated remarks about "Monday morning flu" and "dishpan diarrhea" echoed in her ears as she resolved to pull herself together and carry on. Tomorrow she would go to work.

Tuesday morning when she drove to the *Pennysaver* office on Main Street she noticed the town was ready for the Silver Anniversary Weekend. Banners were flying from the storefronts and silver planters containing blooming hydrangeas and white alyssum dotted the sidewalk. The bandstand on the town green had been decorated with white and silver bunting, and sandwich boards announced the weekend's events, which included an outdoor band concert, fashion show, church service, and dinner dance. When she stepped into the office, she found Phyllis and Ted busy putting the final touches on a special supplement for the weekend.

"How're you feeling?" asked Phyllis, by way of

greeting her. Phyllis was peering at her monitor, copyediting the ads for the supplement.

"Much better," said Lucy, which was all she could manage as she scurried across the office to the safety of her desk. Once she'd seated herself, she switched on her computer and began working through the hundreds of e-mails that had piled up while she was away.

"How was New York?" asked Ted, rubbing his eyes and leaning back in his desk chair, taking a break from the feature story he was writing.

Lucy paused, her finger poised over the delete button. "Okay." She swallowed hard, not sure how much she wanted to reveal, finally deciding she didn't want to talk about it. "I guess I'm not really a city girl. I'm glad to be back home."

"I know what you mean," said Phyllis. "I couldn't stand living in a city, and especially not a big city like New York."

"Did you catch any shows?" asked Ted.

Lucy shook her head, replaying the week's events up until her capture. "I saw my friend Sam, went to the botanical garden, and caught an art show in Soho."

"Sounds like fun." Ted sighed. "Take a look at this story for me, will you, Lucy? It's too long, needs to lose about ten inches."

"Okay."

Lucy was soon immersed in Ted's story, which credited Sylvia as the originator of Silver Anniversary Weekend and provided an account of the planned activities. She found she was able to tighten up the story without making any drastic cuts and soon had it ready for press. Work, she decided, was exactly what she needed, and she threw herself into her job with a vengeance. And so the rest of the week passed and every day she felt a bit more confident and able to control her emotions.

First up on the weekend's program of activities was a Saturday morning fashion show and luncheon at the Quissett Point Yacht Club. Lucy had made arrangements to go with Sue and was looking forward to the occasion. She had carefully chosen her outfit: white slacks, a green and white print tunic, and even a pair of green ballet flats that she was terribly pleased to have found on sale at Old Navy.

"My goodness," exclaimed Sue when Lucy stopped by to pick her up, "that is quite a nice outfit."

"You really think so?" Lucy was so accustomed to receiving a withering critique of her fashion choices from Sue that she could hardly believe what she was hearing.

"I do. You look great," said Sue, grabbing her purse and following Lucy to the SUV. Sue was wearing a similar outfit, though hers had a French flair since she was wearing a striped Breton top and espadrilles.

The two friends reluctantly came to the conclusion that Sylvia had outdone herself in planning the fashion show, which featured a lively narration, a charming musical accompaniment, and a comprehensive selection of wedding dresses that even included a Victorian dress borrowed from the Tinker's Cove Historical Society.

"That was really very enjoyable," admitted Sue, joining the applause when the show was over.

"Are you feeling well?" asked Lucy, somewhat concerned that her friend had not made a single snide remark for over two hours. "You don't seem quite yourself."

Just then Sue grabbed her arm and hissed into her ear. "Look at that woman!"

"Who?"

"The loud one with the Brooklyn accent."

Lucy followed Sue's gaze and noticed a rather tall woman, dressed to the nines in a tight black sheath, stiletto heels, and a necklace made of dinner-plate sized silver discs. "What about her?"

"Honestly, Lucy. She's dressed for a power lunch in New York. She looks like she just got off her private jet. And that makeup! She must scrape it off at night with a putty knife!"

"It's certainly not the sort of outfit you usually see in Tinker's Cove," said Lucy, who was relieved that Sue was back at the top of her game.

"So inappropriate," said Sue with a sniff. "So tell me, how was New York?"

"Captivating," said Lucy, inordinately pleased that she could make a joke about her terrifying experience. How far she'd managed to come in just one week!

"Great," said Sue, plucking a complimentary goodie bag from the table by the door for herself and one for Lucy, too.

Once outside Sue delved inside the bag, then snorted her displeasure. "Nothing but a lot of tissue paper, an Orange Blossom Bridal brochure, and a chocolate truffle. Here"—she dug out the tiny bit of foil-wrapped chocolate—"you can have mine, too."

"Thanks," said Lucy, whose eyes were drawn to the tall woman in black who was walking toward the parking lot. She had the oddest feeling she'd seen her somewhere before.

On Sunday morning Lucy and Bill went to the special service at the Community Church, where Silver Anniversary couples were invited to renew their vows. They weren't regular churchgoers, though they usually managed to go at Christmas and Easter, but Ted had assigned Lucy to cover the service and she didn't want to go alone.

"I don't want to be the only married woman there without her husband. And since it's practically summer you don't need to wear a jacket and tie," she added, to sweeten the deal.

"I'm not going to do that thing. . . . You know, renew my vows," warned Bill, when he'd parked the car and they were walking to the church.

"Fine with me," said Lucy. "I'm not renewing mine either because I haven't broken them. They don't need renewing." She gave him a look. "How about yours?"

"Mine are in good shape, no renewal needed." Not usually one for public displays of affection, Bill surprised her by taking her hand as they climbed the steps to the church door.

"That's good to hear," said Lucy, as they stepped inside the darkened space, where the sun illuminated the stained glass windows but didn't provide much bright light in the interior. As her eyes adjusted, Lucy noticed that the church was quite full, which wasn't usually the case, and she and Bill

were lucky to find a couple of places in one of the
rear pews behind Lucy's friend Franny Small.
Franny wasn't married but she was a faithful member of the church and never missed a service.

The organist, Ruth Lawson, was playing a prelude, and Lucy listened while she got out her reporter's notebook and pen and studied the order
of service. The service was pretty much as usual,
she noted, beginning with a hymn, followed by
readings, prayers, and a sermon. The sermon was
to be followed by the renewal of vows ceremony,
and as Lucy looked around the church, she noticed a good number of women were wearing
dressy pastel suits and dresses appropriate to such
an occasion. Some had even added summery hats
or fascinators.

Reverend Marge Harvey kept the service moving briskly, well aware that it would be longer than
usual due to the renewal ceremony. When the big
moment came, Lucy was amused to see Sylvia and
Warren leading the procession of couples up to
the altar. Sylvia was dressed in a silvery lace dress
with a little tuft of silver tulle tacked on her head
as a sort of mini-veil and was carrying a bouquet of
white roses fastened with a silver ribbon; Warren
was in a gray suit with a silver silk tie.

Lucy smiled to see Pam and Ted in the procession; Pam was wearing the orange caftan she was
married in and Ted was sporting a bright Hawai-
ian shirt. The Shahns, who were following them,
were more sedately attired. Phil was wearing a blue
blazer and chinos and Betty had opted for a summery print sheath. The artists Ben Melfi and Willa
Stout looked quite dashing in matching white

tuxes; she had added a shocking pink tie and cummerbund while his were electric blue.

Lucy was busy trying to capture it all in her notebook—the number of couples, the outfits, the flowers, the music—when Franny Small tapped her arm. "Aren't you going to renew your vows?" she asked, in a tone of voice that struck Lucy as confrontational.

"Uh, n-n-no," she stammered in reply.

"Whyever not?" demanded Franny, whose muddy brown eyes seemed to bore into Lucy's soul.

"I don-n-n-n," was all Lucy managed to say before she began trembling violently. The faces, the walls, the stained glass windows were all a kaleidoscopic jumble, closing in on her. The music was louder and louder and she had to get out of there. Dropping everything, she turned and ran down the carpeted aisle toward the open doors, out into the sunlight.

She was outside, hanging on to the wobbly wrought iron stair rail, when Bill caught up to her. He'd followed immediately, picking up her bag and notebook and hurrying out after her.

"Are you okay?" he asked.

"Crazy, isn't it?" said Lucy, aware of her pounding heart and sweating palms. "It just came over me. Something in the way Franny was talking reminded me, you know, of the cult and the way they were always asking questions."

"It's not crazy. It's a normal reaction. Let's go home, okay?"

"Yeah," said Lucy, allowing him to pry her hands off the railing and leaning on him as he led the way to the car.

"I really thought I'd beat this thing," said Lucy, who was shivering as Bill helped her seat herself in the car. He was careful not to slam the door, but closed it gently before hurrying around to the driver's side.

"I've been studying up on the Internet," said Bill as he started the car. "It's one of those two steps forward, one step back sort of things. You've made a lot of progress but you have to expect setbacks."

"It's so frustrating," confessed Lucy. "I never know what's going to set me off. Poor Franny, all she did was make an innocent comment."

"Well, it really wasn't any of her business."

"That's Franny for you," said Lucy, managing a little smile.

When they got home, Lucy made a halfhearted stab at making lunch, which prompted Bill to take over. He made BLTs, one of Lucy's favorites, but she found it hard to swallow the toasted bread and only took a few bites.

"Maybe later," said Bill, suggesting she lie down on the sofa in the family room for a rest.

That sounded fine to Lucy, and she allowed him to arrange the throw pillows for her and to cover her legs with a light cotton throw. He made sure the TV remote was handy, along with the Sunday papers, and brought her a glass of iced chamomile tea.

"I feel like a baby," confessed Lucy, toying with the tassels on the throw.

"Be a good baby and take a nap," urged Bill.

Lucy was once again filled with doubts and

feared Bill was planning to leave her alone in the house. "Are you going somewhere?"

"No. I'm going to stay right here. I'm going to touch up the paint on the porch railing, so I'll be right outside the kitchen door, keeping you safe."

"What about the front door?"

"It's locked, Lucy. It hasn't been opened in years. I'm not even sure it does open anymore."

Lucy wanted to ask him to shut and lock the windows but knew it would be a ridiculous request since it was such a hot day. "You'll be able to hear me if I yell?" she asked.

"Yup. The windows are open and so's the kitchen door. I'll be right outside."

"Okay." Lucy laughed nervously. "I'm sorry to be such a wreck."

Bill took her hands and bent down, kissing her cheek. "You're not a wreck. You've been through a traumatic experience and you're doing remarkably well. Now do as the doctor ordered and get some rest. Okay?"

"Okay, Doctor."

Lucy flipped on the TV, but found herself yawning as the Property Virgins struggled to find an affordable starter home that met their numerous requirements, which included a master bedroom with an en suite bath, a large kitchen with stainless steel appliances and granite countertops, and a walk-in closet large enough to store the wife's Imelda Marcos–sized shoe collection. She clicked the TV off and, yawning once again, shut her eyes.

Next thing she knew, her cell phone was ringing. She fumbled a bit trying to answer it, thinking it was probably Franny Small calling to apologize for upsetting her, but it wasn't Franny. The voice that came through the tiny device sent chills up and down her spine, and she almost threw the phone across the room.

"Just give me a minute," said Terry. "I called to say I'm sorry."

Lucy didn't believe her for a minute. "Okay. Thanks. Bye." She tried to end the call by pounding the end button, but the phone stayed on and she heard Terry's voice. "I didn't know. Honest. I've been seeing the papers and the news and I'm sick about it. I thought I was saving souls. I really did."

"I find that hard to believe."

"Maybe I was fooling myself. Maybe I wanted to believe so much that I blinded myself to what was really happening." There was a pause. "Well, I just wanted to say I'm sorry for getting you into that mess and everything that happened and, well, I hope you're doing okay."

"I am." Lucy found she had a lot of questions she wanted to ask Terry, and this was her chance. "What about you? Were you caught in the raid?"

"No. I was out at the bookstore. I had a couple of souls I was bringing back to the chapel for the service, and there were all these cop cars and lights and everything. They bolted, and I hung around for a while, watching and trying to figure out what to do."

"What did you decide?"

"I rode the subway all night long. I didn't have money so I jumped the turnstile. I was on the trains for hours, and I was terrified. It was pretty much me and all the homeless people, and then I realized I was one of the homeless people. When the papers came out I stole one. I couldn't believe what I was reading about Father Gabe and everyone. I felt like a fool."

"What did you do? Did you go to the police?"

"I'm too afraid."

"How are you getting by?"

"I'm staying with my brother, in New Jersey."

"That's good. Well, thanks for calling." Again Lucy tried to end the call, but was caught anew by Terry's pleading voice.

"There's something I want you to do for me, okay?"

Lucy couldn't believe what she was hearing. "Are you crazy?"

Terry's voice was indignant. "I'm trying to do the right thing and I need your help."

Lucy was skeptical, but curious. "What do you want me to do?"

"I want you to call the cops for me. Tell them that Father Gabe didn't kill his wife, that Beth woman. The paper said they're investigating him and I know he didn't do it."

"That is exactly the last thing I'm prepared to do, Terry. Sorry. Besides, why would they listen to me?"

"Because I have proof. I was with him that day, the day she fell. We saw the crowd and the ambulance and the cop cars. We'd been proselytizing, handing out pamphlets, and there's even a photo of us. It was in the newspaper. We're far off, down the street, but it's definitely me and Father Gabe. He gave it to me, told me to save it. He said it might come in handy someday. I didn't understand then, but I do now. He wanted proof that he didn't, you know, hurt his ex-wife."

"And you were with him the whole time? He couldn't have gone to see her?"

"No way. We were together all morning."

"Other cult members? Those enforcer guys in the white robes? Could they have done it?"

"No, because whenever Father Gabe went out he made sure the mission was secure. He always ordered them to remain in the front hall to make sure nobody came or left."

Lucy was silent, absorbing this information.

After a bit, Terry spoke. "Are you okay?"

"Pretty much."

"Well, like I said, I'm really, really sorry."

Lucy was suddenly angry, furious with Terry. "That's a whole lot of hooey. It's not enough to say you're sorry—you need to make it right. If you're really sorry you'll go straight to the police and tell them everything you know. And if that means you'll be punished, and I really, truly hope you will be, you deserve it."

This time, the phone went dead.

# Chapter Nineteen

Lucy sat silently on the sofa, her mind in a whirl. Could Terry be telling the truth? Was it actually possible that Father Gabe didn't kill Beth? That he was so busy rounding up homeless kids and trafficking them, transporting illegal drugs, cooking the books, laundering money, and screwing the faithful that he simply didn't have time to commit murder. It was possible, she supposed, especially since they'd been divorced for nearly thirty years. What motive could he have after so many years?

Maybe it really was suicide. Maybe Beth had been overwhelmed by depression, maybe she'd had a bad reaction to prescription drugs, maybe she'd been deadheading some potted plants and reached too far, lost her balance, and fell. It could've happened that way. Maybe it was simply the impulse of the moment, thought Lucy, remembering how quick Beth had been to try new things. Maybe she thought she'd take that final step into the unknown, just to see what awaited her there.

Pretty darn stupid, thought Lucy, pulling off the throw and getting to her feet. She wanted to take another look at that scrap of paper Sam had given her, the purported suicide note that Detective McGuire had claimed was worthless. It was still in her purse, which she always left on the table by the kitchen door that served as a catchall for mail, sunglasses, flashlights, the dog's leash, and pretty much anything that anybody happened to be carrying when they came indoors.

Sue always teased Lucy about the size of her bag, which was roomy enough to hold her reporter's notebook, camera, and a large number of pens as well as a mini-first aid kit, car keys, a pouch for coupons, a wallet with checkbook and ATM card but little cash, pack of tissues, reading glasses, and sunglasses. There was also a zippered pocket in which she stowed important things she feared might get lost in the chaos, and that's where she found the little scrap of gray paper in its plastic sandwich bag. It hadn't changed; the words in Beth's scrawling handwriting were the same:

> *Forgive me. I can't go on like this. It's better this way . . .*

Lucy studied it, wishing there was more. The paper was torn after the word *way*, and Lucy suspected that had been done intentionally by whoever received the note. Beth had obviously continued the sentence to specify what she meant, and Lucy was pretty sure this was a breakup note, not a suicide note. But somebody had wanted to provide evidence that Beth had considered suicide in the past, which would make it seem more likely that she'd actually gone ahead and done it. And she figured that whoever that somebody was, that person who was so eager to claim Beth had killed herself, was in truth Beth's killer.

"You're up," said Bill, coming into the kitchen with his wet paintbrush. "Have you got an old coffee can or something?"

"Check the recycling bin in the pantry," said Lucy, who was still holding the note.

Bill stepped into the pantry and emerged with an empty tomato can, which he filled with water, then added the brush. "All done. It looks nice. You should check it out."

Lucy looked out the window. "Wow. That railing really needed paint."

"Yeah." Bill was at the sink, filling a glass with water. "It's the sort of thing you don't notice, kind of creeps up on you. It's a big improvement." He drank the water. "What'cha got there?"

"It's supposed to be Beth's suicide note. Somebody sent it to Sam."

"Why do you have it?"

"Sam gave it to me."

Bill was silent and Lucy could practically hear the wheels turning in his brain. "Don't tell me you went to New York to investigate Beth's death and that's how you got tangled up in that cult. Did you, Lucy? Is that what happened?"

"Sort of," admitted Lucy.

"You told me you just wanted to get away, revisit

your childhood home, get in touch with the inner you. You lied to me."

"No. All those things were true, but I also wanted to come to grips with Beth's death."

"Coming to grips is different from conducting an investigation, Lucy. And look where it got you."

"I know," admitted Lucy. "It was a stupid thing to do and I'm sorry."

"Sorry isn't good enough, Lucy," said Bill, in a stern voice. Lucy was uncomfortably aware that he sounded quite a bit like she must have sounded when she scolded Terry. "Promise me you'll leave this alone. It's over. Time to move on."

"I promise," said Lucy. "Believe me, I've learned my lesson. I have to accept the fact that I'll probably never know what happened to Beth, and that's okay. I have my own life to live."

"Good." He stepped close and embraced her, stroking her head. "I don't want to have to go through anything like that again. I thought I'd lost you and it was awful. The absolute worst."

Lucy nestled her head into his shoulder. "I'm here. I love you. I won't leave you."

Bill let her go. "I think I got paint on your hair."

"I don't care," said Lucy, raising her face for a kiss when her cell phone rang.

"Leave it," urged Bill, but Lucy was already checking the caller ID display.

"It's Sue," she said, giving him a quick kiss. "Hi! What's up?"

"News flash," said Sue. "I just left Carriage Trade and they've got tunics like that one you were wearing yesterday on sale. I thought I'd let you know."

"Thanks, but even on sale Carriage Trade is too expensive for me."

"Not today it's not. They're ten dollars, down from a twenty-five weekend special. I bet they brought in a bunch for the weekend and got too many."

"Really?"

"Yeah. So if I were you, I'd get down here toot sweet, 'cause at this price they're not going to last long."

"I think I will. Thanks for the tip."

"No problem. Stop by the house after and we'll have some iced tea and gossip. You won't believe what I heard about Sylvia. . . ."

"Do tell."

"No. Not on the phone. It would fry the wires."

"This is a cell phone."

"The tower would crash to the ground."

"Okay," laughed Lucy. "See you later."

"So you're going into town?" asked Bill, as Lucy pocketed her phone. "Are you sure you're up to it?"

Lucy wasn't at all sure. Tinker's Cove was probably still packed with the last of the Silver Anniversary weekenders. She'd never find a place to park, and what if she had another panic attack? "I guess not," she said. "I don't really need another tunic."

"What about Sue? She's expecting you?"

"She'll understand. I'll call her back."

"Don't do that," said Bill. "We'll go together. I could use a new pair of boat shoes."

Lucy was shocked. Bill detested shopping. "Really?"

"Sure. It'll do you good. Get you back in the swim of things. And besides, Sid has a new riding lawnmower and said he'd sell me the old one."

Lucy knew that Bill had wanted a riding mower for some time, and Sue's husband Sid was one of those people who always had to have the newest, latest thing. The old riding mower had only been used a couple of years and Bill could probably get a good deal on it.

"Okay," said Lucy. She tucked the note back into her purse and swung it over her shoulder, ready to go.

The crowds had thinned by the time Lucy and Bill reached town, and they were able to park in the lot by the harbor. The Silver Anniversary banners were still flying, however, and most of the stores were open. They checked out the shoe store, but they didn't have his favorite boat shoes in his size. Next up was the candle shop, which had a sign advertising BUY ONE, GET TWO FREE, which Lucy had to investigate. Bill willingly accompanied her, but when she couldn't decide between Sunfresh Linen and Very Vanilla he began to grow restless. There was a bit of a line at the checkout, so Lucy decided to skip buying the candles and suggested going straight to Carriage Trade, across the street.

Word about the sale had spread fast and quite a few women were pawing through the tunics, which gave Lucy pause. She knew Bill wouldn't be happy in the shop, and the bench outside was already occupied by a couple of husbands, so she decided to send him on his way while she joined the bargain hunters inside. "Why don't you go on over to see

Sid," she suggested. They both knew the Finches' house was only a stone's throw away. "I'll poke around a bit here and bring the car over and meet you there in, say, an hour?"

Bill gave a big sigh of relief, followed by an expression of concern. "Are you sure?"

"I'll be fine," said Lucy. "Go."

Lucy was able to find a pink paisley tunic in her size and bought it. Discovering she still had a half hour before she was due to meet Bill, she continued on down the street to Country Cousins, where she knew they also carried Bill's favorite boat shoes and were advertising 25 PERCENT OFF EVERYTHING!

Dottie Halmstad greeted Lucy warmly when she stepped inside the old-fashioned country store, which drew visitors from around the globe. "It's great to see a friendly face," said Dottie, who was looking rather tired. "The weekend's been a big success, that's for sure. Now what can I do for you?"

When Lucy explained she was looking for a pair of size eleven boat shoes, Dottie had just the thing. "Somebody returned these," she said. "I can let you have them for fifty percent off."

"Great," said Lucy, eagerly snapping up the bargain.

She felt quite pleased with herself and swung her shopping bags as she made her way along Main Street and down Sea Street to the parking lot, where she gave Sally Kirwan a wave. Sally was ticketing cars that had been parked illegally in unmarked spaces. She was a member of the large Kirwan clan that worked in town jobs, especially the police and fire departments. Her uncle, Jim, was the police chief.

"Hi, Lucy," yelled Sally. "Got a minute?"

"Sure," said Lucy, meeting her by a huge Navigator with New Jersey plates that was blocking a driveway.

"Will you look at this?" asked Sally. "I know the lot was full earlier today but there are plenty of other parking places in town."

"Just too lazy to look, I guess," said Lucy.

"Or maybe figures the rules are for other people." Sally ripped the ticket off her pad and slid it under one of the Navigator's windshield wipers, then turned to Lucy. "I heard you had a rough time in New York. How's it going?"

"I have my ups and downs."

"That's how it goes. Don't be ashamed to ask for help if you need it."

"I'll keep it in mind," promised Lucy, amused at the young woman's earnest attitude.

"I've got a story for you, if you're interested," said Sally. "The department sent me to a workshop last weekend on spousal abuse, and Uncle Jim—I mean the chief—has assigned me to spearhead a program to better address the issue."

"Wow, that's great," said Lucy, who knew that abuse was a large but hidden problem in the little town.

"Yeah. I'm going to start meeting with health care professionals to encourage them to ask their patients if they're ever afraid at home. We're working in the department to develop better protocols, and I'm going to be talking at the high school, too. It's not just spouses. It can be boyfriends, too."

"Why don't we set up an interview," suggested Lucy, digging in her purse for her smartphone.

"The sooner the better," said Sally.

When that bit of business was done Lucy continued on her way, taking a moment to enjoy the amazing view from the parking lot. Looking out across the blue water, she could see Quissett Point, with the white-shingled yacht club and the rocky shore dotted with tall pine trees. It was quintessential Maine and it always reminded her how lucky she was to live in such a beautiful place.

She was loading her purchases into the back of the SUV when she heard a familiar Brooklyn accent and turned to see the tall woman Sue had remarked upon at the fashion show. No longer dressed in city black, today she was wearing a formfitting and extremely low-cut silver dress that sparkled with sequins. This time Lucy's memory clicked and she realized the woman was Dr. Fine's receptionist, who'd insisted she pay the $240 copay. And the man with her, who was unlocking the expensive sports car parked next to her CRV, was no one other than Dr. Fine himself.

"Hi!" she exclaimed. "Imagine seeing you here. I was in your office last week. I'm Lucy Stone. You gave me an adjustment."

"Right, I remember you," said Dr. Fine. "How's that back?"

"Just fine," said Lucy. "Did you come to town for the Silver Anniversary Weekend?"

"We did," said his companion, chiming in so enthusiastically that her bosom jiggled and Lucy wondered if she'd had a drink or three with her lunch. "I saw the ad in the *Times* and I thought how this is our twenty-fifth year of being together, if you know what I mean. We've only actually been married for twenty-three years; he had a wife to get rid of and she didn't make it easy, did she?"

Dr. Fine seemed a bit uneasy at the direction the conversation was taking and jangled his car keys. "We better be going. We've got a long drive ahead of us."

"Are you going back to the city?" asked Lucy.

"I hate to leave. It's so nice here. We stayed at this gorgeous B and B, the Queen Something or other," said Mrs. Fine. "I'm Ronnie, by the way."

"So you're married and work together, too?" asked Lucy, slamming down the rear hatch door. "You really deserve to be congratulated."

"It hasn't been easy, that's for sure," said Ronnie, eager to chat with her new best friend.

Lucy saw that Dr. Fine had opened the passenger door for his wife, but Ronnie was ignoring him, unwilling to drop a favorite line of conversation.

"Second marriages are hard—everybody says so—because there's not just the two of you in the marriage, but the ex and the kid and, in our case, the ex's first and second husbands." She rolled her eyes, which were heavily made up with plenty of gloppy mascara, dark eye shadow, and dramatic swoops of black eye liner. "You'd think he'd have better sense than to get involved with a woman going on her third marriage, wouldn't you?"

Lucy shrugged and attempted to step past Ronnie so she could get in her car, intent on escaping what was fast becoming an awkward situation. "What is it they say? The heart wants what it wants—something like that."

Ronnie grabbed her arm and leaned close, so close that Lucy could smell the alcohol on her breath. "He wanted me, the naughty boy. But that wife of his, she simply wouldn't accept the fact that their marriage was over. She was always after him. At first it was for more alimony, even child support, which was crazy since Colin here wasn't even the kid's father. And then, wouldn't you know it, she married that billionaire Jeremy Blake and moved into the same apartment building as Colin's mom. Talk about awkward—they were always bumping into each other, at least that's what she claimed, but I know better. She used to lie in wait for him, peering out the little peephole in her door, trying to catch him when he visited his mother."

That was interesting, thought Lucy. Dr. Fine's mother lived in Beth's building, apparently on the same penthouse level. Now she wanted to hear more, but Dr. Fine had other ideas.

"That's enough, dear," he said. "We really have to go."

Dr. Fine took his wife's arm, attempting to guide her into the car, but she was having none of it. "She was one crazy bitch, that woman," she said, planting her feet and digging in. "Do you know what she did? Here she was, living on the penthouse level, married to a billionaire, had everything a woman could possibly want, which in my case would be not having to work in my husband's office tracking down those weasly insurance companies and deadbeat patients. . . . Well, to make a long story short, Madame Blake just took it into her head one fine day to jump off her balcony, up there on the twenty-second floor." She gave a sharp nod. "With predictable results."

"Okay, dear. That's very interesting, but I don't think we should hold up Mrs. Stone. . . ." The doctor raised himself to his full height, then bent down and took his wife quite firmly by the shoulder, attempting to shove her into the low-slung sports car. The doctor's shape, bent over, flashed in her brain, superimposed over a similar image. It was the shadowy shape of the intruder, who'd broken into her apartment in New York.

Of course, she realized, picturing the note in her purse. Beth's supposed suicide note. It was written on a prescription pad. That's why the paper had looked so familiar. It had been torn off a prescription pad. Suddenly, it was as if her brain was on fire. Everything was falling into place. He had a motive: The newly assertive Beth was threatening to reveal his profitable sideline writing prescriptions for painkillers. He had the means: Beth's penthouse balcony. And he had the opportunity: after paying a visit to his mother he would have the freedom of the building without being caught on the CCTV in the lobby. Lucy was seeing Colin Fine with new eyes and her reaction was to run, to get away as fast as she could. She yanked open the car door and practically leaped inside, starting the engine.

Colin had noticed her reaction and was desperate to get away, so he grabbed Ronnie by her shoulders and manhandled her, roughly shoving her into the car and banging her head in the process. Ronnie yelled and next thing anybody knew, Officer Sally Kirwan had stepped in front of the sports car and was taking control of the situation.

"Hold on there," Sally ordered, legs apart and right hand on her gun, which was still holstered.

Faced with the officer blocking his escape, Colin turned and yanked Lucy's door open.

"Move over!" he yelled.

"Wha?" Lucy wasn't about to budge, but then she felt something pressed into her side. A gun? A knife? He prodded her again and she scrambled awkwardly over the console and into the passenger seat, allowing him to take the driver's seat. Then they were off, narrowly missing Officer Kirwan and tearing through the parking lot, clipping the tail of the last car in the row as he swung wildly into the turn and roared up Sea Street.

"You can have the car, just let me out," begged Lucy, as he took the turn onto Main Street so fast it felt as if the SUV was on two wheels. Lucy saw the startled expressions of pedestrians, and the desperate look on a woman's face as she yanked back the stroller she was about to push through the crosswalk, as Colin drove through the red light, pursued by a cruiser with siren blaring and lights flashing.

"You can't get away," Lucy told him, as another cruiser joined the chase. "They'll have every cop in the state chasing you."

"Shut up!" he snarled, sailing through the stop sign and taking a left onto Shore Road. "I'm not going to jail. No way." He gave a harsh, cackling laugh. "Beth'd just love that. She always did her best to wreck my life."

Lucy knew Shore Road only too well. She'd covered numerous crashes that had taken place on the twisty road that ran atop a cliff and offered spectacular ocean views. "Oh, no, you don't want to go here. Take the next right—it'll bring you to Route One."

"No way." The car was climbing up the steep incline, going much too fast. The sirens were screaming behind them, and when Lucy turned she saw flashing blue lights as far as she could see.

"Honest. This road . . ." She protested as he drove past the turn. "You've got to slow down, there's a hairpin . . ."

It was too late, she realized, as he pushed the gas pedal to the floor. He was almost to the turn and she knew they'd never make it. The car would crash right through the barrier and fall onto the rocks and seething sea below.

Belatedly realizing his danger, Colin hit the brakes and Lucy shoved the door open and threw herself out of the car, hitting the tarmac hard and rolling onto the grassy verge. Her shoulder slammed painfully against a wooden fence post, inches from the edge. Cradling her arm, she pulled herself up in time to see her car go right through the barrier and sail into thin air. Brakes squealed as the cop cars halted and sirens silenced. They heard the awful sound of metal hitting rocks and a single, piercing scream.

# Epilogue

It all seemed like a dream, actually a nightmare, thought Lucy, who was struggling to make sense of everything that had happened. The fact that her mind was muddled by the painkillers they'd given her at the hospital was only adding to her confusion.

She was pretty banged up from her leap from the car, but she'd only broken her arm, which the ER doctor thought was remarkable, especially considering the speed of the car. Her hands and elbows were scraped. She had bruises all over and whiplash from crashing into the barrier, but she would eventually make a full recovery. And for the moment, anyway, she wasn't really in any pain, but she didn't expect that situation to last. Once these drugs wore off, she would have to get by on over the counter painkillers now that the opioid epidemic had put an end to generous prescriptions for drugs like oxycodone and Vicodin.

Now she was tucked up in a corner of the emergency room, waiting to be released, while Bill went to the billing office with her insurance information. She'd been pleased when her friend, Officer Barney Culpepper, had popped into her curtained cubicle, eager to fill her in on the latest developments.

"Hell of a thing, Lucy," he'd said, standing awkwardly beside her gurney and swinging his blue cap in his hand. "Good thing you jumped when you did, otherwise you'd be sleeping with the fishes."

"I kept telling him about the curve, but I guess he didn't believe me."

"Maybe he figured he'd rather die than go to jail, something like that. NYPD checked the tapes from your friend's apartment building and it turns out he was there when she died. They've got video of him exiting the lobby, dressed like a woman and carrying a little dog. And it seems he's been under investigation for being a regular Dr. Feelgood, writing prescriptions for cash."

"I suppose it was Beth, his ex-wife, who fingered him."

"Mebbe. Or mebbe they just got into a fight, like people do. Mebbe she had a habit of playing loud music that bothered his mother, or mebbe she complained about the mom's dog or something and he lost it and flipped her off the terrace."

"It's too horrible to think about."

"Well, he got his, that's for sure." Barney had nodded sharply, his face set in a bulldog expression. "And his wife's no sweetheart, either. The dispatcher heard her arguing with his life insurance company, furious that they're withholding payment pending an investigation."

"She was bragging about it being their silver anniversary," Lucy had said.

"Oh, that reminds me. While we were fishing the doctor out of the drink, the county sheriff had to respond to a domestic here in town. It was the Bickersons—I mean the Bickfords—and this time he swears he's going to divorce her."

Lucy had started to laugh, but ended up groaning in pain. "It'll never happen," she finally said.

"You said it," said Barney, setting his hat on his graying brush-cut head. "Well, I gotta go. Get well soon."

Now, left alone, she kept thinking about that CCTV recording and how it had initially fooled the New York cops. Dressing as an old woman was a clever disguise—didn't they say that old women were practically invisible for all the notice people took of them? But was that how he was dressed when he attacked Beth? Lucy hoped not. It was too creepy.

She shifted cautiously, trying to get comfortable, and wondered what was taking Bill so long. She wished briefly she had something to read, anything to distract herself, but found herself yawning and dozing off. She began to dream, a dream so vivid it seemed absolutely real. In her dream she saw Beth standing on her balcony, wearing a beautiful white dress, like a wedding dress. She wasn't smiling, like a bride; she was frightened. Someone was with her and she was fearful. But why? It was only her neighbor, elderly Mrs. Feinstrom.

But then the angle switched and the focus was on Mrs. Feinstrom, only she'd changed. Now she was revealed as a man, a man who was screaming abuse at Beth, yelling at her and hitting her. Beth put her hands up to protect herself and he grabbed her by the shoulders and pushed her hard. She should have fallen. All the laws of physics demanded that she should have tumbled over the railing and dropped twenty-two floors to the concrete sidewalk below.

But she didn't. He grabbed her shoulders and pushed her over, but instead of falling, Beth floated upward, buoyed by the ballooning skirt of her white wedding dress. Her head was covered by a white veil, but it lifted in the breeze and wafted around her, revealing her face. She was radiantly happy. She looked like a Botticelli angel, with an expression of exquisite rapture on her face.

A noisy cart rattled past the cubicle and there were voices, which wakened Lucy, but there was none of the fear and anxiety that had gripped her lately. Someone had covered her with a heated blanket and she was filled with a sense of peace and contentment as she relaxed in the warm bed and drifted back to sleep.

*With family tensions intensifying in Tinker's Cove, part-time reporter Lucy Stone could really use some time off the grid. But after she RSVPs to an unconventional celebration on remote Holiday Island, Lucy realizes that disconnecting from reality comes at a deadly price . . .*

Lucy doesn't know what to expect as she arrives on a private Maine island owned by eccentric billionaire Scott Newman, only that the exclusive experience should make for a very intriguing feature story. An avid environmentalist, Scott has stripped the isolated property of modern conveniences in favor of an extreme eco-friendly lifestyle. A trip to Holiday Island is like traveling back to the nineteenth Century, and it turns out other residents aren't exactly enthusiastic about living without cell service and electricity . . .

Before Lucy can get the full scoop on Scott, she is horrified to find one of his daughters dead at the bottom of a seaside cliff. The young woman's tragic end gets pinned as an accident, but a sinister plot unfolds when there's a sudden disappearance . . .

Stuck on a clammy island with murder suspects aplenty, the simple life isn't so idyllic after all. Now, Lucy must tap into the limited resources around her to outwit a cold-blooded killer—before it's lights out for her next!

**Please turn the page for an exciting sneak peek of Leslie Meier's next Lucy Stone mystery INVITATION ONLY MURDER coming soon wherever print and e-books are sold!**

# Chapter One

The little bell on the door to the *Pennysaver* newspaper office in the quaint coastal town of Tinker's Cove, Maine, jangled and Lucy Stone looked up from the story she was writing about the new recycling regulations—paper, glass, and plastic would not be accepted unless clean and separate, no more single stream—to see who had come in, and smiled broadly. It was her oldest and best friend, Sue Finch, looking every bit as stylish and put-together as usual with her dark hair cut in a neat bob and dressed in her usual summer uniform: striped French fisherman's jersey, black Bermudas, espadrilles, and straw sun hat. Skipping a greeting, Sue pulled an envelope from her straw carryall with a perfectly manicured hand and declared, "Guess what came in today's mail? It's an invitation to die for!"

Lucy, who was used to playing second fiddle to Sue, raised an inquisitive eyebrow. She was also dressed in her usual summer uniform: a freebie T-shirt from the lumberyard, a pair of cutoff jeans, and neon orange running shoes. She hadn't bothered to style her hair this sunny June morning, thinking that it looked fine, and had missed a stubborn lock in back that curled up like a drake's tail feather. "Do tell," she said, leaning back in her desk chair.

"Just look at the paper," cooed Sue, pulling a square of sturdy card out of the velvet-smooth lined envelope. "Handmade. And the lettering is hand-pressed. And, oh, the address on the envelope was done by a calligrapher," she continued, handing the envelope to Lucy. "Trust me, something like this doesn't come cheap."

"Is it a wedding invitation?" asked Lucy, admiring the elaborate, swirling script on the front of the envelope. Turning the envelope over and studying the back, she recognized the formally identified senders: Mr. and Mrs. Scott Newman. Everybody in town had heard of the Newmans, who had recently bought an island off the coast and proceeded to hire every contractor in the county to restore the property's long-abandoned buildings, including spending a fortune to save the magnificent barn that was considered an architectural masterpiece.

"No, it's for a 'night to remember,' that's what they're calling it," replied Sue, handing Lucy the invitation. "It's to celebrate the Newman family's donation of the island to the Coastal Maine Land Trust and to thank all the people who worked on the restoration."

"I bet we're invited, too, then," said Lucy, whose

husband, Bill, a restoration carpenter, had been the lead contractor for the project. "The invitation's probably in the mailbox at home."

"It's going to be fabulous, if this invitation is any indication," said Sue. "No expense spared and believe me, the Newmans have plenty of expense to spare."

Lucy knew all about Scott Newman; she'd written a profile of the billionaire venture capitalist when rumors started floating that he was interested in acquiring Fletcher's Island for his family's summer vacations. When she interviewed him, she'd been somewhat surprised to learn that he was a keen preservationist who was interested in keeping the island completely off the grid and was refusing to install modern innovations, allowing only the original nineteenth-century technology. He planned to collect rainwater in a cistern, use a primitive electric generation system, and cook on an enormous woodstove, all of which were considered wonderfully advanced when the island was developed by lumber tycoon Edward T. Fletcher. When Lucy asked if this wasn't rather impractical, Newman had replied that it was modern life that was impractical, citing scientific studies linking climate change to human activity. "The old ways were much kinder to the environment, and face it, we've only got one planet, there's no planet B," he declared. "We've got to take care of Earth, or we're all doomed."

Some of the locals hired to work on the restoration project had a good laugh over Newman's proclaimed environmental stewardship, as restoring the nineteenth-century structures required using thousands of kilowatts of electricity, provided by gas-greedy portable generators. His insistence on using authentic materials such as lath and horse-hair plaster rather than sheetrock, and searching out recycled flooring, windows, and doors, not to mention hardware, had required lots of workers who had to be ferried to and from the island on power boats that burned gallons of fossil fuel. "It's like the cloth versus disposable diapers thing," Bill had told her. "Sure, the disposables fill up the landfill, but washing the cloth diapers uses water and energy. It's kind of six of one and half a dozen of the other when it comes to the environment."

Most controversial was the restoration of the im-mense barn, which alone was estimated to cost at least two million dollars. The huge number of cedar shingles required for the roof and siding had created an industry shortage that sent the price sky-rocketing and shook the commodities market. The *Pennysaver* had received numerous letters to the ed-itor protesting the shingle shortage and arguing that there were better ways to spend so much money. One writer proposed restoring the sprawl-ing local elementary school, for example, which he claimed was a prime example of 1960s architec-ture.

Locals had also refused to be bamboozled by Newman's supposed generosity in donating the is-land to the land trust, while reserving his right to retain it for his own use during his lifetime. It was true that he'd also preserved the rights of the Hopkins family, long-term residents of the island, to remain there, but again, only during his lifetime. And while the agreement set limits on how the island could be used, and was intended to preserve the island's environment in perpetuity, the gift had come with plenty of strings attached and had garnered a large tax deduction for the Newmans, a fact that many writers of letters to the editor had also pointed out.

Despite the controversy, however, the party was eagerly anticipated by everyone who received an invitation, and that included land trust board members, contractors, local officials, and media, which was pretty much a who's who of the entire town. The question that was on everyone's lips as the big day drew closer was, how were the Newmans going to pull off such a big party while preserving their nineteenth-century lifestyle? Sue Finch wasn't the only one to wonder, "Are we going to have to swim there? And are we all going to be sitting in the dark, huddled around a campfire, toasting wienies on sticks?"

Lucy was pondering that very question when she drove home from work a week or so later and found a rusting and dented old Subaru parked in her driveway. The car was missing a couple of hubcaps, had a crumpled front fender, and the glass on a rear window had been replaced with duct tape and a plastic grocery bag. Continuing her examination with the keen eye of an investigative reporter, she noticed the registration tag was out of date, and so was the required state inspection sticker.

Climbing the porch steps of the antique farm-

house that she and Bill had renovated and entering the kitchen, she was greeted by her aging black
Lab, Libby. Arthritis didn't stop Libby from rising
stiffly from her comfy dog bed and wagging her
tail in welcome, earning her a treat and a pat on
the head from Lucy.

Voices could be heard in the adjacent family
room and Lucy stuck her head in, curious to learn
who owned the Subaru. "Oh, hi, Mom," said her
daughter Zoe, quickly disentangling herself from
the arms of a shabby-looking fellow with a stubbly,
three-day beard. "Mom, this is Mike Snider."

Mike didn't bother to get up from the comfy
sectional where he was reclining, or even to lift his
head from the throw pillow it was resting on.
"Hiya," he said, raising one hand and giving a little
flap.

Lucy glared at him, taking in his shaved head,
tattooed neck, and torn jeans that clearly needed a
wash. Worst of all was the T-shirt with a message
that was clearly unprintable for a family newspaper
like the *Pennysaver*. "Hiya, yourself," said Lucy,
turning on her heel and marching out of the
room, leaving no doubt that this was a situation
that did not meet with her approval.

Back in the kitchen, Lucy got busy on dinner,
noisily pulling pots out of cabinets and slamming
them down on the stove. She was filling a pasta pot
with water when the couple appeared, holding
hands, and were met with a low growl from Libby,
who watched Mike through narrowed eyes and
flattened ears from her doggy bed. She was clearly
considering getting to her feet, painful though it

would be, when Mike reached for the knob and pulled the door open. "Catch ya later," he said, before stepping through the doorway. Moments later, Lucy heard the roar of the Subaru's unmuffled engine, which sputtered out a few times before catching and carrying Mike away.

"Who is he? And where did you meet him?" Lucy demanded, turning to face Zoe. Zoe was her youngest, at twenty, and every bit as pretty as her older sisters, Elizabeth and Sara. She shared Elizabeth's dark hair and petite build, but had Sara's peachy skin and pouty lips. Today she was glowing, no doubt the result of her aborted activities on the sectional.

"At school, Mom," she answered, referring to Winchester College, a local liberal arts university where she was a junior, currently majoring in French after trying political science, psychology, and art history. She had hopes of joining Elizabeth in Paris, where her older sister was working as an assistant concierge at the toney Cavendish Hotel. "Mike's a TA in the computer science department. He's really smart. Even Sara says so," she added, bolstering her case with a reference to the family's doubting Thomas, who was a grad student at Winchester.

"He might be smart," admitted Lucy, "but he's certainly not socialized. Libby has better manners, and she's a dog."

"He's a little rough around the edges," said Zoe, beaming, "but Libby only gets up to greet you because she knows you'll give her a treat."

"That was unkind," retorted Lucy, bending over

the dog and scratching her behind her ears. "You love me, you really, really love me, don't you?"

The dog yawned and settled her chin on her front paws.

"And that car," said Lucy, reverting to the subject at hand. "The registration's elapsed and so has the inspection, which is understandable since I doubt it would pass. It definitely needs a new muffler."

"Mike's got better things to think about than bother with stuff like that. He's working on a computer game that's going to be revolutionary, that's going to change everything."

"Well, if you ask me, he'd be better off taking a shower and changing into clean clothes."

"Oh, you don't understand anything!" declared Zoe, storming up the stairs to her room, where she slammed the door.

"What was that all about?" asked Bill, stepping into the kitchen and kissing his wife on the cheek, before depositing his empty lunch cooler on the counter. Lucy smiled, noticing that Libby didn't get up for him, but did manage to thump her tail a few times.

"Zoe's got a new boyfriend," explained Lucy. "A real loser."

"She'll learn," said Bill, opening the refrigerator door and extracting a can of beer. "She's got to figure these things out for herself."

"Just you wait until you meet him," said Lucy, tearing up lettuce for salad. "I bet you'll change your tune then."

Bill sat down at the round, golden oak table and

popped the tab on his beer. "Whaddya think about this island shindig?" he asked, with a nod at the invitation that was stuck to the refrigerator door with a retro magnet advertising Moxie soda pop. "I'm not gonna have to wear a jacket and tie, am I?"

"No jackets, no ties," said Lucy, repeating the verdict Sue had handed down when Lucy called for advice. "It's resort casual."

So Bill was togged out in a navy polo, Nantucket red shorts, and boat shoes, and Lucy was wearing de rigueur white jeans, embroidered tunic, and sandals when they joined the assembled guests at the appointed day and hour at the harbor in Tinker's Cove. It was a balmy evening, but these Mainers weren't fooled by the thermometer and were carrying windbreakers for the breezy boat ride.

"How are they getting us out there?" wondered Ted Stillings, Lucy's boss at the *Pennysaver*. "Newman is a big fan of sail."

"Yeah, he's got a beautiful restored yacht, a cutter," added Sid Finch, Sue's husband, with a hint of envy in his voice. "But it's not gonna hold all these people."

The dock was indeed crowded. It seemed as if most of the town had been invited, and spirits were high with anticipation. They were all expecting the promised night to remember, but weren't sure exactly what that might be. When two of the puffin watch boats that carried sightseers out to view the colorful birds that were the Maine version of penguins hove into view and chugged up to the dock, there was a heightened sense of excitement.

"Well, we're off!" sang Sue, as they settled themselves on wooden benches for the ten-mile crossing to the island.

Ninety minutes later, the boats had crossed the ten miles between town and the Fletcher's Island dock, where Scott Newman and his wife awaited them. Lily Starr was Scott's second, much younger wife, and before her marriage had a rising career as a country-western singer. Even in flats she was slightly taller than Scott, who was a slight man with very short, very dark hair who seemed barely able to contain his intense energy. "I trust you had a pleasant crossing," he said, as the gangplank was lowered and the guests began to debark from the boat. "Welcome to Fletcher's Island."

The couple stood together by the gangplank, taking each guest by the hand and helping them negotiate the steep incline, welcoming them, and instructing them to follow the illuminated path that led from the landing up to the barn. Dusk was falling and Lucy was grateful for the lighted luminarias, most probably constructed of biodegradable paper bags and soy candles, that lit the way along the gravel road that gradually ascended to the island's summit. As they rounded a bend, the massive, newly restored barn came into view, causing people to catch their breath at the amazing sight. Light glowed in the many windows of the huge structure, which had a unique sloping roof topped by five illuminated cupolas and two soaring silos at either end topped with conical roofs.

The barn was surrounded by a cluster of outbuildings, including an icehouse, creamery, henhouse,
as well as the modest stone house occupied by the
Hopkins family. The Turner mansion, which had
also been restored and was now the Newmans'
summer home, was on the south end of the island,
some distance from the barn, and the party.

Continuing along the road that circled the barn
and outbuildings, Lucy entered the barnyard, where
she joined the other guests, who were oohing and
aahing over the spectacular view and the gorgeous
sunset.

"Not too shabby," said Sue in an approving tone
of voice, taking in the expanse of rosy sky and silvery ocean dotted with small, pine-covered islands.

"And the barn, just look at it," said Lucy, sighing. The roof alone was sixty feet at its highest
point, and the thought of the slippery slope the
roofers had to negotiate gave her the shivers. The
huge doors stood open invitingly, so they went into
the large space that was illuminated by old-fashioned
lanterns. Enormous arrangements of daisies, grasses,
and meadow flowers decorated tables covered with
blue-and-white checked cloths, and bales of hay
topped with matching checked pillows offered
plenty of seating. "Is that a bar?" asked Bill, interrupting her thoughts.

"I believe so," said Sid, and the two men strode
off purposefully, followed by their wives.

The bartender was a remarkably good-looking
young man with blond hair and a neatly trimmed
beard, wearing a black T-shirt printed with a map
of the island and the words QUAHOG REPUBLIC. A

name badge announced his name was Wolfgang, and a slight German accent indicated he wasn't a local.

"Are you working here for the summer?" inquired Lucy, aware that the plentiful summer jobs in Maine attracted college students from all over the world.

"I'm from Berlin," he said. "I was hoping to work in one of the craft breweries. I heard there are a lot of them in Maine, but this came up and I like it here." He nodded, looking around at the island in approval. "What can I get you?"

The two couples had no sooner been supplied with drinks, beer for the men and white wine for the women, when they were approached by two attractive young women offering trays of hors d'oeuvres: tiny crab cakes, chicken wings, and deviled eggs. "I'm Parker, and I just want to let you know there's cheese and crackers and crudités on the table over there," said the first, who appeared to be in her late twenties and was dressed in a bright pink Lily Pulitzer style shift and bare feet.

"And I'm Taylor," said the second server, who appeared to be an identical twin of the first, dressed in a blue and green Lily Pulitzer and bare feet, adding, "and there's a raw bar next to it."

"Thank you," said Lucy, taking one of the crab cakes. "Are you girls going to be here all summer?"

"We sure are," said Taylor. "Dad's really keen on having the whole family together for this first summer on the island. He's put us to work monitoring a puffin colony on the back side of the island."

"That must be really interesting," said Lucy, who had realized the girls must be Scott Newmans' daughters, probably from his first marriage.

"And important work," added Sue, surprising Lucy by taking one of the proffered crab cakes. Sue rarely ate anything that could be classified as actual food, and seemed to exist on a diet of black coffee and white wine.

"You should try the deviled eggs, they're from our own chickens," said Parker.

"And the wings?" asked Lucy, with a mischievous smile.

"I'm not sure about those," said Taylor, with a little smile. "But Dad does want the island to become self-sufficient. We're starting with the chickens and goats, and there's a big vegetable garden, too."

"Don't miss the raw bar; it's over by the milking parlor," added Parker as she too drifted off, carrying their offerings to the other guests.

"What cute girls," said Lucy. "Fancy a bit of cheese?"

"Are you out of your mind?" snorted Sue. "Cheese is full of fat and calories, while oysters, on the other hand, are nothing but sea water and lean protein."

"Oysters it is, then," said Lucy, as the two made their way to the raw bar, where their husbands were already working on second helpings. Another good-looking fellow, this one dark-haired and brown-skinned, was shucking oysters, and Lucy wondered if an attractive appearance was a requirement for working on the island. The shucker was also wearing a Quahog Republic T-shirt, and his name badge gave his name as Ben.

"Are you also a foreign student, like Wolf?" asked Lucy, plucking an oyster from its bed of ice.

"Not unless you think Brooklyn is a foreign country," he replied, smiling and revealing very white teeth.

"It almost is, to us Mainers," said Sue, nibbling on a huge shrimp. "I suppose you wanted to get out of the city and get some fresh Maine air?" Sue's daughter, Sidra, lived in Brooklyn, and Sue was forever complaining about the air, which she said smelled of diesel exhaust from the busses.

"Yup," replied Ben, cocking an eyebrow and adopting a bit of an attitude. "I'm just a big Fresh Air kid, straight off the bus."

"I think you mean straight off the boat," said Lucy, trying one of the shrimp. While chewing she noticed a distinct chill in Ben's attitude, and was quick to make amends. "I really didn't mean that the way it sounded. All I meant was that you can't take a bus to an island."

"Don't miss the clambake," advised Ben, with a rather curt nod toward a column of smoke that was rising outside on a grassy area behind the barn. "It ought to be just about ready."

"Thanks for the advice," said Lucy, grabbing Sue's hand and looking for their husbands, who had wandered off in the direction of the bar. "We've got to get the guys; they won't want to miss it."

Word had quickly spread among the guests, who were streaming toward the clambake, which was just being uncovered by two young men also wearing the black T-shirts. Lucy recognized them as

Will and Brad Hopkins, lobstermen she'd often seen unloading their catch at the lobster pound in Tinker's Cove. The two were taking instruction from an older man she suspected was their grandfather, Hopp Hopkins. She'd never met him, but had heard of him, as the legendary paterfamilias of the Hopkins clan. The family had stubbornly remained on the island after other members of a once-thriving fishing community had sought greener pastures elsewhere, and Lucy wondered what the Hopkinses really thought of Scott Newman and his family. Were they pleased to work for the billionaire, or did they resent taking orders from a newcomer? Whichever it was, the Hopkins men were too busy to think about it, raking off the steaming seaweed and fishing out steaming net bags containing the traditional clams, lobster, corn, and potatoes. Soon everyone was seated at long outdoor tables covered with checked cloths and lit with glowing oil lamps, cracking open their lobsters and clams, and dipping the meat into melted butter. The wine and beer flowed, and the atmosphere was lively and friendly, since nothing breaks down social barriers like the messy process of eating lobster in the rough.

The lobster was followed by dessert, a choice of strawberry shortcake or hand-churned goat's milk ice cream, both made by Susan Hopkins. Susan, Hopp's daughter-in-law and Will and Brad's mother, was rarely seen in Tinker's Cove, but did come to town a couple of times a year to see the dentist or shop for supplies. Lucy had tried to catch her on one of those visits to interview her about her island life, but Susan had demurred.

"I've really nothing to say," she'd said, "and I do have to get back home." She'd then glanced anxiously toward the harbor, where Hopp was waiting for her in the family's lobster boat, and Lucy had wondered if Susan was a victim of domestic abuse. Tonight, however, she seemed at ease in her black apron with the white Quahog Republic logo, smiling as she doled out the delicious desserts.

People were just finishing up the last of their cake and ice cream when music could be heard. "A live band?" wondered Lucy aloud, as they tossed their biodegradable paper plates and bamboo forks into the trash and headed toward the dance floor, lured by the sound of a bluegrass band. The dance floor was located in the former hayloft, which was reached by climbing a flight of stairs that had been cleverly constructed in one of the silos.

"I know you want to work off some of that dinner by dancing," said Scott Newman, speaking to the gathered guests. "But first we have some official business to take care of." He then introduced the board members of the Maine Coast Land Trust, including Roger Wilcox, the board president. Wilcox then took over, producing a deed for the transfer of the island to the trust, which both he and Scott signed with great ceremony. The men shook hands, and Lucy used her phone to take a grin-and-grab photo for the *Pennysaver*, then everyone settled in for the obligatory speeches.

Wilcox was brief, saying the addition of Fletcher's Island to the trust's other properties was a significant step in preserving Maine's unique history and island ecology, and would provide an important habitat for local wildlife such as seals and the threatened population of puffins. He then turned the mike over to Jonathan Franke, the trust's chief executive. Lucy remembered him as the long-haired and Birkenstocked environmental agitator who had been instrumental in creating the Association for the Preservation of Tinker's Cove. That organization of earnest citizens had continued to maintain the town's conservation area, but without Franke. He had now cut his hair and shaved his beard, and was dressed in business casual befitting his new role with the trust.

"I'll be brief," promised Franke, "but I do want to say how grateful we at the trust are to be the beneficiaries of Scott Newman's incredible generosity. It's thanks to his foresight and his commitment to the environment that Fletcher's Island will become a natural preserve, providing habitat for a large variety of seabirds, including the threatened Atlantic puffins. I know there has been some controversy about the nature of the gift, and I want to assure everyone that Scott Newman himself was insistent that the island eventually be restored as closely as possible to a natural condition. The buildings, including this magnificent historical barn, will remain and will be used for educational and research purposes. So, in closing, on behalf of all the members and officers of the trust, I want to express once again our gratitude and appreciation to Scott Newman."

Led by Franke, the gathered company joined in giving Scott an enthusiastic round of applause as he took the microphone and held up his hand in a modest protest at the applause.

"Thank you so much," he said, again signaling that the applause should end. "As I'm sure you all know, the donation of the island was only possible because of the success of my company, New World Capital. We venture capitalists often get a bum rap, and I admit we must accept our fair share of blame for putting money ahead of environmental concerns, but I am happy to say that we at New World are taking a different tack, and our success has been built by investing in environmentally conscious and beneficial technologies. The experts, the economists, and the guys at Wharton and other top business schools said it couldn't be done, but we proved them wrong. New World Capital has done very well, you could even say exceptionally well, by committing to following tough environmental standards, and I attribute a good portion of that success to my daughter, Parker. It was Parker who came home from kindergarten one day and asked, 'Dad, what are you doing for the environment?' At that time, I simply didn't have an answer, but I looked at my little girl and promised myself that I was going to do everything I could to preserve her future and the future of millions of other little children like her. That's how New World Capital came to be and tonight, on this very special occasion, I'm happy to announce that Parker Newman will become a full partner in the company." He signaled to his daughter to join him and she did, bowing her head bashfully as everyone applauded.

This news struck Lucy as surprising, since she had rather patronizingly, she now realized, considered Parker a rather pampered, overprivileged rich girl who was doing a nice job serving hors d'oeuvres.

After the polite applause died down, Newman went on to praise his other daughter, Taylor. "She's an absolute PR whiz, and you can all thank her for this fabulous party—it was her idea."

The appreciative guests' applause was somewhat more enthusiastic for Taylor, who encouraged everyone to stay and dance to the music. The band took the cue and struck up a lively tune, prompting a few brave souls to take to the dance floor. Bill and Sid headed over to the bar, which had been moved to the loft, and Lucy decided she really ought to check with Taylor, making sure she had her facts straight for the story she would write about the party and the transfer to the land trust.

Taylor was standing with her father when Lucy approached and introduced herself. The pair greeted her warmly, asking how they could help. "I just need to check some facts, make sure I've got everybody's name spelled right," said Lucy.

"Of course. I've prepared a press packet," said Taylor. "It's downstairs in the office. I'll be back in a minute."

Taylor dashed off, leaving Lucy standing rather awkwardly with Scott Newman. "This is quite a party," she said, breaking the ice.

"I'm glad you're enjoying it," said Scott.

"I'd love to interview you sometime about your lifestyle choice here," said Lucy. "I know you're very interested in environmental stewardship and historical preservation."

Newman was thoughtful, gazing off in the distance. "That's a good idea. Why don't you come and stay here with us on the island for a few days? Then you'd get to see what we're doing firsthand. How about it?"

"That would be great," said Lucy, as Taylor trotted toward them, a folder in her hand. "I'd have to check with my editor, of course. How can I get back to you?" Lucy was aware that the island was off the grid, and presumably that meant no cell phone service.

"Taylor will get in touch with you . . ." he said, turning around rather abruptly and greeting another guest.

"Don't mind Dad, he's always thinking," said Taylor, returning and presenting her with the folder.

Lucy smiled and took the folder. "This will be very helpful. I probably ought to mention that he invited me to the island so I could experience the lifestyle and write about it in more depth for the paper."

Taylor's eyebrow rose in surprise. "Did he, now?" She smiled warmly. "I guess that means I'll have to work out the details and get in touch with you."

"I'll be looking forward to hearing from you," said Lucy, fingering the folder.

"Great." Taylor nodded, dismissing her. "Don't miss the music," she urged. "It's the Brian Brown Blues Band," she said, naming a group Lucy vaguely remembered from her college days. "And Lily's promised to sing."

This really is a night to remember, thought Lucy, turning and looking for Bill. She spotted him standing on the edge of the dance floor, holding a beer, and joined him, taking his hand. The song was ending and Lily took the stage, dressed in a flowery, diaphanous dress with many fluttering layers, and stood behind the mike. She began to sing, a sad song about love lost, and Bill slipped his arm around Lucy's waist. They stood together, swaying slightly to the music, and Lucy thought nothing could be more perfect than that moment. Not ever.